WHEN CIVILIZATION BROKE DOWN, THE GANGS TOOK OVER . . .

They came through the bushes and took their final cover, behind a hedge of hydrangea. Lawrence looked through first and turned away, sickened. Matthew moved forward, and peered through the gap between two plants. The grotto was in front of him, and about twenty yards away.

There seemed to be a lot of men there, but when he counted them there were only five. Five, and Archie. They had tied his hands and feet and he was lying on the ground on his back. He still had his shirt on, but his trousers had been pulled down. His body looked small and pathetic, very white against the sunburnt arms of the men bending over him. One had what looked like a pair of pliers, the other a lighted taper. Nausea rose in Matthew's throat. From sadistic schoolboys to savages, the objectives were the same. The eyes and the genitals, particularly the genitals . . .

A Wrinkle in the Skin
JOHN CHRISTOPHER

SPHERE BOOKS LIMITED
30/32 Gray's Inn Road, London WC1X 8JL

First published in Great Britain by Hodder and Stoughton Ltd 1965
Copyright © John Christopher 1965
First Sphere Books edition 1978
This edition published by arrangement with the author and his agent
Reprinted 1979, 1980, 1983

Printed in Great Britain by
Hazell Watson & Viney Ltd
Aylesbury, Bucks

ONE

A POPULAR newspaper called it the Quaking Spring.

The first disaster, in New Zealand, killed upwards of thirty thousand people, leaving Christchurch badly shattered and Dunedin almost destroyed. Two weeks after that there were tidal waves in Malaya and North Borneo, and a chain of volcanoes rose, steaming and smoking, out of the South China Sea. A fairly severe quake took place in the Bolivian Andes, and a milder one in Jamaica. Russia reported a quake in the Turkmen, and China, according to the seismologists, concealed a very big one that happened shortly afterwards in Tibet.

The vagaries of nature with which Matthew Cotter was most concerned, though, were nearer and more ordinary. A series of cold fronts rolled in from the Atlantic, bringing squally winds and unseasonable chill rain to the island. It was the crucial time of year, when the trickle of early tomatoes was turning into a more profitable flood, and his fuel consumption in keeping the greenhouses hot enough was dismaying. Matters were not helped when, on successive weekends, the squalls blew up into gales which damaged the glass. On the second of these, after a day spent patching, he remembered with mixed feelings he had been asked to supper by the Carwardines. He did not look forward with any pleasure to making his own supper, but the prospect of putting on a suit and a social face was not tempting, either.

The Carwardines lived a couple of miles from him, in Forest. John Carwardine, who was in his early sixties, had retired five years before from a post as geologist with a Middle East oil company. Matthew and he got on quite well, playing snooker together at the Club once or twice a week. They were good-natured people but that in itself did not, he thought, account for their persistence in hospitality to a solitary male. As he had expected, Meg Ashwell's blue Mini was in front of the house when he drove up.

Meg Ashwell and Sylvia Carwardine were old friends; it was largely because of this that the Carwardines had retired to Guernsey. They were much the same age—Sylvia was a good twenty years younger than her husband—and had similarly sanguine and easy-going temperaments. Physically they were in contrast, Sylvia being small and blonde and rather plump, and Meg tall and dark with a springy gait. She had been married to an advocate who had died three years previously, leaving her with two children. She was attractive and capable, and clearly would make a very good wife for a divorced grower, whose daughter had grown up and gone to the mainland. Sylvia was tactful about this, not pointing up the obvious but putting the two of them in each other's path so that they might recognize it. Matthew thought that occasionally he detected a touch of humorous complicity in Meg's glance, an invitation to be amused by the whole thing. He supposed that if he were to start taking it seriously, so might she, but that at present she was unconcerned. She seemed to lead a full and satisfying life with her home and children.

The sitting-room had a roaring fire in the grate: the climate, after the Gulf, was the only drawback the Carwardines had found to the island. John poured him a powerful whisky, and Sylvia asked him about Jane. He must, she said, as she had said before, feel lonely without her. Matthew agreed.

'But she's a good correspondent, and she telephones every week. And it's a good thing for her to get away.'

Meg said: 'Yes. Very important, I think. A wonderful place for children, but narrowing for a late teen-ager. I'm determined mine will go to the mainland after school, whether they make university or not.'

Her boy was sixteen, the girl twelve, handsome and likeable children. Sylvia said:

'You will find it worse than Matthew, I should think. After all, he has the vinery. An empty house, for a woman, is much emptier.'

Meg said briskly: 'I don't worry about that. There are plenty of things one can find to do, if one looks for them. I don't imagine I shall find time hanging heavy.'

She spoke honestly, not trying to make an effect, and Matthew admired her for it. She was, he saw again, an admirable woman altogether, and Sylvia's project was clearly a sensible one. He doubted, though, if he would ever bring himself to co-operate in it. He was contented as he was.

Sylvia was a good cook. She served them a rich lobster bisque, followed by a daube of beef with celery and spring greens from their garden and floury buttered potatoes. They drank a claret, which John imported by the cask. Afterwards there was a flan, made with damsons bottled from the previous summer, and then they went back and had coffee by the fire. It was all very satisfying and comfortable, an eminently suitable time and place, Matthew thought, to discuss the world's disasters. They were talking about the latest earthquake. Rumours had begun to reach the west, chiefly through Hong Kong, that it had been a spectacular one, more destructive even than the one in South Island.

Sylvia said: 'I can't think why the Chinese want to keep quiet about it. There's nothing to be ashamed of in an earthquake, surely—not like a crop failure. It isn't an indictment of socialist planning.'

'Habit, probably,' Matthew suggested. 'And a reluctance to admit any kind of weakness.'

Meg nodded. 'People do that, too. It must be a terrifying thing—to find the earth no longer solid beneath you. And there have been so many of them. Might it happen here? I suppose there's no reason why not.'

She looked at John, who said: 'It's unlikely.'

'Why? Because we haven't had earthquakes in the past?'

'It amounts to that. Most quakes come in two specific areas—in the great-circle round the Pacific, or along the Caribbean–Alps–Himalaya axis. Those are the unstable regions. We're quite a bit outside them.'

'There was a small one about ten years ago,' Meg said. 'I remember being wakened by it. Helen was in a cot still, and at first I thought she was shaking the bars, and then I realized the whole house was shaking.'

'Three or four on the Mercalli scale,' John said. 'We do get little shocks occasionally—there's a place in Scotland that has them quite regularly—but not the big stuff.'

'What's the Mercalli scale?' Matthew asked. 'Something like the Beaufort?'

'Yes. It's done on a one to twelve basis, at any rate. One is imperceptible, except by instruments. At the top end, ten's Devastating, eleven's Catastrophic, and twelve's Major Catastrophe, with just about everything flattened. The South Island one rated eleven.'

'Thirty-five thousand dead,' Meg said. 'I should think that would qualify as a major catastrophe.'

'What causes earthquakes?' Sylvia asked. 'I've never understood.'

'Nor will you now,' her husband said. 'Most of them are due to slipping along faults, and the faults themselves are due to stresses and strains which may have been building up for thousands of years. Those two regions I mentioned are unstable because they are the relics of the last period of mountain-building, which is a long time ago. The earth still settling down.'

'But so many of them lately,' Sylvia said.

'I don't think that means anything. Coincidental, probably.'

Meg said: 'What if the mountain-building starts all over again? It would make life pretty uncomfortable, wouldn't it?'

'Very. I don't see any reason why it should, though. There's nothing in what's happened this year to make one apprehensive. It's been catastrophic enough for the poor devils who've been caught up in it, but on a global view it doesn't add up to much. One or two wrinkles in the skin of an orange—the orange very big and the wrinkles very small.'

'Have some more coffee,' Sylvia said. She busied herself with the Cona. 'Well, as long as our bit of orange doesn't wrinkle. It would be awful if it did. For Matthew, especially.'

'For me?' He smiled. 'All the glass, you mean. Yes, I must say things are bad enough, without earthquakes.'

'Mind you,' Sylvia said, 'I'm not sure a shock of some kind might not be a good idea as far as Matthew's concerned. He's a little bit complacent.'

8

'More indifferent than complacent, I think,' Meg said. 'He's a very self-contained person.'

The two women watched him, smiling. John said:

'They're gunning for you, Matthew. I think you'd better have a brandy with that coffee.'

On the way home, Matthew reflected that it had been a pleasant evening, and that it was pleasant, too, to be going back to his home and his own company. It would, of course, have been even more pleasant if Jane had been there, but her going away was something he had accepted as inevitable long ago. To some extent he had schooled himself against it in advance. Because he loved her, he had let her go—encouraged her to go. In his life he had known, by normal standards, relatively few people, and loved only one. For her own sake he was ready to lose her—it would not be long before she was married—and he did not expect to make that sort of contact with anyone again. Not complacent, he thought, but resigned. And self-contained? Possibly. He had independence, and the memory of good times. Not many had as much.

Moving on to the crown of the road to avoid an ambling hedgehog, he considered the charge of indifference. He was, he knew, more detached from his fellow human beings than most people appeared to be. There was something of a case history there, of course. A happy early childhood that ended, at five, with his mother's death. Her funeral was the first thing he could remember well—she was no more than a hazy image, a warm laughing thin face and comforting hands—the clucking aunts and the minister groaning his way through incomprehensible prayers. And the long cold winter after that, with Mrs Morris looking after the house in which his father spent less and less time. In the spring had come the sudden change—his father whistling before breakfast, stomping cheerfully into the house in the evening, even visiting his room at bedtime. And the summer of Miss Arundel, who became Aunt Hilda and who would next, he realized before he was told, become Mummy. A tall woman with cold delicate fingers and warm scented breath.

After the wedding there was the move to North Wales—

Hilda's country, and beautiful, he thought, but harsh and un-friendly after Kent. In the years that followed he grew to love the place, but with an austere, almost fearful love. And there were the children: Angela and Rodney, and Mary, born when he was twelve. Matthew had gone away to school the following year, and from school, the war having started the previous autumn, to the Army. His contacts with the family had been brief and infrequent, and after his father died while he was in France in '44, ceased almost entirely.

Demobilized, he had drifted to London and to a series of not very well-paying jobs in journalism. Also into marriage with Felicity, a colleague in the first of them. It was very hard, looking back, to see what had motivated either of them. He had not thought, after the first few months, that it could last long, but it had lasted twelve years before she left him for another, more successful journalist, and took Patrick with her. Patrick, from the beginning, had been Felicity's child in every way. Mat-thew's chief feeling had been one of relief, at being able to keep Jane.

The legacy from his uncle came between the nisi and the absolute. It was more substantial than he had expected; thou-sands where he had thought there might be hundreds. He took Jane on holiday to the Channel Islands, and realized, while they were there, that there was no need for him to go back. He found what he wanted in Guernsey, in St Andrew's: fifteen hundred feet of glass attached to a granite farmhouse tucked into the side of a hill. He paid his deposit, and resigned his newspaper job two days later.

And the good years had followed the bad, nine of them by now. Jane had gone to school on the island, and so to university in London. He, for his part, had made mistakes as a grower, bad ones at the beginning, and had had his share of natural disasters —one whole crop ruined by fusarian wilt—but on the whole he had modestly prospered. He had made no real friends, but he was happy in his work, and reading, or snooker and whisky at the Club, gave him the relaxation he needed.

He was, he thought, a reasonably contented man. Indifferent? Well, he knew the limitations of happiness, the penalties attaching to human affections. Because, he admitted to himself as he put the car away, he missed her, missed her badly. He was grateful for what there had been, and what was left. But he would not want to put his reasonable contentment further in hazard.

The weather improved during the week that followed. There was quite a lot of rain still, but the temperature shot up ten degrees, and between showers the sun came out strongly enough for Matthew to be able to cut the boilers out altogether. Prices at Covent Garden were staying quite high, and the new soil additive which the fertilizer company had talked him into appeared to be justifying its cost. The trusses were heavy and the fruit had a good colour. It seemed also that the Dutch growers were concentrating their main effort in the German market. It might be a good year, after all.

Jane telephoned early on Friday evening. The operator said: 'Will you pay for a call for Miss Jane Cotter,' and he said: 'Gladly. Put her through.' She sounded cheerful, a little breathless. Matthew asked her if she had been running.

'Not *exactly*, Daddy. Moving fairly fast, though. I'm at Charing Cross, on my way down to Aunt Mary's.'

Mary, the younger of his half-sisters, was the only one of the family he kept in touch with. She had been in London, trying to be an actress, during the latter years of his marriage, and had visited them at the high-ceilinged gloomy flat off Cromwell Road. Although she had not said so, he had known that she disliked Felicity and sympathized with him. She had also been fond of Jane, and had several times had her down since she had gone to university. Married six years to an East Sussex farmer, she had no children of her own.

'That's good,' Matthew said. 'Much better than a weekend in London, I should think.'

'My God, yes. One of the chaps is writing a novel—about, you know, life here. He couldn't think of a title, and Mike suggested one for him: "Bugger Sunday". He thinks it's terrific—it's really got him past the block.'

Matthew laughed. 'How is Mike?'

He knew of him as a boy, reading Chemistry, who had begun

to figure fairly largely, though innocently, in her accounts of university life.

'Oh, pretty fair.'

'And work?'

'Ghastly, darling. How about the tom-toms?'

'Mustn't grumble.'

'Which means things must be pretty good. We may be able to get that winter sports trip after all.'

'Might manage it for you. I'm not going.'

'Oh yes, you are. Even if you only sit and sozzle. You're getting too dull on that island.'

He was pleased by her insistence, and said mockingly:

'Well, there speaks the cosmopolitan. One's allowed a bit of dullness in middle age.'

'Not while I'm around. Uncle Harry's meeting me at St Leonard's. In the new Jaguar. Do you think he'll let me drive?'

'No. And you're not to pester him.'

'As if I would. But there's nothing wrong with being terribly admiring, and then looking a bit sad. I mean, is there?'

'I think I'll ring Harry and warn him.'

'You wouldn't do that. Damn! The pips.'

'I can afford another three minutes.'

'Darling, I can't. My train's due off in two. Tell you what—I'll ring again in the morning.'

'Good. Bye, love.'

'Bye.'

Matthew got himself supper, a casserole of pork steak which had been simmering all afternoon in the Aga oven, watched television for an hour and, after making a final round of the vinery, went early to bed. He read for a time, and fell asleep easily. In the early hours he was awakened by a dog barking, and sat up and switched on the light.

He kept a couple of dozen hens on free range, to provide a supply of non-battery eggs, and there had been trouble with a dog disturbing them at night. It was apparently a small dog which got into the hen-house and chivvied them off their perches. Matthew had got up one night and heard it dash away as he approached. That had been over a week ago, and since then he had kept a shotgun in his bedroom. It would do no harm, he thought, to give it a peppering. He put on socks and shoes, and trousers and a guernsey over his pyjamas. Then he loaded the gun and, picking up a torch, went out quietly in the direction of the hen-house.

It was a clear, fairly cold night—no clouds, a quarter moon, and light sifting out across the sky from the great arc of the Milky Way. He heard the dog again as he went down the path, and stopped short. It was not barking any longer but howling, and he could tell that it was not in with the hens. It sounded like the cross-bred collie on the Margy farm. But there was a disturbance among the hens, all the same, a nervous clucking which was, at this time of night, more unsettling than a positive sound of outrage would have been. Matthew tightened his grip on the gun, and went on towards them.

He became aware of other noises, carried on the still air. A second dog took up the howling of the first, and he thought he heard a third, more distant. Cows lowing, and the bray, hideous and ear-splitting even at a quarter of a mile distance, of one of Miss Lucie's donkeys. The sounds, familiar though they were, had a touch of horror in their present context: this otherwise quiet night, with no breath of wind, the sharply delineated peace of the middle hours of darkness. Then came another sound, as mild, as well known, but now the eeriest of them all. The chatter of birds, awakening from their sleep. One or two first, and then more and more, until Matthew felt that all the birds in the island were awake and shrieking their unease. He stopped again, abreast of the cane brake at the end of his kitchen garden.

Then, after one swift, barely perceptible shudder, the earth heaved beneath him, slammed him like a rat against itself and, heaving again, tossed him bruised and winded through the air.

TWO

MATTHEW felt the canes whip against his face and body, and reached out convulsively to anchor himself. The earth subsided and he began to slip down, then rocked as violently as before, throwing the stars into a lunatic gyration across the sky. This time he went deep in, the canes yielding to the thrust of his body. His left leg and the left side of his body up to his shoulder were wedged painfully between the shafts of bamboo.

There had been a hush at the first shock, a silence that almost rang in the ears. The noise reached him with the second one, a bellowing rumbling diapason that dwarfed his memories of the Caen bombardment, that sounded, he thought crazily, as though the world were being torn from its orbit and sent grinding and skittering through space. It died away only to start again, and by this time the earth was heaving for the third time, the canes that held him tilting violently in defiance of gravity. From that point, the shocks were successive—lurch and roar, lurch and roar, in a hideous phased rhythm. Once he thought he heard a dog howl, but for the most part a sound so small would have been lost in the brutal crescendoes of the torn and protesting earth.

When a new noise did break through, it was altogether different but on as gigantic a scale. It swelled into the ebb of one of the shock waves, and Matthew realized that he had been hearing it without distinguishing it for some moments. It was the howl of a storm and the bellow of an avalanche mixed up, along with the whine and scream of the sea in tempest. It rose to a high, scarcely endurable pitch of savagery, and subsided from it. But, subsiding, it changed its pitch, like the whistle of a railway train which has passed the station and is racing away into the distance. As it died, the earth heaved again, and roared, and heaved and roared, a stupendous theme and variations, orchestrated by demons, and a great gale of wind almost plucked him from his perch.

He had no idea how long it was before the first real lull came. He had the impression that the shocks had been going on for hours, but that was not to be relied on; all his senses had been thrown out of gear by the physical and sonic buffeting he had endured. At some time he had heard the splintering crash of glass, shattering into a hundred thousand pieces, but he was too confused to remember whether it had come at the beginning or the end. But at least he was conscious of the fact that the earth was still, that the agony of its mutilation was fading in far-away groans and squeals. The silence which came was not of expectancy but exhaustion, a silence following pain, a terminal quiet. The crackle of bamboo was loud in his ears, as he struggled to free himself and get down. It was not easy, he was so firmly wedged, and he was sweating in the cold night air by the time he managed it.

And even though he was on firm ground, something was subtly wrong. His balance? Could the battering have affected it? He was not standing quite straight, he thought, and when he started to walk along the path towards the house he stumbled and nearly fell. He halted, looking up. The sky was serene, unchanged, the bright stars and the quarter moon. Matthew shifted his feet, and realized what was wrong. Here the ground had been level. Now it rose a little, towards the greenhouses, towards the west.

The thought stunned him. He had known this was an earthquake, a series of earthquakes, of frightful severity. He had known his glass was gone, and expected his house would be badly shattered. But the earth itself twisted out of shape?

He had dropped the torch he was carrying (switched off, he recalled with wry surprise, because he had been hoping to surprise the dog among his hens) when he grasped for the support of the canes. He looked for it but there was no trace, and he abandoned the search. Instead he walked back in the direction of the house. It was light enough to see a little way in front of him. Surely, in fact, to see the house from here? He ran a few paces; then stopped. When he walked forward again, he did so slowly.

The moonlight and starlight showed him the pile of rubble. It covered a fairly extensive area, but it did not rise very high from the ground. The highest features were a door, somehow still upright, and the television aerial, sprouting from a hillock of shattered bricks. Matthew was staring at this when the shock hit again, flinging him to the ground.

It was less violent than the earlier ones, and the one that came as he struggled to his feet was milder still, shaking him but not throwing him down. At the same time, he was more consciously aware of fear than he had been before, possibly because, his mind being less severely bludgeoned, he could think more clearly. The cane brake had protected him, and might do so again. There was no other refuge.

He went back and crawled in among the lances of bamboo. By breaking them and twisting them underneath him, he was able to make himself a kind of cage or nest; not comfortable, but better than nothing. In the next shock it creaked, but did not collapse. He settled down as well as he could, to wait for the night to pass. His watch, which had been on the table beside his bed, was somewhere under the rubble. It might have been any time between midnight and four o'clock.

There were other shocks, but they were not very strong and the intervals grew longer. He thought about Jane, and was glad she was so far from the island. Close on two hundred miles—more than enough, surely, for safety. Later he thought about his own future: all his capital had been tied up in the vinery and the house. He tried to remember what his insurance policy said about earthquakes. Still, he was lucky. He was alive. He realized with chill certainty that most of his neighbours would not be. There was no sound anywhere. Even the dog had stopped howling.

In the east the sky turned from black to purple and, as the stars faded, to light-flushed blue. The earth was quieter, trembling from time to time but with no great violence; almost gently. Matthew came down, cold and cramped, from his perch, and stretched his stiff limbs.

The path that ran past the vinery led to the Margy farm. The glass lay like a frozen lake, laced with driftwood that was the shattered structure of the houses. Beneath it, like drowned vegetation, lay the crushed green plants, spotted and splotched with red. Just beyond was the smashed heap of the packing-shed in which, the previous afternoon, over fifty trays of fruit had been left ready for picking up this morning. More than a quarter of a ton of tomatoes. Matthew averted his head and carried on down the path.

Somehow the sight of the Margy farmhouse was more shocking than his own had been. It was the same idiot's heap of bricks and granite blocks, rising only a few feet from the ground. Matthew walked slowly forward. There had been some idea in his mind that he might be able to help, to rescue someone trapped. The sight before him disposed of that. He walked round the pile, finding no reference point that he could recognize. All sorts of things were jumbled together—curtains and crockery, smashed furniture, the gaunt finger of a standard lamp, a book lying open, one page weighted down with a fragment of slate. And, towards the centre, a human arm stretched out, in protest or supplication. It looked very young and white. The daughter, probably—Tessie, who was to marry the young chap from the garage at the end of summer. Matthew turned and walked away.

He was aware, reaching the ruins of his own home, of cold and numbness, and also of the sharp pangs of hunger. He stared at the tangle of stone and torn wood, working out where the kitchen had been. He climbed gingerly over the rubble and saw the cream top of the refrigerator just under the surface. He heaved a couple of broken beams away, and started to clear away in front of the door. It was fairly easy to start with, but became progressively harder as he got down to the more compressed layers. At last he reached something quite beyond his power to move—one of the oak roof beams that had wedged itself under the handle. He straightened his back, sweating. Hunger gnawed at him, more viciously for the disappointment.

As he glanced down, he saw the coloured label of a tin. He scrabbled and unearthed it. A tin of frankfurter sausages which had been in the house for some time—Jane liked them but he did not. He felt more than ready to eat them raw. He looked wrily at the tin in his hands. All he needed was an opener.

There had been one, he remembered, in the cutlery drawer of the kitchen cabinet, and at his feet a fragment of glazed green glass, part of the cabinet, stuck out of a chunk of plaster. Matthew got down and worried the rubble like a terrier. He found odd things—knives, a battered saucepan, part of the coffee percolator, a breakfast cup incredibly intact—but no opener. He went on looking for a long time, only desisting when he came on more tins of food. Baked beans, asparagus, and sardines. He threw the first two aside. The sardines had an opener attached to the tin.

A couple of stone mushrooms, perches for the Guernsey witches, had stood in his front garden. One had fallen, but the other was still upright, more or less. Matthew sat on it, and carefully wound the lid off the sardines. He picked the fish out with his fingers, and ate them one by one. Afterwards he lifted the tin and drank what remained of the oil. He looked automatically for somewhere to dispose of the empty tin; in his housekeeping he had always been meticulous about not attracting flies. Then he thought of the arm reaching from the ruins of the Margy farmhouse, and with an angry motion tossed the tin away from him.

It was quite light now. The sun was almost up, the landscape clearly visible. The weirdness lay not only in the devastation of house and vinery, but in the lie of the land itself, the horizon dipping to the west, strangely rising to the east. For the first time, he took this in properly. My God, he thought, the whole island must have been tilted, twisted. He saw a trail of wire and identified it—the telephone wire. Jane had said she would ring again this morning. Was it going to be possible to get in touch with her that day at all? Or were all the lines down, throughout the island? It seemed more than likely.

There was no point, anyway, in staying where he was. There was nothing he could do for the people in the Margy house, but he might be able to help elsewhere. The Carwardines, for instance. He felt better equipped to deal with things after the sardines. The hunger had probably been more psychological than real, a need for reassurance. Matthew looked again at the debris. Was there anything useful he could take with him, anything he could pick up without too much effort? Catching sight of something else, he smiled. It was the silver cup he had won for boxing, as a subaltern. He supposed looters might get it, if any were left alive and active enough to loot. He did not think it was worth either taking or hiding.

But before he left he found something which he felt was worth taking—the shotgun, its stock embedded in soft earth. It was still loaded. He checked the safety-catch, and tucked it under his arm. He did not know why, but it seemed a sensible thing to do.

Matthew walked down the slope of land, towards the brightening east. There were a few hundred yards of lane, leading to the main road. Near the top, a clump of trees had been uprooted and had fallen, barring the way; he climbed the bank to get round them. Their exposed roots thrust towards the sky, on the edge of a fissure several feet deep. He could see the empty road now, and the remains of a couple of cottages. The same total destruction, the same silence. The dawn was well advanced, but there was no twitter of birds. He wondered what had happened to them all. Plucked from their roosting twigs and dashed against the earth? Or flown away, seeking refuge in distant safer lands? Or simply stunned into silence? He trudged on, listening to the sound of his own footfalls on the ground.

The road was empty; there would have been very few people driving at the time the earthquake struck. It curved back on itself on this stretch; he was traversing an arc of circle with his home as centre. He heard the familiar noise with an uprush of relief—the bray of a donkey. One of the four Miss Lucie kept, and had done for years. Jane, on her way to school, had stopped to feed them with pieces of bread, cake and stale apples. There was life still. He hurried towards the sound.

The house was a heap of stone and dust and oddments. He went on past the ruin where the stables had been, and came to the paddock. The body of one of the donkeys was lying against a twisted stretch of fencing, and he saw another dead one a little further on. He could still hear the braying, and went up the field. It was L-shaped, containing a thicket—sloe and elderberry and willow—which was also bounded by a douit.

The donkey brayed more loudly and pitifully when it saw him. It was lying with one leg folded under it, at such an angle that it was plainly broken. Matthew went to the animal, and patted it on the head. The long face and big liquid eyes stared at him, and it groaned hoarsely. He placed the muzzle of the shotgun near it, slipped off the safety-catch, and pressed the trigger. The shot crashed across the stillness and the shaggy head dropped back.

He was walking back to the road when he heard braying again, turned, and stared incredulously. The noise came not from the field but the thicket, and looking there he saw the fourth donkey. It was helplessly caught in the spiky tangle of sloe branches. The sight had a comic grandeur that made him want to laugh. He crossed the douit, and forced his way into the thicket.

The donkey was stuck, but seemed unharmed. Presumably it had been thrown up there by one of the early shocks. Its struggles had enmeshed it more fully in the cocoon of thorn, and the cocoon had preserved it as the cane had done with him. All that was necessary now was to free the animal. He tried wrenching at the branches with his bare hands, but only succeeded in scratching himself. He needed a tool—an axe or something. He might find one, he thought, in the wrecked stable. He backed out, and the donkey brayed at him. Matthew recognized it now as the light-coloured one, Cobweb—the four donkeys had been named after Titania's fairies.

'Don't worry, old girl,' he said. 'I'll be back.'

The search was, at the outset, discouraging. It had been a typical Guernsey stable, built with heavy beams of wood and granite blocks, and he found himself sweating and straining and not getting far. The sun came up over his labours, and soon after there were more earth tremors—mild ones, but enough to make him take refuge for a time in more open ground.

Eventually he found a spade. It had been kept in good shape, and the edge was keen. He took it to the thicket and attacked the branches, driving the blade down as a cutting edge with what strength he could muster. The donkey struggled at first, but went quiet as he continued. The work was not easy: the thorn branches were springy and the blade frequently skidded off. After half an hour's work, he did not seem to have made a great deal of progress. He paused, and wiped the sweat from his face.

It occurred to him that he had got his priorities all wrong. There might be other human survivors needing help or rescue. It was ludicrous for him to be bending all his effort to the release of a donkey from a thicket. The donkey brayed again. Matthew shrugged, picked up the spade, and returned to the attack.

He had no idea how long it was before he got the animal free. He loosened the last leg from a snare of twisted branches, and it stepped forward, showing little sign of distress. He rubbed the furry head, the soft silky nose. Cobweb went to the douit, and lowered her head to drink. Matthew realized that he was thirsty, too. He hesitated; even under normal circumstances, douit water was not regarded as fit for human consumption, and there was no knowing what pollution existed now. But there was, anyway, no alternative. He knelt beside the donkey, cupped water in his hands, and drank deeply.

Unconcernedly, Cobweb cropped the grass a few yards from her dead companions while Matthew rested and thought what to do. He was aware again of the enormity of having spent so much time and effort on an animal when people—the Carwardines, possibly, or Meg Ashwell and her children—might need help. The least he could do was get on to their place as quickly as possible. He would have to leave the donkey, of course. He remembered a coil of rope he had thrown aside in his search of the ruins of the stable, brought it to the field, and tied a noose round Cobweb's neck. He attached the other end to one of the willows. It would keep her from wandering, but was long enough to give her a fair grazing range.

Further down the road, he came on the ruins of more houses. He stood and called out, listening after each call for a sound that might indicate that someone was still living. But there was nothing. Surely in earthquakes some survived inside the wreck of their houses? But he remembered how shock had followed shock during the endless night; it was all too likely that those who had merely been trapped by the first had been battered to death by the ones that followed. Matthew looked up into the empty sky, where the sun was already high. He was searching for something, without at first understanding what it was. It came to him: aeroplanes. The island might have been beaten almost to death, but surely help would be coming from the mainland? He remembered the television pictures of the other disasters, taken from helicopters. They should be here by now. And if they weren't, what could it mean? Only that the devastation stretched further than he had guessed, that what had happened to a small island was not reckoned important in the great canvas of disaster.

Jane, he thought. Had the damage reached as far as East Sussex? He shook his head. Even if it had, it could not have been as severe as here. This must be the worst. Here, on the bend, the houses, shaken to pieces, had been spilled out over the road. He could see a leg in the rubble, a grotesque bunioned foot projecting. He called again, but did not expect any reply.

He knew then why it was he had stayed to free the donkey. Because he could not believe that, himself apart, there was any survivor on the island. He would go through the motions of looking, but he would not find any. The disaster was total.

Something moved on the edge of his vision, and he turned his head quickly. Not just the donkey and himself. Many, probably most, of the smaller animals, might have survived. The rat, a large one, stopped, then skittered on across the mound of ruin. Loathing it with all his heart, he found a stone and threw at it. The stone fell short, and the rat stopped again, squatting on its hind quarters. He read defiance into the gesture, picked up more stones and lunged towards it, throwing as he went. The rat disappeared, under a pile of wood and plaster.

There was something else he could see from this new vantage point. It squatted as the rat had done, looking at him, but provoking horror and nausea, not anger: the head of an old man. Eyes and mouth were open, frozen in a gasp of agony. There was a beam behind it, dried blood on the plaster in front. Matthew bent over and was sick: the noise of his vomiting tore at the stillness of the morning. When he had done retching, he went away, keeping his eyes from seeing it again.

He could only guess the position of the road from its continuation in the distance. Here it was lost beneath the debris. Glass and cloth and metal—a child's toy car, a hat stand, a Victorian family portrait, a splintered piano. And broken bottles and a strong and familiar smell. There had been a pub here, on the corner. He almost tripped over the projecting edge of a cardboard crate exuding whisky fumes. It had been sliced across and the bottles broken. All broken. It was a pity. A moderate intoxication, he felt, would have been preferable to sobriety in the world in which he found himself.

From time to time he stopped and called, and his voice echoed emptily back at him. The wall at the Vauxbelets was shattered, the old monastery a grey tumulus in the distance. He went down the dip and up the other side, then climbed over a flattened hedge and headed across a ploughed field towards the airport.

The field was tilted, but the landing-strip, in addition, was buckled and twisted, and riven by huge fissures. Near one of the hangars a Viscount sprawled, starboard wing crumpled, fuselage broken in two. Matthew stared at it. To him, as to most islanders in recent years, it was the airport rather than the harbour which was the link with England. No planes would land here again. Hangars might be rebuilt, and cracks filled in, but what would be the point, with the ground itself at this angle? Standing in the middle of the sloping emptiness, he shouted:

'Is anyone there? I'm here. I'm here! Is anyone alive but me?'

The emptiness drowned his voice. He walked on across the field, towards the Forest Road. There were houses, crumbled like the others, and he kept away from them. He headed down towards the valley of the Gouffre, where the Carwardines lived. Had lived—he had no hope now of finding them alive.

Even so, when he came to what was left of the house he set to work, pulling away bricks and plaster and wood and broken sticks of furniture. He found them at last. They were huddled in the remains of their bed, clutching each other as they must have done when the shock woke them and, in almost the same instant, killed them. Matthew stared at their bodies unhappily. They were to have come to him for a drink on Sunday—tomorrow morning. There ought to be something he could do. Dig a grave, perhaps, and bury them. But he was tired, drained of energy, and the spade was back at Miss Lucie's. All the same, he could not leave them exposed like that. He heaped broken plaster over them, till they were hidden again.

He went on, with no particular aim except that he was not far from the sea, and the idea of its vastness and changelessness appealed to him. In the garden of one of the ruins he passed, bees swarmed in the sun, dipped down to take nectar from a flowering bush that seemed to grow out of stone, and danced again. Matthew stood for a while, listening to the somnolent murmur of their buzzing. He wondered about seagulls. As near the sea as this, one usually heard them mewing and shrieking. Had they gone, too, like the land birds? He would have thought that they could live out any cataclysm by taking to their own element.

He stared in disbelief as he came down the last stretch of hill, steeper now, and looked out to where the sea should have been. It was like a glimpse of another planet, a strange savage and barren world. He could see the tangled green of the great weed beds, the rawness of exposed rock and sand. Here and there the glint of water; light thrown back from pools trapped in hollows. But the blue sweep of wave was gone. A sunken land was drying in the early summer sun.

THREE

MATTHEW went out on to the cliff path. There were several shallow stretches of water—lakes or ponds—but as far as the eye could see, the sea-bed lay open to the blue sky. Far to the south-east a higher hump of land was Jersey; they could scarcely have fared any better than Guernsey. He remembered the great noise, the rushing and whining and howling, which had changed its pitch in mid course. The sea, draining back past the island, rushing to the west to find its new level. The island . . . Not any longer. He strained his eyes to the north, looking for the vanished gleam of the sea.

He turned from that at last, and made his way back inland. He felt empty and light-headed. He supposed he should try to find something to eat—it must be late morning, and he had vomited up the few sardines he had had. But the hunger which had been ravenous then was as markedly absent now. The feeling was something like drunkenness: he contemplated his state with mingled pity and grandeur. The last man left alive? The Robinson Crusoe of planet Earth? It might be so. The silence went on, and the sky stayed blue and vacant.

He went across a field to avoid more ruins and, stumbling over broken ground, almost fell. He used the gun to keep his balance, and the muzzle went into the ground. Matthew found a piece of stick, and cleaned it out. Doing so, he thought of Jane, with a clear and biting lash of grief. If she had been here on the island she would have died all the same, but at least he could have given her burial.

He stared at the gun in his hands. He had fired one barrel, to put a crippled donkey out of its misery. The other remained loaded. It would be a simple thing to do; simple and, surely, sensible. What point was there in surviving in a charnel house? On this hillock, rising from a drained and lifeless sea? Peace, he thought, and turned the gun towards himself.

A small sound stopped him. It came from a distance, and might have been no more than one of the shattered houses settling in further on itself, but his first thought was that it was the donkey braying. He remembered that he had left her tied up. If she were freed, she could forage for herself, and survive the summer at least. He put the gun under his arm, and set off across the field.

He traversed the airfield well to the west of his original path. The ground had been cut and twisted here like modelling clay; there was one gap where a plane could have rested without its wings touching the sides. The walls of the cleft gaped rawly, showing earth and stones, and there was water at the bottom, a spring welling up. In a hundred years, when grass had grown over the nakedness and trees had taken root round about, it would be a pretty spot.

He heard the cry as he slithered down the bank from the airfield to the road. It was very faint, and he could not judge the direction properly. He stood, listening and waiting, for what seemed a long time. At last it came again, weak and indistinguishable but, he was sure, from the west. He walked that way, calling out as he walked.

'Who's there? Give me a shout if you need help. Let me hear you. Shout so that I can hear you, and find you.'

There was no reply, and he thought that he might have imagined the voice. Hallucinations would not be surprising, in this loneliness. He came to the wreckage of a house, and stared at it. It had been shaken to pieces, like all the others. What could possibly have survived in such as that?

But the cry came again, and louder. He hurried towards it, up the road and round the bend. There had been three or four houses together; they were collapsed into a single mound of rubble. Matthew stood at the edge, and called:

'Shout! Give me some idea where you are.'

The voice was muffled and sounded girlish: it came from somewhere at the far end. He began to terrier his way into the mound, but cautiously. Disturbing the mass too much might make it shift and settle.

'Hang on,' he shouted. 'I'll have you out soon.'

There was no reply. He wondered if, ironically, it had been the final cry for help he had heard, the last gasp before death claimed this one, too. He strained and shifted a beam, and saw there was a figure beneath it. A girl in a flowered nightdress. Then that was it, he thought. She was dead all right. The nightdress was torn, showing one of her breasts. Matthew touched it: cold, quite cold. He straightened up. Then it could not have been she who cried, only a few minutes ago. He called out, and dug with his hands, and called out again.

When he came to the small foot, he thought it was another corpse, but this time the flesh was warm to his fingers, and he thought there was a tremor in the limb. A section of the roof ridge had crashed onto a bed and wedged across it. It had trapped the child, but also protected. Matthew began clearing away the stuff over it.

'You're all right,' he said. 'There's nothing more to worry about. We'll have you out in a jiffy.'

It was a boy about ten, semi-conscious. His head and face were thickly covered with plaster; it was a wonder he had been able to breathe, let alone call out. Matthew wiped it away, as best he could, with his hands and the sleeve of his guernsey. He bent to lift the child, but he cried out in pain.

'My arm . . .'

It was the left one. Matthew felt along it gently. A slight fracture—greenstick. He said: 'All right, old chap.' Pain had made the boy fully conscious; he looked up, groaning. 'A bit of damage to the arm, but we can fix it.'

He had not done First Aid since his Army days, and he had to think about it before going to work. Forearm at right angles to upper arm, thumb up and palm in. He eased it into position; the boy winced, but did not cry.

'Pretty good,' he said. 'Can you hang on like that while I find some splints?'

There were plenty of pieces of wood about. He managed to break a couple of roughly the right length and blunted their jagged ends by rubbing them against a block of stone. He padded them with pieces ripped off the bed's cotton coverlet, and put them in position along the arm. He tore the top sheet up for bandages, and fixed the splints with one bandage above the fracture and a second figure-of-eighting from the wrist. The boy stayed quiet while he was doing it.

'Right,' Matthew said. 'An arm sling, and you're ready for action. What's your name?'

'Billy. Billy Tullis. What happened? Was it an explosion?'

'Bigger than that. An earthquake.'

The eyes widened. 'Was it?'

Matthew tied the ends of the triangle in front of the shoulder; he really ought to have pinned the third point, but he had no pin and it would not matter for the time being. He asked:

'How's that? Fairly comfortable?'

'Yes. What about Mum and Dad? And Sylvia?'

He presumed that Sylvia was his sister, that hers was the body he had first found. He said: 'Hang on a minute. I won't be long.' He went back to the body, and covered it up. When he came to the boy again, he said:

'That's something else you're going to have to be brave about.'

'They're dead?'

'Yes.'

'I thought they must be.' He had dark, rather nondescript features, and brown eyes with something of a slant. 'I called to them. I called a lot, and when no one came I thought they must be dead. Was it a big earthquake?'

Matthew picked the boy up and carried him across the wreckage to open ground. He said:

'Very big. About the biggest ever.' He set him down. 'Can you stand up, do you think? Can you walk?'

The boy nodded. He stared at the wreck of his home. Then he looked at Matthew.

'Where are we going?'

'I don't know yet. I haven't given it much thought. You're the only person I've found alive so far. There are just the two of us. Well, three. But the third's a donkey.'

'One of Miss Lucie's? Which one?'

'The light grey one. Cobweb.'

'I know.'

'I've left her tethered. I think we should go back and see how she is.' He looked at the boy, standing in thin pyjamas, with bare feet. 'I wonder if we could find some of your clothes before we go.'

'I'm not cold.'

'You will be, later. You stay there and get yourself uncramped, while I look.'

Matthew found the boy's bedroom slippers under what was left of the bed and, searching further, discovered a shoe. Hunting for its pair, he lifted the edge of a broken door and was looking at the body of a man. The face had been badly damaged, and there was a lot of blood. There was another body, he could see, beside it. From behind him, Billy called:

'Can I come and help?'

Matthew eased the door back. 'No. I'm coming now.'

He took blankets with him from the boy's bed, a left slipper and a right shoe. He put them on the boy's feet.

'There. That's better than nothing. We'll rig one of the blankets round you like a cloak, and I'll carry the others. You'll need them tonight.'

'Where shall we sleep?'

'I don't know. It will have to be out in the open. I shouldn't think there's a roof standing, and there may be more shocks.' He rubbed the boy's head. 'You're going to have to live rough for a few days.'

Billy said earnestly: 'I don't mind. I was supposed to go to scout camp in August.'

'Well,' Matthew said, 'you're all right in that case. Come on, let's be going.'

They headed back towards Miss Lucie's. Matthew continued to call from time to time, and Billy joined in, but there was no response. He was concerned about the boy's reaction to his first sight of death, but when it came—a man's body, only partly covered by rubble—he appeared to take it calmly. Matthew kept their course well clear of the horror of the head.

Cobweb brayed a welcome as they approached. Billy ran to her and wrapped his free arm round her neck. He said:

'I suppose she thought I was bringing her something. I used to, quite often.'

So did Jane, Matthew thought. He smiled with difficulty.

'We'll get her something. I want you to hang on here and look after her. I'm off to do a little foraging, for us as well as for her.'

'Can't I come with you?'

'Not this time. You stay here. She can do with some company.'

Matthew heard him talking to the donkey as he went away. He would have to do some planning, he realized. They could not stay in the field, with three dead donkeys, and he had no intention of wasting precious energy burying them. Death was all round; in a very short time there would be the stink of putrefaction in the air. There was no way one man and a crippled boy could cope with that except by retreating. They must make themselves a camp, well out in the open but within reach of food. Food was the most immediate need. The little general shop at the end of the lane. He came to a place where the ground had buckled into a ridge five or six feet high, a sycamore fantastically projecting out of it, and climbed over. The heap of bricks and wreckage beyond would be the cottages; the shop had been on the far corner.

It was hard work and, to start with, unrewarding; then he began to get lucky. He hit on the small hardware section and discovered a couple of undamaged saucepans, and next matches. Several gross packages were mashed and scattered, but he found almost a dozen individual boxes in fair shape. Then a kitchen knife, and an aluminium soup ladle. Immediately after that, the best find of all. The cardboard container was battered and torn, but the object inside was undamaged. A tin opener. One of those elaborate ones, meant to be screwed on the wall of a neat modern labour-saving kitchen; he was surprised that Mrs Triquemin had stocked anything so advanced. But the important thing was that it would open tins. All he needed now were the tins to open.

He found Mrs Triquemin first. Her face had the look of faint surprise which had been habitual, as though she were about to open her mouth and say: 'Why, it's Mr Cotter—what can I get for you this morning?' The lower half of her body was buried under heavy granite blocks. Matthew covered her up, and went on with the search.

Suddenly he hit treasure trove, a mine of tins of all shapes and sizes underneath the shelves from which they had cascaded. Nearly all were battered and quite a few had burst open, spreading a paste of meat and fruit syrup, processed peas and concentrated soup and other unidentifiable components all round. But there was a great deal to be salvaged. Matthew carted them in armfuls to the place where he had put the saucepans. There was enough here for him and the boy to live on for a week at least. He went back to his digging. It would be nice to find something special for the boy.

A large rectangular object was the deep-freeze chest. The front had broken open, but the top was still in place. He recognized melted ice cream in the mush. The boy would have liked ice cream: he wondered when, if ever, he would taste it again. For the first time he thought of the long-term aspects of survival. The aeroplanes had not come. It was going to be a hard world—there was no telling how hard.

He rescued various polythene-wrapped meats and vegetables. They could be eaten right away, and the tinned stuff kept. The thing to do, he realized, was to dig out as many tins as possible during the next few days, and then to stay clear of the ruins until the bodies buried under them had rotted down into the cleansing earth. How long would that take? A few weeks? Or months? One could mine them again after that.

But what about next year, and the years to follow? There were crops in the fields—one could plant potatoes. It might be possible to find corn, and grow it. Protein was going to be the difficulty. He was brought up short by the shocking awareness of just how great a difficulty: no cattle and, the sea having left them, no fish. Rabbits might have survived—rats, he recalled with distaste, certainly had. He abandoned the speculation. The only thing to do was concentrate on the present and let the future take care of itself.

Shattered glass and scattered sweets told him he had reached the part he was looking for. Burrowing on, he found bars of chocolate, and took an assortment for Billy. He found an old sack, too, which he could put the tins in for carrying. That was a relief, but also a reminder of the depressing number of essentials they lacked. He dropped the things into the sack, and humped it on his back.

In the field, he put bricks together to form a rough field kitchen, and he and Billy found dry wood and made a fire. He made a stew in one of the saucepans, from a mixture of meat, peas and sweet corn. When it was ready, he poured some into the other pan, set it in the douit to cool for a few minutes, and gave Billy the ladle to use as a spoon. He said:

'What does it taste like? Can you eat it?'

'Jolly good.'

'And how's the arm?'

'It hurts a bit. Not much, though.' He stared past Matthew. 'Look!'

A white cat was treading its way through the grass towards them, presumably attracted by the smell of food. It came to Matthew, arched its back, and rubbed against his leg. It was very much a house-cat, sweet-natured from pampering. Billy offered it a piece of meat and it went to him, sniffed delicately, and took it to eat.

'There are other things alive then,' Billy said.

'Some. I don't think many.'

'Perhaps people?'

'Not so likely. Dogs and cats were more likely to have been out in the open when the earthquakes started. And the smaller the animal, the more likely it would survive without having bones broken.'

Billy finished his stew. Matthew said:

'No pudding, I'm afraid. Will this do?'

He produced the chocolate and saw the boy's face light up.

'*Thanks!* Can I give Cobweb some?'

'A little if you like. There probably won't be any more after this.'

Matthew poured some stew for himself and ate it. It was not bad, though the sweet corn was a little hard. There was meat left in the pan, and he put it down for the cat. It ate with small growls of pleasure. If one cat had survived, there were likely to be others. They would go wild, but they would breed. He was not particularly keen on cat as a source of protein, but it was better than rat. And there would almost certainly be hedgehogs, too. The Romany, he remembered, baked them in clay.

He was going to the douit to wash things when the ground moved sharply beneath him. He heard Billy cry out, and saw him lying on the ground. As he ran to him, there was a new tremor and he threw himself down beside him.

'My arm . . .' His face was twisted with pain. 'I think it's all right, but . . .'

'Let me look.' Matthew felt the arm gently; the splints were still in place. 'Have another piece of chocolate to take the taste away.'

The earth was quiet. He helped the boy up. Billy said:

'Are there going to be earthquakes all the time?'

'You get little ones for a while after a big one—the earth settling down. And last night's was pretty big. You'll have to be prepared, and train yourself to fall on your good arm.'

Talking to the boy helped him also. Each new tremor brought an instinctive fear which seemed as severe as those in the night. Without the boy, it could have been paralysing. The urge had been to roll himself into a ball, close eyes and ears—forget everything.

The boy was sobbing, his slight body shaking. Matthew put an arm across his shoulders.

'The pain will go soon. You're not eating your chocolate.'

'It's not that . . .'

'Then what?'

'The cat?'

Matthew looked and could only see the pieces of meat on the grass. He asked:

'What about the cat?' The sobs continued and he could not make out what the boy was saying. 'Slowly. Take it easy.'

'She's gone . . . I thought she would stay with us, but she's gone. I wanted her to stay.'

He was not weeping for the cat, but for his parents and sister,

33

for everything that had happened since he snuggled down peacefully in bed the night before. Matthew said:

'She'll come back. She was frightened, that's all. I was frightened, too. Don't worry. She'll feel better after a time and she'll come back.'

Billy went on sobbing and Matthew stood close by him. He felt a tightness and misery inside himself which would not disperse; in a way, he envied him.

In the afternoon, Matthew set up camp. The need to be out in the open clashed, he found, with a fear of the open, a longing to huddle against some protecting thing. He finally settled on a corner of a field, on high ground. Most of the surrounding hedge was down, but a clump remaining on the corner itself gave an illusion of security. A douit came from the next field into this along the bottom of the hedge. He was able to trace it back and found that it ran about a quarter of a mile, apparently uncontaminated, to an underground spring. It was as safe as any water on the island would be.

From his garage he had rescued a tarpaulin. It was stiff and cracked, but would shelter them from the rain. Not that there was any sign of that, at the moment: the day had all the calm and golden peace of summer. He secured the ends of the tarpaulin to stakes of wood driven into the ground, making a forward-sloping roof, and tied blankets up for sides. In the end he had a square tent-like construction which could house the two of them fairly comfortably. He used Cobweb as a beast of burden, and got a couple of mattresses up to the field, taking them from the ruins of the Lucie house. He found Miss Lucie's body while doing so, and, after covering her, drove an upright piece of wood in to mark the spot. He decided he would do that in future, to avoid turning bodies up again in later salvaging operations.

The light faded, the sun setting in a cloudless sky. Matthew made another stew with foods from the broken freezer, and afterwards opened a tin of peaches. He had found spoons during the afternoon; he was beginning to build up his supply of useful articles. He would have liked a cup of coffee, but had not come on any yet. And cigarettes. He was not a heavy smoker, but he could have done with one now.

Their tent opening looked south. It was full dark when they settled down, and they could see out to the starry sky. And a horizon that glowed faintly. In France? A town burning, or a new volcano? The latter seemed a little more probable. There had been no sign of fire here; probably the successive shocks had put out any that might have started.

'Are you all right, Billy?', he asked.

'Yes, Mr Cotter.' There was a pause. 'She hasn't come back, has she?'

'The cat? Give it time. We'll find her again. Go to sleep now, Billy.'

Matthew himself lay awake for some time. The lift which had come from finding the boy, from the need to look after him, was lost in the quiet dark. Depressed and wretched, he stared at the glow on the horizon. It varied in intensity, flickering, flaring up and dying down. A volcanic fire, he supposed, would look like that, but so might a burning city. He tried to feel something for all the others, the millions, who had died or were still suffering. But it was no good: there was no projection. Except for one.

It seemed that as soon as he fell asleep, he was dreaming. It was all happening again, the shock and roll of the earth, the crash of bricks, the giant's howl of the withdrawing sea. But in and through it all he could hear Jane's voice, calling him. He struggled and woke in a sweat to find that the earth was indeed in shock, but only with one of the mild tremors they were becoming used to. Billy was sleeping. Matthew lay awake, remembering the sound of his daughter's voice crying out.

FOUR

In the early morning there was a quite violent shock which woke them both. It lasted for something like half a minute, and in the field outside Cobweb brayed her distress. Matthew reached out and gripped the boy's hand.

'Easy. Easy, old son. It's not really a bad one. In fact, it's just about over.'

There was very little light, but he could see that Billy's face was white. He said:

'I thought it was happening again.'

'Nothing like that. It's stopped. You see? How's the arm feeling?'

'Stiff. It's not bad, though.'

'Good.' Matthew pulled himself up out of the blankets. 'Look. Now that the alarm clock's gone off, I'm going to get moving. I'll make us some breakfast, and then I want to go out foraging. I want to get hold of as much stuff as I can during the next day or two.'

Billy sat up, too. 'I'll come with you.'

'No need.'

'But I'd like to.' He hesitated. 'I don't want to stay on my own.'

'Fair enough. Can you manage to wash yourself with one hand?'

Matthew had put kindling—paper and wood—under cover in the tent, and he took them out and set about making a fire. The moon was paling in a sky from which the stars had faded. There was a small fresh breeze from the east. The donkey, at peace again, cropped the dewy grass. He made the fire, opened a tin of pork sausages, and cooked them. They speared them on slivers of wood and ate them. Matthew was reminded of a recent cocktail party, the little sausages on toothpicks being carried round on a silver plate, the atmosphere of slightly

36

vicious chatter and tasteless luxury. Only ten days ago? It seemed much longer.

They tethered Cobweb in a new patch—this was a hayfield and had been almost ready for cutting—and set out. St Peter Port was the first objective Matthew had set himself. It had obviously been terribly damaged but the shops there, if he could get to them, would provide all sorts of things that they needed. He had given some thought to the best way of approaching the town and decided that the south, the Val de Terres, offered this. They could reach it by way of mainly open country, avoiding the need for climbing over rubble and then, going down the hill, get into the town itself from the Esplanade. Once there, he had a mental list of priorities: chemist, hardware, food, footwear. He would get as much out as possible and stack it in a cache. Later he could bring Cobweb in to help get it all back.

Going past ruins they called out as before, but not expecting any reply. They saw three dogs in all, and a couple of cats, but not the one that had visited them the previous afternoon. There were some strange sights: in one place a wall had survived, all of eight feet high, and in another a television set, apparently undamaged, showed them its blank screen from the top of a small pyramid of debris. And some unpleasant ones. A case where a man seemed to have got halfway out of a window before the house collapsed and the frame crushed him. An arm, bleached of blood, lying in grass like a branch fallen from a tree. A baby that, though dead, seemed untouched until, coming nearer, he saw that rats had been there during the night. He turned away, sickened, and managed to prevent the boy seeing that.

He made a short detour to take in Meg Ashwell's house. It had stood in a dip, surrounded by quite a large garden. A chasm gaped across the neat lawn and continued through to the house itself. The fragmentation and destruction were so great that there could be no hope of anyone having survived beneath it. Matthew stared at it for a time, but did not call. Billy said at last:

'Did someone you know live there, Mr Cotter?'

'Yes.' He turned away, not wanting to disturb the sunlit silence. 'We'd better get on.'

So they came up the hill to the jumble of bricks that, like a high water mark, outlined the Fort Road. This was the point which offered one of the finest views in the island—the Fort George headland, green and wooded, on one's right, ahead the expanse of sea, broken by the other islands, Herm and Jethou and the more distant Sark and, on good days, Alderney, its cliffs bright in the sunshine. And the town below, the huddled terraces dropping, layer on layer, towards the waterfront and the harbour.

He saw the islands first. They stood where they had always stood, but islands no longer; between and round them lay the rock and sand and banks of weed of the sea bed. In the middle of the Russell a cargo boat sat, broken-backed, on an upthrust shoal. Nearer, Castle Cornet was broken, leaving a few bits of wall. It looked, on its rocky eminence, like a shattered tooth. Nearer still . . .

He had expected total ruin, even a desert of smashed brick and stone, all salient features destroyed. But the reality had power to amaze and shock him. The town had gone completely. Where there had been houses and shops one saw raw earth and rock, the contours, exposed again, of the time before history. All that remained was a vague outline of front and harbour; at one point the twisted stub of one of the big cranes stood out. As he looked more closely, he saw that the bed of the Russell, as far as the eye could see, was speckled with debris. What he had seen before on the island had been ruin: this was obliteration.

Billy stood beside him. He said, in a quiet voice:

'What did it?'

'The sea.'

'All that?'

'Like a wall,' Matthew said, almost to himself. 'A wall of hammers, battering rams, bulldozers, beating and scouring. My God! And to think I thought there might have been fire there.'

They were silent, looking down. It was possible to trace the course of the tidal wave by the great smear of erasure, running along the sides of the hills on which the town had been built, to the north spilling inland. There would be nothing left of St Sampson, either, very little of anything on the far north of the island.

Billy said: 'Are you going to go down there, Mr Cotter?'

He shook his head. 'Not now.'

But he continued to stare, trying to force eye and memory to come to terms with each other. Billy turned away. He said suddenly:

'Mr Cotter!'

'Yes, Billy?'

'A man.'

He spun round himself. The figure was approaching them, and not more than fifty yards away. He seemed to be about sixty, but his condition made it difficult to judge his age with any accuracy. His feet were bare, black with dirt, and he was wearing only a pair of pyjamas of torn and stained red cotton. His long thin face was blackened and bruised, his hair thick with dust. His hands, Matthew saw, were scarred and bleeding.

The extraordinary thing was the way he came towards them without any sign of recognition or greeting. Matthew wondered if he could be blind until he noticed the assurance with which he walked over the uneven ground. He called out to him:

'So you've survived, too! What part are you from?'

The man made no reply. He was not walking direct to them, but to a spot a few yards away. He stopped, gazing at the abraded slopes where the town had been.

'God looked at them,' he said. It was a normal, educated voice. 'The saints and prophets had warned them, but they took no heed. Then in the night God looked down and wept for their iniquity. And his tears were like thunderbolts, and his sigh was a tempest.'

Matthew said: 'You look as though you've had a rough time of it. Have you eaten anything since it happened? You'd better come back with us, and we'll get you some food.'

He walked over to the man and touched him on the arm. The man did not turn his gaze from the scene below.

39

'Down there,' he said. 'Down there they lived. Down there they ate and drank, lied and cheated, danced and gambled and fornicated. And in a second, in the twinkling of God's eye, they were swept away.'

'You ought to eat something,' Matthew said. 'Come back with us.'

He took hold of the man's arm, to guide him. He brushed it away, but looked at Matthew for the first time.

'Then why spare me?' he asked. 'I lied and cheated, I lusted and gluttonized and blasphemed. Why was I spared the terrible vengeance?'

It was not the madness which was disgusting, Matthew thought, but the self-obsession. Though one could argue, perhaps, that this was what madness was. But the melodrama, the note of ham that crept in as the voice went on? He thought: there is nothing I can do for this man, and it is bad for the boy. He said quietly:

'We need to be getting back, Billy. There's no point in staying here.'

Billy, who had already backed warily away, nodded eagerly. They began to retrace their steps. The man called:

'Wait!'

Matthew turned round. He took a step in their direction.

'I must confess my sins,' he said. 'Before God looks again, I must confess my sins.'

'Confess them to God, then,' Matthew said. 'I'm not a priest.'

He touched Billy's shoulder and they walked on. There was a scrabbling of loose stones behind, and he realized that the man was following them.

'Listen,' he said, 'listen. I blasphemed. I took the name of the Lord God in vain. I cheated. When I was in business in England, I put money in my own pocket that should have gone to the company, to the shareholders. I drank, and I did not observe the Sabbath. I lusted after women . . .

He was walking at about ten paces distance, calling out. As Matthew stopped, he stopped also. Matthew said:

'Shut up. We don't want to listen. We don't want to hear

what you did, or anything about you. Go away and find peace in your own way.'

He started walking on again, with Billy beside him. The voice resumed:

'You will listen.' There was petulance in it, as well as melodrama. 'You must listen so that I can save my soul. Because I have been a great sinner, as great as any of those who were killed by God's wrath. There was a woman. She is dead now, with all the others. She had a mouth like honey, breasts like sweet soft fruits. She looked at me and I was tempted . . .'

Matthew stooped and picked up a loose stone. 'Go away,' he said. 'Shut up and go away. I mean it.'

He stood looking at Matthew, and laughed. 'You must listen to me. I was the only one saved, and now there is you and the boy. You to listen to my confession of my sins, the boy to carry my message to future generations. For I lusted after this woman, and one night . . .'

Matthew threw the stone, but it missed him. He began to laugh again, and Matthew picked up half a dozen stones and threw them, feeling an insensate violence, a need to maim and kill. Stones struck the man on his arms and body, and he went on laughing. Then a stone hit him on the cheek, and the laughter stopped. He put his hand up to his face, and the blood trickled through his fingers. He stood still, staring at them.

Matthew said: 'Stay away from us.'

He gathered Billy again, and walked on. There was no sound of footsteps behind them. When they had reached the crown of the hill, he glanced back. He was standing there, not moving.

Billy said: 'He was mad, wasn't he?'

The disgust was with himself now. He did not know how one was supposed to cope with a lunatic in a world broken down to the bed-rock of existence, and he had the boy to look after. But this was, perhaps, the one other survivor, and he had stoned him. Worse than that was the recollection of how he had felt, of the deep joy welling up at the sight of blood.

'Yes,' he said, 'he's mad. It's not his fault, you know. I think he was trapped somewhere and had to dig himself out. He can't help the way he is.'

Billy said with satisfaction: 'You drove him off, all right, Mr Cotter. You really hit him with that last one. I bet that hurt him.'

He wanted to say something to the boy that would explain it, but could not find the words. And if he had, would there have been any difference between himself and the man back there? Both of them hawking their consciences and self-concern to an unwilling, uncomprehending audience. He said:

'We'll head for St Martin's, Billy. There's a chemist's shop there. I'll have a dig and see what we can find. There's a hardware shop, too, and foodstores. It will be better really than St Peter Port would have been. We shan't have to carry things so far to our camp.'

'It is a camp, isn't it, Mr Cotter?' He paused. 'Shall I build a pile of stones up by the tent—in case he comes there?'

'No,' Matthew said. 'I don't think that will be necessary.'

They saw the group of people when they were some distance away from them. They were coming up from the Hubits valley, and the people were at La Bellieuse. There were at least half a dozen of them, a couple digging in the rubble and the rest standing by. One of them saw Matthew and the boy about the same time, and waved an arm in greeting. Billy clutched Matthew's hand.

'Is it all right?'

'All right?'

'They won't have gone mad, too, will they?'

'I shouldn't think so.'

He was thinking about his own reactions. From the moment of finding Billy, there had been the feeling in the back of his mind that there would be others. It had been something to hope for, a protection against the otherwise hopeless loneliness of their future. The man they had met at the top of the Val de Terres had made him sure of this. Others would have survived, and in due course they would find them; there would be people to live and work with, to take some of the weight of responsibility for the boy off his shoulders. Now the hope, the conviction, had become reality, and he wondered why he was not overjoyed. He walked towards them, Billy at his side, and felt disturbed in a way he could not explain to himself.

The two who had been digging broke off as they came up. There were seven in all. Three were female—a thin dark ugly woman of about sixty, a plump fair stupid-looking girl in her early twenties, and a girl a year or two younger than Billy. They seemed to be in good physical shape, apart from cuts and bruises. Of the four men, one was quite old, one around Matthew's age, and the remaining two, he thought, about twenty-five. One of these, weedy, with curly blond hair, was sitting down, his right leg, splinted and bandaged, stretched out in front of him. The old man had his head bandaged with a dirty-looking cloth and seemed to be running a fever. The man Matthew's age was apparently unhurt but looked dazed and a little sick. The only one who showed any sign of real vigour was the second of the young men. The others wore an odd assortment of clothes which did not match and in many cases did not fit, either. He was wearing blue overalls which, although stained and dusty, gave him an air of efficiency, and high leather boots. He looked at Matthew and the boy thoughtfully, and put his hand out.

As Matthew took it, he said:

'My name's Miller, Joe Miller.'

'Matthew Cotter. And the boy is Billy Tullis.'

He ran his hand roughly through Billy's hair. 'Hello, Billy. Had a bit of an accident with your arm, then?'

'It got broken in the earthquake. Mr Cotter fixed it.'

'Good for Mr Cotter.' He turned his attention to Matthew. 'We can do with someone who can be useful. There's not a lot of usefulness in this bloody bunch.' He had thick, quite long hair, and his chin was blue with a heavy beard stubble; he was powerfully built, handsome in a conventional way, and looked at Matthew with steady grey eyes. 'I'll be glad of someone who can lend a hand with things.'

The hour threw up the man, of course, and Miller, as far as this group was concerned anyway, was undeniably the man. It was also something that he was aware of and determined to maintain: there had been assertiveness in his voice, a challenge to the newcomer.

Matthew said: 'Are there any others, do you know?'

'Alive, you mean. Haven't seen any. Have you?'

'One man, but he was—well, unbalanced.'

'Off his nut?' He regarded his companions with contempt. 'So are most of these. Their brains are still addled from that shaking they got. You've seen the town?'

Matthew nodded. 'Just now.'

'First place I headed when I managed to get clear. What a bloody mess. St Sampson the same. This is the only sizeable shopping centre that hasn't been swept away.'

'That's why we came here,' Matthew said. 'I was thinking of the chemist's, in particular.'

'Great minds, eh?' He chewed his heavy lower lip. 'The chemist's, yeah, I didn't think of that. We're still after food and clothing. But you're right, though. We ought to give that priority. Things like bandages and stuff. Need to get them out before it rains.' He looked at Matthew sharply. 'Where did you kip last night?'

'We rigged up a tent in a field, not far from my place. That's St Andrew's.'

'We're fixing ourselves a site up above Saint's Bay.' He grimaced. 'Some bloody bay it is now, too. Handy for this part, and it should be out of stink range. You'd better bring your gear over.'

He had a crude intelligence, or, at least, shrewdness. Matthew nodded slightly. Billy said:

'We've got a donkey.'

'Have you, now!' He looked at Matthew. 'In good shape?'

'Yes. Not all that young, though. One of those Miss Lucie kept.'

'As long as it's got four good legs. I've seen a few cows alive but too crippled to last. Mother Lutron'—he jerked his head in the direction of the older woman—'says she saw one up and grazing. But she's seen angels, too, and Jesus Christ coming in his glory. Tell you what—we'll go and get your animal now, before it gets knocked off.'

'By whom?'

'You never know. Or strays. We can load your stuff on it.' He spoke to the middle-aged man. 'Harry, try and keep them at it till we get back. I'll want to see how much you've got out.'

Matthew said: 'You can stay here, if you like, Billy.'

'I'd rather come with you, Mr Cotter.'

Miller gave him a friendly pretended punch to the chin.

'You stay and look after little Mandy. She needs someone to play with.' The boy looked reluctant. 'Go on then, lad. Do as you're told.'

Billy looked inquiringly at Matthew, and he nodded. Billy went over to where the girl was standing. They were looking at each other uncertainly, as Matthew and Miller moved away.

'The younger generation,' Miller said. 'I like kids, providing they do as they're told. And we'll need them.'

Matthew said: 'You're thinking in terms of long-range planning, then?'

'Long-term, short-term—the one thing certain is that things have got to be worked out. We've got to know what we're doing, and do it right. There's one thing we need to get straight, by the way.'

The eyes looked at Matthew intently from under the heavy black brows. Matthew said:

'What's that?'

'Shirley.' Matthew showed his surprise. 'The little blonde. She's mine.' He paused, but Matthew made no response. 'I can see you're a hell of a lot more capable than that lot I've got myself lumbered with. You and I can work together. I don't see any reason why we shouldn't get on, but I don't want any trouble about the girl.'

'There won't be,' Matthew said, 'as far as I'm concerned.'

'Right!' He spoke with confidence, but looked relieved. 'I just wanted to make sure we understood each other. Now let's go and get that donkey.'

They had their mid-day meal not far from the diggings. The two women made a stew in a big pan—a jamming pan, Matthew thought—and ladled it out into various receptacles: smaller pans, a couple of empty tins which had held fruit, a battered cake tin. There was one unbroken soup plate, which was given to Miller. They had a mess of defrosted strawberries afterwards, with tinned cream. Later they sat in the sun, smoking cigarettes. The one Matthew had was a bit squashed, but tasted good.

They had acquired another person during the morning. His name was De Portos and he had the typical Guernsey physique: short and stocky build, round cheeks, a strong nose and slightly protruding eyes. He was in his early thirties, the son of a Vale farmer. Miller, who was sitting apart with Matthew, nodded in his direction.

'We're doing well for men. Useful as far as the work is concerned—if I can get the bastards working, that is—but it might not be so easy later on. We could do with more women.'

Matthew realized that he was being built up as the lieutenant to the chief. He regarded this with indifference, tinged with a wry amusement. He said:

'Ought we not to do something more positive about looking for survivors? I thought at first I was the only one, but more and more are turning up. I suppose it's difficult, even with a disaster on this scale, to make an entirely clean sweep of forty-five thousand people.'

'Where do you start looking?' Miller asked. 'We dug the kid out, and Mother Lutron, and Andy.' Andy was the one with the broken leg. 'But how do you know where to dig if you don't hear them shout? And the few that are still alive have probably got their mouths covered with muck.'

'We could make a sweep,' Matthew said. 'Spread out like a line of beaters. Call, and see if we get an answer.' He looked up at the sun, hot and innocent in a cloudless sky. 'If there are any still trapped, they won't last long. The food and stuff will keep better.'

Miller lit a new cigarette from the stub of the old, and offered one to Matthew, who shook his head. The cigarettes were kept with the rations and doled out as appropriate, but Miller had his private supply. He said:

'I think you've got something there. And this bloody lot can walk, and listen, even if they can't work. We'll lay off the digging here. We've got enough out to last us for a few days, and, as you say, it will keep.'

'Talking of which,' Matthew said, 'I don't think we ought to rely on the stuff from the frozen food chests after today. It's a bit risky.'

'It's wrapped in that plastic stuff—poly what-you-call-it.'

'All the same, I think it would be taking a chance.'

Miller puffed smoke out. 'You're probably right. And we're not short of tinned stuff.' He looked at Matthew, grinning. 'I like you, Matty. You've got your head screwed on. What a relief to have someone with some bloody sense around! Sure you won't have another fag?'

'No,' Matthew said. 'Not now, thanks.'

Miller planned the operation. His idea was that they should head for Torteval by way of Forest, coming back through King's Mills. Matthew had reservations about the possibilities of completing a sweep of this extent, but kept them to himself. They left Mother Lutron, Andy and the two children behind: Billy protested about it but Miller cut him short. He was right, Matthew thought. If they had to dig for survivors they were likely to turn up the ones who had not survived also. However accustomed to horrors the children had become, there was no point in adding to them.

In fact, they did not get much more than halfway to Torteval. They had the first response to their calls from the ruins of a large house just past the airport: a woman's voice, moaning. It was about an hour before they reached her. During that time she moaned occasionally but made no coherent reply when they spoke encouragingly to her. They found her finally pinned down by a beam resting across her thighs; she was a woman about thirty, buxom, with long dark hair matted round her face and breasts. She shrieked in pain when they came to lift the beam. They got it away from her, and she went on shrieking, though less piercingly.

Miller said: 'What do we do about this?'

'I don't think there's a lot we can do,' Matthew said. 'Broken pelvis for a certainty, spine maybe damaged, and God knows what internal injuries. Morphine is the only thing that might help, and we haven't got morphine.'

'She's dying, isn't she?'

'I think so.'

'I bloody know so. If we'd brought that gun of yours along . . .' He looked at Matthew challengingly. 'Except that we can't spare that solitary cartridge.'

Matthew said: 'I'll see if I can get her to take some codeine. Not much good, but better than nothing.'

Codeine was one of the things they had found in the tangled litter that had been the chemist's shop. Matthew pounded half a dozen tablets up, and mixed them with water in one of the empty fruit tins. They lifted her head, the shrieks rising to a new pitch. To his surprise, though, she made an effort to drink the liquid. Instinct, probably, rather than co-operation—after thirty-six hours she must be suffering acutely from thirst. They gave her some ordinary water afterwards and she drank greedily. She stopped shrieking, but groaned continuously.

Miller had been standing back, watching. He said now:

'That's no good. And we're wasting time. Ashley!' This was the old man. He was white-haired, tall, running to fat, and had been complaining about having difficulty in walking. 'Stay with her. And give her a sip of this from time to time.'

He produced the stone bottle of gin, which was the only liquor that had been retrieved so far. Miller had taken it in his personal charge. He handed the bottle to Ashley.

'This is more likely to keep her quiet. But don't overdo it, and for Christ's sake don't spill any. I need a spot of that to keep me going.'

They found another survivor in a house near St Peter's church. This was a man called Mullivant; apart from shock and a nasty gash in his upper arm, he seemed all right. But they had trouble with him because of his family. His wife and two daughters were under the rubble, and he would not come away without them.

Miller said: 'They're dead. You're not the only one. Every single one of us has lost his family. Don't be bloody stupid, man. There's nothing you can do for them.'

'They may be alive.'

'We've been yelling our heads off the last couple of hours.'

'I mean, unconscious.'

'They're dead, I tell you.'

He said desperately: 'I don't believe you. You've got to help me dig them out.'

Miller stared at him for a moment. He said: 'Come over here.'

They had found the children's bodies while digging for the man, and had covered them with blankets from their beds. Miller took him to the nearer one, and pulled the blanket back. This was the child whose face had been badly crushed; Matthew did not know whether Miller had forgotten it, or whether the act was deliberately brutal, an intent to shock. While Mullivant stared, Miller said:

'Do you want to see the other?'

Mullivant shook his head and, bending down, covered the battered face again. Miller said briskly:

'All right, then. Let's be going.'

'My wife . . .'

'She's dead, too.'

'You didn't find her body, did you?'

Miller stared at him with exasperation that seemed only just short of breaking into violence. Then with a swift gesture of impatience, he said:

'If you want to have your nose rubbed in it! We'll find her.'

They came on her quite soon, a young auburn-haired woman, her face peaceful, unmarked except by the plaster dust which had settled like a white mask on her. Mullivant, gazing at her, wept, with shuddering sobs that racked his body. Miller allowed this to continue for a time, and then said:

'Cover her up, and we'll go.' When Mullivant made no response, he shook him by the arm. 'You'll feel better when you get away from here.'

Mullivant said: 'I'm not going.'

'What the hell good do you think you can do by staying? They're dead. You're alive. You've got to look at things straight.'

'You go,' Mullivant said. Tears had streaked lines down the grime of his face. He looked at Miller in an agony of blankness. 'Thanks for getting me out. I'll be all right now.'

'You want some nourishment,' Miller said. 'You'll feel better when you've got food inside you. And a drink! We can give you a tot of something on the way back. That'll set you up.'

He gave no sign of having heard anything. He said, in a reasonable voice:

'I'll be all right. I'd rather you left me.'

Miller looked at Matthew, who shrugged. He said:

'Righto. It's your own concern. We're at the top of Saint's Bay. You know how to get here?' Mullivant nodded. 'Come in your own time, then.' Miller turned to the others. 'Time for us to be getting back, too. We'll cut a bit north—make it a slightly different route.'

They found no more survivors, but in one place the body of a man clear of the patch of rubble which had presumably been his house. Matthew thought he had been thrown clear and killed at the same time, but Miller corrected that.

'Look at his watch,' he said.

It was a gold Omega; the pyjamas, Matthew now saw, were silk. It had a sweep-second hand which was moving round steadily. Miller eased the bracelet, an expander, over the dead hand, and held the watch to Matthew's ear.

'Automatic. Still going, so it must have had movement in the last twenty-four hours. And look at his hands, fingers. He dug his way out, and then collapsed. Tough.'

'Yes,' Matthew said. The man had been in his fifties; he could have been a heart case. 'Shall we cover him up?'

'Does it make any difference?' Miller slipped the watch on to his wrist and looked at it admiringly. 'Time's too valuable.'

They came back to the place where they had left Ashley with the woman. He was sitting on a chunk of granite, and as they came up, he said, without looking up:

'She's dead.'

'Thank God for that,' Miller said. 'I'll have the bottle, then.'

He put his hand out and, after a momentary hesitation,

Ashley gave it to him. Miller took the stopper out and wiped the rim on his sleeve. Then he hefted the bottle in his hand, weighing it. He shook it, listening to the slosh of liquid.

'It's bloody near empty!' He stared at Ashley, and said quietly: 'There's getting on for half a bottle gone. What happened to it?'

'She was in pain—moaning and groaning all the time.' He looked up at Miller helplessly. 'It was the only thing that quietened her a bit. I couldn't stand her being in all that pain.'

'When did she die?' Miller asked.

'Not long ago,' Ashley said. 'Quarter of an hour, maybe twenty minutes.'

'Stand up,' Miller said. 'You can stand, can't you? Here, I'll help you.' He transferred the bottle to his left hand, and assisted Ashley with the other. They were about the same height. Standing close to the older man, Miller said: 'How long ago did you say she died?'

'Half an hour, perhaps.'

'You lying bastard!' His voice was still calm. 'She's been dead since just after we left you, hasn't she? You drank that gin yourself. You sat there and guzzled my bloody gin, didn't you?'

'I only had one drop. It was when I realized she was dead. It just got me . . .'

'Shut up! You stink of it. You can't even stand straight.' Without warning, he swung a savage open-handed blow which caught Ashley on the jaw and sent him flying to sprawl on the bricks a foot or two from the dead woman. Miller went over after him. 'Stand up.' Ashley groaned, but made no attempt to rise. Then Miller kicked him viciously in the side. He kicked him twice more, and turned away. He said to Matthew:

'That's what I call a good afternoon's work. One man who won't leave his corpses, one woman dead, and half a bottle of gin gone. Let's get home.'

The rest followed him obediently. When they had gone about a hundred yards, Matthew looked back. Ashley had got up, and was limping after them.

Clouds came up late in the afternoon, but they were high and did not threaten rain. They had their evening meal at the camp; while it was being prepared, Matthew wandered away and stood on the cliff top. If one looked directly down one might think, seeing the sand, that this was just low tide, but the eye went out, looking for the familiar peace of the waves. And finding only jagged rocks and desolation, a moon landscape. The tide had gone, far out and forever.

He was not in a mood for company, and sat apart from the others after supper as well. He could hear their voices, and catch occasional snatches. Most of them seemed to be back on the subject of the earthquake—they went on, over and over again, telling their own experiences, how they had felt, how they had managed to get free. It was something they could not leave alone; they probed it like tongues feeling cavities left by a dentist. They would tire of it in due course, presumably. Matthew fought down a feeling of contempt. One must face realities, he told himself, make the best of what one had. For some time at least he must remain among these people; perhaps he would have to live out his life with them. He thought, with a frisson of pain, of Jane, of her freshness, her bright honesty. That was a reality he ought to face, too, and turn his mind away from the memory. But it was too good. Even though it hurt, he could not do without it.

The reverie was broken for him by a new scene of violence. Miller had gone off somewhere along the cliffs, and in his absence their most recent recruit, De Portos, had gone to sit with the girl, Shirley. After a time, De Portos apparently persuaded her to go with him for a walk. They were heading away from the cluster of ramshackle tents which formed the camp when Miller met them on his way back. He wasted no time in talking, but swung at the shorter man. De Portos dodged the main force of the blow, and hit back. The two men grappled and punched at each other while the girl looked on, her silly podgy face showing mingled pleasure and alarm.

Miller was much the stronger and slightly the more skilful and the fight ended with De Portos on the ground, displaying no inclination to get up. Miller went over to the girl and slapped her face hard enough to make her cry out. She ran back to the tent she shared with him, weeping, and disappeared inside. Miller looked after her, and came over to sit by Matthew.

'Stupid little sow,' he said. 'Mind you, I'd have had to do it eventually to one of them. Probably have been Andy, except for his broken leg—I've seen him looking at her. But I reckon I ought to give her a proper lacing as well, to drive it home.'

'How long do you think you can keep it up?'

'Keep what up, Matty?'

'I wouldn't have thought she was the kind you could keep indefinitely in purdah.'

Miller was silent for a few moments. Matthew wondered whether the remark had offended him, whether, despite the way in which he spoke to her and of her, he was genuinely fond of the girl. But he said:

'Not indefinitely, maybe, but long enough.'

'Long enough for what?'

He looked sideways, grinning. 'To make sure she's up the spout, and to make sure it's mine.'

'And after that, you don't mind?'

'After that, I'll see. I'm a realist, Matty. After all, six men and only one girl that's ripe—four even if you count out yourself and Ashley. But there's got to be the kid first.'

'I suppose you want a boy?'

'By God, yes!'

'A son for King Miller the First.'

There was another pause. Miller's gaze went far out to the empty horizon, the darkening sky. It had been a cloudy sunset, and there were bars of black and vivid red in the south-west. Miller said:

'What do you reckon's happened everywhere else?'

'I don't know. Things must be pretty bad.'

'That's the way I see it. Or there would have been planes, wouldn't there? We can reckon Europe's been pretty well knocked out, and America, too, I suppose.'

Matthew remembered the evening at the Carwardines, the

quiet friendly talk with civilized people in front of a fire. He said:

'Not so long ago . . . someone was talking about the earthquakes. About the British Isles being outside the area where the big ones were likely to happen.'

'The laugh was on him.'

'He said the regions where they did happen were the ones where the last lot of mountain-building had taken place, places like the Alps and the Himalaya, and all the way round the Pacific. Perhaps this is a new lot of mountain building. How much have we been lifted? There's no way of knowing, is there? There may be another Everest in Norway, or New England. What I mean is, it's possible that we've got away comparatively lightly.'

'Do you think there's more to come?' There had been the by now customary earth tremors at intervals throughout the day, but nothing big. 'I mean, anything like that last lot?'

'Who knows? I wouldn't care to sleep inside a building for the next few months.'

'Not much hope of our having the chance, is there?' He took a cigarette and gave one to Matthew. 'Have one while they last. Things aren't going to be the same again, are they? Not in our lifetimes, anyway.'

'No.'

He took a light from Miller's cigarette. The man of roughly his own age who was called Harry was watching them hungrily. He would rather have given him the cigarette than be the subject of that melancholy stare, but there was no point in trying to do that—Miller would not have permitted it. Puffing smoke into the still air, Miller said:

'Better it happened now than winter.'

'Yes.'

'We can do things. We can get the place organized. We've bloody well got to, haven't we? A certain amount of hard sweat, but it's worth it. Then in twenty years' time or so the kids can take over.' He looked towards the tent from which the sound of heavy, artificial weeping still came. 'By God, she'd better have boys! And the first one had better be mine.' He called out towards the tent: 'Shut up! Shut up, you silly bitch.' Getting to his feet, he said: 'I think I'd better go and sort her out. Be seeing you, Matty.'

Matthew stayed where he was, smoking. There was Miller's raised voice inside the tent, the sound of a blow, louder wailing, and eventually quiet. Billy came over just as he finished the cigarette. He said:

'Mr Cotter.'

'Hello, Billy. How's the arm feeling?'

'Not so bad. Mr Cotter?'

'Yes?'

'I wish we could have stayed in our own camp.'

'It isn't possible. And you've got Mandy to play with here.'

The boy shrugged, but said nothing. He was still, of course, in the male-oriented world of the pre-pubertal boy. That would change. The two of them would grow up together and in due course . . . No, nothing so simple as that. The story-book days were over. The girl would be nubile when the boy was still too young to stake an effective sexual claim. One of the other men would take her if Miller did not. She would be a woman at twelve or thirteen, a mother within the following year. Billy might, if the dim-witted Shirley had the succession of boys Miller demanded of her, have to wait for Mandy's daughters to grow up. It was probably as good a pattern as any, he thought. It was just that he felt nothing for it, for the future, but indifference and distaste.

Billy said: 'We can't go back, then?'

'No. And even if we could, they wouldn't let us take Cobweb.'

It was a child's face, trying to comprehend adult perplexities. Would he take his own place as Miller's lieutenant, the guardian of his sons, or would there be conflict within the tribe, the old tyranny of greed and hate? No, Matthew thought, however it turns out, I don't think I want to see it.

'Better get to bed, Billy,' he said. 'We need to be up early in the morning.'

FIVE

THE next day was a good one.

It started with a confused alarm in the grey pre-dawn light, which Matthew became aware of as the sound of raised voices mixed with another noise which at first he thought was a foghorn. He stumbled out of the tent, half asleep, knowing that something was wrong with this, but uncertain what. He walked into a scene that might have been part of some bucolic slapstick film. Two of the tents had been knocked over and figures beneath one were trying to disentangle themselves from the blankets. Mother Lutron, in a nightgown plus guernsey, her feet enormous in men's grey woollen socks, was yelling powerfully for help. And the cause of the trouble stood gazing at her, counterpointing her distress though in a much lower key—a cow.

Things settled into perspective as people became more positively awake. Mother Lutron stopped having hysterics, and the others were helped out of the collapsed tents. Miller, in pants and shirt, came out to take charge, first sending a nude Shirley scuttling back into the tent. He stared at the cow with a greedy joy.

'That's lovely!' he said. 'Isn't she lovely, Matty? I didn't believe the old bag when she said she'd seen one, alive and uncrippled, but by God, she was right. And it came here, looking for her. Maybe she's a witch. Hey! Are you a witch, Mother? Better watch your step, or we'll build a little bonfire for you.'

It was a joke now, too feeble for anyone to laugh at, even though Miller made it. Matthew wondered whether it would go on being a joke in the hard years ahead. The island had a tradition of witches, and the fear of witches.

He said: 'It's fairly clear what she is looking for. See those udders.'

56

'Poor bloody beast,' Miller said. 'It must be like wanting a slash and having to bottle it up. Well, who's the prize milker round here? What about you, Matty?'

Matthew shook his head. 'I never acquired that skill.'

De Portos, in the end, admitted to having done a bit of milking in his young days, and on Miller's orders he got to work on the cow. He had to kneel to do it; he jetted the milk into one of the heavy plastic buckets which had been rescued and were kept for water. He made heavy weather of it at first, but gradually got into a rhythm. The others stood watching, and cheering him on.

'That's your job from now on, Hilary,' Miller said. 'Daisy's your responsibility. God help you if anything happens to her. Who knows, we may find a bull yet.'

After breakfast, the men set out on another search for survivors, this time concentrating on that part of St Martin's between Sausmarez Road and the cliffs. They found no one, but where a small garden had been converted into a dell by collapsed buildings which surrounded it, four hens scrabbled, throwing up sun-warmed dust. In one corner of the garden there was a clutch of three eggs, and in another, two. Miller ordered Ashley to look after the eggs, and threatened him with dreadful penalties if any was lost or broken. The hens were captured and their legs tied with string. He said to De Portos:

'You can take them back, Hilary. We'll make a run for them later on.' He looked more thoughtful as De Portos began tying the strung legs of the chickens together. 'No, second thoughts. You take them, Harry. Ashley can go back with you and give the eggs to the women to look after. We'll meet you again up towards Fort George.'

Even after the beating he had given both of them, Miller clearly did not trust De Portos near Shirley when he himself was away. The price of chastity, Matthew reflected, was going to have to be eternal vigilance. Rolling on her back was an instinctive reaction as far as Shirley was concerned, and De Portos, he suspected, was one of those natural lechers you sometimes found among short tubby men.

They saw the mad man as they approached the Fort headland;

he probably confined his roaming to the same small area in which Matthew and Billy had first met him. He kept his distance, contenting himself with bellowing vaguely apocalyptic phrases at them. Miller, in return, cursed him, colourfully and with vigour, but was content to leave it at that. He said:

'I suppose we might as well cut over towards the Vardes. It looks as big a mess as this lot, but there's no harm in checking.'

They each of them carried sacks, into which they put anything worthwhile which they happened to turn up. Matthew, while keeping his eyes open for objects of general usefulness, was concentrating on clothes, and particularly footwear, for Billy and himself. It might be a very long time before the community produced its first shoemaker. He was glad to be able to put away a couple of stout pairs of shoes, one pair Billy's size and the others which he would soon grow into, and a pair of boots for himself. He also found a single Wellington, a couple of sizes large for himself, and, after a little thought, took that as well. It was bulky, and pretty useless by itself, but there was the chance of finding a pair to it later on. Being too big was not important; he could always wear extra pairs of socks.

But his more important find was in one of the big houses off the Vardes. He was twenty or thirty yards from the others, poking about in a tangle of leather-bound books, shattered crystal glass, smashed wood and brick, when he saw the corner of a box and cleared away the surrounding rubbish. He knew what it was even before he saw the printing: this particular dark heavy oily cardboard was unmistakable. Number eight shot. Two dozen cartridges.

Matthew looked back towards the others. They were facing the opposite way; Miller had apparently caught sight of De Portos and Ashley and was yelling to them to hurry up and come along. It was something he would have to decide quickly. Miller had not actually commandeered the shotgun; with only one cartridge available he probably did not think it worth while antagonizing a man whose support he regarded as important. But if more ammunition turned up . . . Matthew had very little doubt as to what his reaction would be.

On the other hand, did it matter? The one thing certain was that he was not going to challenge Miller, for leadership or anything else. In which case, it would do no harm to let him have the cartridges and the gun. He listened to Miller shouting: 'Get a move on, you pair of idle buggers! I didn't tell you to take all day about it.' There were clouds in the sky, but the sun was shining at the moment. It was warm, and the air was heavy with the sweet rotten smell of death.

Matthew reached into his sack and pulled out the rubberized mackintosh which he had picked up earlier in the morning. He wrapped the box carefully in it, tucking it round so that there was a double layer of protection. Then, with a quick look to make sure he was still unwatched, he dug a hole in the rubble and wedged the box down into it, covering it with trash. He memorized the general position as well as he could, and then stuck in a broken thistle decanter as a marker.

They went back for their mid-day meal, and in the afternoon Miller said they would carry on the search, this time in the upper and inland parts of St Peter Port, which had escaped the tidal wave. Ashley protested; he said his feet were not up to it, that he had not yet found a pair of shoes which did not cripple him.

'You're not likely to find them, either, sitting on your arse, are you?' Miller asked him. 'All right, you can stay behind. But you're going to be useful. You can make a run for the hens. There's that chicken-wire we found in the ironmonger's. See you do a good job. I'll inspect it when we get back.'

Ashley took Matthew on one side before they set out. His face, naturally weak and flabby, looked a good deal worse with the addition of a two-day beard, though Matthew did not suppose that he himself looked much better, if at all. Ashley said:

'Would you have a look for a pair for me, Matthew? Ten and a half, if you can manage it. Broad fitting.'

His querulousness, and the way he added the last two words, tempted Matthew to ask him: 'Brogue or suède?' He said:

'I'll see what I can do. It's not the easiest size, though.'

'I've always had difficult feet,' Ashley said gloomily, 'even as a boy.'

The great tide had plunged through the Charroterie, and sucked back out again. They crossed a drying river bed, littered with the by-now familiar scourings, and with the bodies of people and domestic animals, swelling and putrefying in the sun. It was a relief to climb the hill on the other side, and to be surrounded by the more normal forms of destruction. The going was not easy. Litter from the houses formed a kind of scree which gave way beneath their feet. They made their way up slowly, sweating and cursing and from time to time slipping back. At last they came to more open ground and were able to make better progress. The sun was very hot again, and the stink of death seemed stronger here.

There was quite a severe shock, lasting about ten seconds, and to their horror a stretch of rubble immediately in front of them collapsed in on itself, leaving a gaping depression from which dust drifted up like smoke. After the tremor had died away, they stayed where they were, unwilling to risk advancing from the relatively safe ground on which they stood. Matthew was not sure whether the fear was in himself or whether it was communicated from the others, but he felt a reluctance to move which was, for a time, almost a paralysis. His muscles ached with the strain of his immobility.

Eventually, Miller said: 'Seems all right now. We can get moving again.'

Harry and De Portos objected. De Portos said:

'The only way I want to move is back. We've done enough looking. There's no one alive up here. The place looks as though it's been through a mincer. We're wasting our time.'

'Come on!' Miller said. 'Move when I tell you.'

They were still reluctant. He said, appealing, to Matthew:

'We can turn back at the top of the Grange. There's a repository down the Rohais which we ought to have a look at—should have plenty of tinned food in it. And we can head back through the Foulon.'

Matthew nodded. 'That's sensible. It's hardly any further, is it?'

He began walking forward, and the others followed.

Miller came up beside him. He said:

'How dangerous is it, do you think?'

'Because of that last quake? It looked worse than it was.'

'I was thinking of the bodies.' He sniffed the air. 'They're bloody ripe now, aren't they? What about disease?'

'I suppose it's a risk. But we're more likely to get things like typhoid from our drinking water than from this sort of jaunt, I should think. It ought to be boiled.'

Miller said: 'I'll get the women on that. All the same, I don't see we're doing a lot of good. Not much hope of finding anyone alive.'

The part they were traversing did give the impression of having been even more severely mangled than the others they had seen; in the immediate vicinity, Matthew could not see one brick still standing on another. In the distance a dog stood and silently watched them for a few moments before loping away. It looked like an Alsatian cross. Matthew said:

'The dogs will need thinking about, won't they? If we don't do something, they're likely to go wild, and if they do they might be dangerous.'

'I hate bloody dogs,' Miller said. 'Always have done. If I had a gun, I'd settle the buggers.'

'You can borrow mine.'

'With one cartridge? We'll hang on to that. In case there's a mutiny.'

They failed to find the repository Miller had mentioned. There were no landmarks left, no signs of anything but splintered ruin. From time to time they called out, as they had been doing all along, but the calls were increasingly perfunctory as they became discouraged. They were on the point of turning away towards St Andrew's, when De Portos said:

'What was that?'

'What?' Miller asked.

'Thought I heard something. Listen.'

They listened, and heard it. It was feeble and muffled, but unmistakably human. Miller called again, bellowing: 'Who's there?' and the response was immediate. A girl's voice. At a signal from Miller they fanned out and started covering the ground in the direction from which it had come. Matthew found himself at the right hand end of the line. He advanced cautiously, feeling his way. It would not do the person trapped any good to walk over her.

Miller found the point at which to begin digging, and they got to work. It was not easy: the wreckage here was matted, impacted on itself. Matthew did not see how the girl or woman could have survived. The answer lay in a stoutly-built cellar, with a particularly strong wooden floor protecting it. It had buckled in one place, but it had held. The stairs leading down to it were, of course, choked with rubbish, and that took further clearing. The sun was quite low by the time they got through it. Miller did the final burrowing, breaking a hole through. It was only then, in the confused outcry of relief and gratitude, that Matthew understood what had been troubling him about the voice from inside all along. It was not just one voice. There were two girls down there.

They staggered out with Miller's help, blinking and shading their eyes against the sun. They were dirty and dishevelled, and looked exhausted, but otherwise seemed to be all right. Miller gave the first girl water from the plastic bottle Harry had been carrying, and had to take it from her to prevent her drinking it all. She watched, gasping, as the other girl gulped down the rest.

The first girl was called Irene, the second Hilda. They had a flat, ground floor and basement, and had been sleeping in the basement when the shock came. It was an odd and unhealthy design for living, but it had saved their lives. The ceiling of the basement had collapsed on them, but that was only plaster, and one wall had collapsed. Hilda was clutching a broken pair of spectacles and crying continuously. Both girls were in their middle twenties. Irene, Matthew saw, would be attractive once she had a chance to clean and tidy herself.

He thought of Jane, bedraggled like these, being rescued perhaps from similar imprisonment, and felt a wave of sickness and misery. For a moment he hated them for being alive.

They found things chaotic at the camp. As a result of the fairly heavy shock, Mother Lutron had retreated again into delusions and babbling; she was staring at the sky and seeing, she proclaimed in a loud flat monotone, angels marching with spears of fire and shields brighter than diamonds. Andy was complaining that he had been thrown—that his splints had shifted and his leg was hurting badly. Billy had got the fire going, but nothing had been done about supper. Miller said to Ashley:

'Why the hell haven't things been got ready?'

'I've been making that run for the hens. You told me to do that.'

Miller looked angrily at the ramshackle arrangement of wire and bits of wood. He kicked the nearest post and it fell over.

'And a bloody fine job you've done on it, too. Anyway, where's Shirley?'

'In the tent.'

Miller yelled for her, and she came out. She had been crying and looked even less attractive than usual. Miller said:

'What about supper?'

She pointed at Mother Lutron. 'She wouldn't help. And I was frightened by the quake.'

Miller hit her with the back of his hand, and she cried out and started sobbing again. It had not been a hard blow but delivered, Matthew thought, with a more conscious arrogance. It was meant to impress the two newcomers who watched in silence.

'Now,' Miller said, 'get on with it.' He turned on Ashley. 'And you can help her, you useless old bugger. We'll fix up this chicken run you were supposed to have done.'

While the men were working on the run and Shirley and Ashley were preparing supper, Irene and Hilda went down with Mandy to the douit. They came back tidier and considerably cleaner. Irene was a very good-looking girl, with thick dark hair that was pretty now the dust had been brushed or combed out of it, large brown eyes, and regular open features. In a normal world, she would have been a girl most men would

63

have given a second glance, and her effect on them here, even on Harry and old Ashley, was unmistakable. Hilda, although nothing like as attractive—she had slightly protruding teeth and the blind stare of the myopic deprived of spectacles—was also wholesome and seemed pleasant. Shirley was a very ordinary little slut against either of them, and from her depressed look and sniffling whimpers appeared to be aware of it.

De Portos, in particular, was very attentive to both girls during supper. Miller, on the other hand, after an initial show of interest, was abstracted. He gave the impression of being engaged in working out a problem. Matthew guessed what the problem was and wondered how he would go about solving it—or rather, how he would go about presenting his solution to the rest.

At the end of the meal, Miller stood up abruptly. He said to Irene, in a clipped voice:

'I'd like to have a chat with you.' She looked up from the grass and nodded. 'We'll have a little walk.'

She stared at him without answering, and did not get up. With a gesture compounded of impatience and anger, he turned to Matthew.

'You come along, too, Matty.'

Matthew was amused by his apparent role of chaperon, but the girl seemed satisfied. They walked along the cliff top in the direction of Jerbourg. It was a blue glimmering evening, and there was a hum of midges in the air; the catastrophe, plainly, had not harmed them. Miller did not say anything, but there was a brooding quality to his silence which communicated to the girl—she started talking, rapidly and nervously, about the earthquake, and being trapped: the compulsive re-telling of disaster which had affected almost all the survivors. She broke off abruptly, when Miller said:

'It's all new. You realize that? Laws, and everything else—all gone. So there's got to be someone who decides what's going to happen.'

She said, with a touch of defiance: 'Oughtn't we to decide things among ourselves—I mean, all of us decide?'

'Listen,' Miller said, 'you're an intelligent girl. You know better than that. If it hadn't been for Matty and me organizing things, you'd still be down in that cellar. You don't think the rest of them would have bothered, do you?'

He was nervous, more nervous than Matthew had seen him before. The girl was much more self-possessed. Whatever the immediate outcome, Matthew had an idea she was going to be an important figure in the group.

She said, with a touch of coldness: 'We're very grateful for being rescued. I wouldn't like you to think anything else.'

Miller said: 'It's just that things have got to be done quickly now. And we can't have—well, loose ends. There's got to be someone in charge, and it happens to be me. The others have got to do as I say because it's the only way things will work.'

Irene said: 'I'm sure Hilda and I won't cause you any difficulties.'

'Hilda won't, but you might.' She looked at him inquiringly. 'You're a girl.' He looked away in embarrassment. 'A very pretty girl, too. You're likely to have trouble with De Portos, and maybe Harry—and Andy as soon as his leg's better.'

'I can handle any trouble there is.'

'No, you can't,' Miller said flatly. 'You don't realize yet, the way it's all changed. And I can't risk there being trouble in the camp. So I'm telling them, when we go back, that you're my girl.'

She gave him a cool look. She was someone who would be unlikely to make a wrong step out of rashness. She said:

'Hilda and I are going to fix up a tent to share.'

Miller said quickly, eager for the compromise: 'We'll fix up living quarters for you. I know the sort of girl you are. I'm not rushing anything. But you've got to be under my protection—the rest of them have got to understand that.'

'And Hilda?'

'She can do as she likes. As you like.'

There was a pause before she said: 'What about Shirley? I got the idea she was under your protection, too.'

'She's a slut. You can forget about her.'

Irene stopped. She said: 'I'm very tired. I'd like to go back now.'

It was a tacit and provisional acquiescence, which intrinsically left her free, even dominant. She was a strong-minded person. Were they heading, Matthew wondered, for a matriarchy? It could depend on this moment.

Miller talked forcefully, laughing a lot, on the way back. He was plainly relieved to have come through a delicate situation. His own role, Matthew saw, had not been merely that of chaperon, but also of validating authority. He hoped Miller was not coming to depend on him too much.

Halfway back to camp, he said: 'Listen.'

They all stood still, and Miller broke off what he was saying. It came out of the deepening blue, and Matthew wondered how such a sound could ever have been taken for granted, scarcely listened to. So one, at least, had survived. The bird sang a few more notes, and then was quiet.

SIX

FIVE days after the first shock, the good weather broke. Clouds gathered during the morning, and rain poured down torrentially in the afternoon and evening. They had a damp night of it—the tents leaked and in due course became almost useless as protection against the elements. In the early hours, the wind began to rise, and dawn broke over a wet and windy and generally wretched scene.

By ten o'clock they had abandoned their attempts to do anything with the tents and retreated from the camp site to a less exposed spot. This was found a quarter of a mile away, in the shape of an escarpment covered with the stubs of uprooted trees, whose position offered some defence against the wind and a little against the rain. Matthew made the tentative suggestion of taking to the caves at the foot of the cliffs, but this was not received well. It would be a difficult climb down, especially with Andy's broken leg, and an even more difficult climb back ... one could not set up a permanent camp in so inaccessible a place so why bother? ... and it would be dark there, and the smell of rotting weed ... The real objection, Matthew thought, was not stated: their intense fear of being surrounded and covered by anything more substantial than a tent. He felt it himself, a chill paralysing anxiety at the idea.

So they huddled miserably together for the rest of that day and the following night. Efforts to build a fire failed, and they were made more depressed by having to eat food cold out of the tins. Mother Lutron relapsed into mania, and from time to time went stalking off, shouting prayers and curses to the tattered streaming sky; but she did not go far and came back soon. First Shirley and then Hilda had crying fits, which died away into sniffling sobs only to break out with greater violence. Little Mandy cried, too, but more quietly. Billy did not, but Matthew saw his lip trembling now and then. He tried to keep the children cheerful by talking to them and getting them to play games like 'I Spy', but, Jane apart, he had never been particularly good with the young. It was a woman's job, really, but three of them were plainly worse than the children, while Irene had withdrawn into a prickly, non-communicative moroseness to which Miller danced an unavailing attendance. They slept fitfully through the long hours of darkness, and woke to a day as cold and blustery as the previous one. It was not actually raining, but obviously would rain again soon.

Mullivant joined them in the later afternoon of that day. He had been seen, after his rescue, when one of the last search parties passed close to the ruins of the house; he was standing near three newly-dug graves. Miller had called to him not to be a fool, to come with them, and he had shaken his head in silence, and looked away. Now he came to them, gaunt and soaking, and although he hardly spoke at all he accepted food from them, and, as evening turned into a third squally night, he lay down shivering with the others.

In the morning they were all cramped and cold and unhappy, and Harry and Mandy appeared to be running temperatures, but the wind had slackened and the clouds showed signs of breaking. They managed to get a fire going, and cooked tinned sausages and heated up beans with them. The invalids were dosed with codeine, and the rest set to work to re-organize things. They worked better—more purposefully and more willingly—than they had done in the immediate aftermath of the earthquake. It was as though the rain and privation had washed away some of the marks left by the shock. They accepted Miller's orders more readily, too, Matthew noticed. They had come together for mutual help and comfort, but it had been in a spirit of desperation. Now there was something else: the beginning of hope, perhaps.

When they resumed foraging again they found the repository Miller had spoken of. They made panniers for the donkey, and she and the men carried load after load of tinned foods back to the camp. A lot had been damaged in the collapse of the building, but what remained would see them comfortably through the winter and well into the following year. They also found, on the same site, several tarpaulins, in good condition, measuring twelve feet by eight. With these they made two large community tents, one for dining and one for general purposes. They were constructed and erected with more care than the earlier tents had been, and on the new site which afforded some protection from the north-easterly winds. It was tempting, Matthew thought, to imagine that history was beginning here, that the years ahead might bring to this spot a council hall, a palace, perhaps a temple to strange gods, but he did not think it likely. Even though it was no longer an island, he doubted that the trails of the world's commerce would lead here. And even on a local scale, when it came to building towns they would look for a more sheltered and more convenient place than this.

The small tents went up alongside the bigger ones, and patterns of relationship were established, or re-established. Part of the acceptance of Miller's position as leader lay in the acceptance of Irene as being outside the reach of the other men. She did not allow Miller any familiarities, and slept in a tent with Hilda, but she took the general deference for granted. Hilda was courted by De Portos and Harry and Andy—most assiduously by the first but with more probability of success, Matthew thought, by the last. He was still crippled by his leg, and she spent a lot of time looking after him. There was also the fact that both De Portos and Harry had resorted to Shirley for sexual release. The former had made no secret of this. Harry had been more furtive but everyone knew about it. They did not go to her tent, which she shared with Mother Lutron and Mandy, but took her out along the cliffs. She seemed contented enough, in her sluttish way.

The community developed in other ways. Three more lots of poultry were found, so that altogether they had fifteen hens and—an even greater blessing—a couple of roosters. One of these was a poor specimen and apathetic, but the other trod his subjects with great vigour. Two of the hens went broody, and sat on clutches of eggs. Everyone was delighted by this. The tinned foods, on which they chiefly lived, were a dwindling

69

asset; the chick embryos growing inside the warm eggs were an earnest of the future.

They had a feast of celebration, and drank canned beer on Miller's dispensation: a few crates had been found, their contents battered but in most cases not actually leaking, and in a moment of largesse he shared them out. (A few more unbroken bottles of spirits had turned up, which he was holding on to.) It was from the general noise and confusion and cheerfulness of the feast that Hilda looked up and saw the stranger. She called out in wonder, and they followed her pointing hand.

At first Matthew thought it was the mad man, who had not been seen since the storm. But this man was younger and taller and red-haired. He had obviously been living hard—harder even than they had. He was painfully thin, and dirty, and his clothes hung in tatters. They made a place for him near the fire, and gave him some of the stew which had been left over, and he ate ravenously. While he ate they questioned him, and between gulps he answered.

He was not from Guernsey at all, but Sark. He had wandered about that island after the catastrophe, searching for some other survivor without success. Then for some time he had lived a stuporous, almost vegetable existence, eating and drinking and sleeping, hoping vaguely that help would come from outside. On the previous day, though, he had woken to a sudden clarity of understanding that this was not going to happen. He had survived out of a few hundred on Sark; it was reasonable to believe that more had survived from the much larger population of the parent island. The sea had gone: there was nothing to stop him walking the nine miles to Guernsey.

He had set his course in the first place for the smaller islands of Jethou and Herm. Reaching them he had seen, in the clear level light of late afternoon, the devastation of the Guernsey east coast, the naked scar where St Peter Port and St Sampson had once been. This ruin, on so much larger a scale than the things he had seen on the other islands, had upset and depressed him. He had stayed the night on Herm, and not until late in the morning of the present day had he nerved himself for the final three mile stretch. He had reached Guernsey, made his way up the stinking ragged slopes of earth and rock which had been the capital of the bailiwick, and come out at last on to the southern plateau, all hope abandoned. It was then, in contemplation of his state as perhaps the last man left alive, that he had heard their voices in the distance, and staggered unbelievingly towards them.

He thawed as he talked from a frozen caricature into humanity. He was, Matthew thought, a naturally garrulous man, and it must have been hard for him to have no one to listen to him. As with several of the others, his sense of perspective was wildly out of true. He had been one of the Sarkees engaged in the carriage business, and he continually reverted to the fact that he had recently acquired an extra equipage for a season which was now going to be completely devoid of tourists. 'What about the winter, eh?' he asked. The winter was the lying-up time, in which the Sarkees lived on the fat of the previous summer. 'What will we do in the winter?'

When the novelty of his arrival had worn off, Matthew got the newcomer to himself, and asked him questions which had been in his mind since he became aware of his origin.

'What's it like, crossing the sea bed? Is the going very rough?'

'It varies. Good where there's sand, and where the reefs are not too spiky. Some nasty mud flats, but they're drying up. And the weed, eh? God, how it stinks! Worse than corpses, I reckon.'

'What sort of time did you make?'

'Time?'

'In getting across. A mile an hour? Less?'

'More. I got to Jethou in about four hours, I reckon. That's guessing by the sun. I picked up a watch but a day or so later I threw it away. Didn't seem to make any sense to know what time it was.'

'There's some water left out there, isn't there? One can see stretches of it.'

The Sarkee shrugged. 'Pools. You could call the big ones lakes, maybe.'

'How big?'

'One about a quarter of a mile long. She had mackerel in her. But they're drying up, eh? You can see where they're drying up—rings along the sides where they're shrinking.'

'So altogether you didn't find it too difficult?'

'Not once I'd got started. It was starting that was hard. Even after looking out and seeing it dry all that time, it still seemed wrong to be walking out there. Like I was frightened, eh? Of the sea coming back. I kept looking over my shoulder for it, and I was glad to climb up on Jethou. Though there's nothing there now except a bit of grass at the top. The big wave cleaned everything else off. The same with the harbour buildings in Herm . . .'

He went on talking, and Matthew let him ramble on, nodding from time to time as seemed appropriate. He was thinking of Jane, with a resurgence of hope he knew to be irrational but which he nurtured as the most precious thing that had happened since he had known the full extent of the disaster. Bemused by the holocaust of death and destruction in which he found himself, all he had been conscious of was the fact that no help had come from the world outside, from the mainland. The possibility of similar survivors out there had been beyond imagining. And even with the sea gone, the ingrained sense of insularity had remained. One thought of leaving the island in terms of the mailboat or the morning Viscount. The shock of someone coming from outside was two-fold—other communities might, almost certainly must exist on the mainland . . . and might be reached. Sark was only nine miles distant, Southampton over a hundred, but the *possibility* was there.

And from that possibility his mind went irresistibly to others. He could have had no hope if she had been in London, a speck in the biggest ant-heap of all. But at Mary's, in Sussex . . . It was an old staunchly-timbered house, on high ground, and she would have been sleeping, as she always did in the gabled room under the roof-tree. She might have come through it. The odds against might still be measured in hundreds, but he could visualize it now, could see her being helped out of the ruins as

72

the two girls here had been. She came alive to him again and the grief which had surrounded his thoughts and actions ebbed away. To be replaced by an anxiety and impatience. Once it was conceivable, reaching her became the one thing worthwhile. Matthew checked himself deliberately. There would have to be preparations. It was a long journey, through a land made unknown by total change. He must make his plans carefully.

Matthew thought about it during the night, lying awake for a long time and watching the stars through the tent opening. In the morning, he spoke to Miller. Miller was inattentive at first; De Portos had come back from milking with the idea that the cow might be in calf, and he was wrapped in visions of the herds of the future. Matthew had been talking for some while before he snapped into a response.

'What was that? Go to the mainland? Have some sense, Matty! You'd never bloody well make it, and if you did what good would it do?'

'It's my daughter,' Matthew explained again. 'She may be alive. I know the chances are small, but I want to make sure.'

Miller stared at him. 'You're off your nut.'

Matthew shrugged. 'Perhaps.'

Miller put an arm on his shoulder. 'I don't mean to be nasty. We've all been a bit off our nuts since it happened. We don't all rave like Mother Lutron and that silly old sod up by the Val de Terres, but we rave inside. I know I do. All the same, you've got to see the sense of this. You wouldn't do any good, on a crazy thing like that. Le Perré . . . it was different, him coming from Sark. He was on his own there, going crackers, running short of food probably—and only nine miles to go. You see what I mean?'

'Yes, I see. But it makes no difference.'

'I tell you, it's like committing suicide!'

'That's a matter of opinion. At least, it doesn't concern anyone else.'

'Doesn't it, by God! A little group like this, we need every pair of hands. We can't spare anyone. You least of all. You're my right-hand man, Matty. I depend on you to keep things running, help organize them. You know I depend on you.'

'You don't need anyone now. It may have been different at the beginning, but it's all running smoothly enough.'

'Because you're here, it is.'

'I can't accept that.'

Matthew did not put his thoughts into words: that while it might be true that Miller was that kind of strong man who must have someone to lean on, the replacement was already present in the person of Irene. Miller did not see this because, although he acknowledged strength in a woman, he did not understand either the strength or his own deference to it.

Miller said, blustering: 'I don't give a bugger if you accept it or not, Matty. I'm telling you that's the way it is. I need you here.'

'You'll learn to manage without me.' He smiled. 'You won't find it very difficult.'

'No!'

He had the forced, nervous, in a way desperate look that Matthew remembered from the time he had half-pleaded with, half-bullied Irene into accepting him as her protector. That situation could have gone badly if the girl had thwarted him and so, Matthew saw, could this. He said, trying to keep it light:

'Are you telling me I shan't be able to get an exit permit?'

Miller said heavily: 'You're not leaving, Matty. It's for your own good as well as ours. We're all a bit rocky still—you'll feel different in a few weeks. But get it in your head that you're not going away. If we have to, we'll tie you up to stop you.'

Matthew wondered if the others would follow him in such an enterprise. Perhaps, perhaps not. But it would do no good to provoke conflict, which would either leave him frustrated of his one objective, or else Miller defeated and the group disorganized. He saw that some of them, attracted by Miller raising his voice, were listening—De Portos, Hilda, little Billy. He said submissively:

'You're the boss. But I hope you'll change your mind. We'll talk about it again some time.'

Miller squeezed his arm, nervously laughing. 'Talking does no harm, Matty! As long as you realize that we can't spare you.

74

Come on, then. Let's have a look at that bloody cow. How do you tell when a cow's pregnant? You got any ideas about that?'

Matthew did nothing for a couple of days, in case Miller was watching him, and thereafter went about his preparations carefully and in secret. In the store of things which had been accumulating he found a camper's rucksack. He took this to a cache—one of the old German bunkers further along the cliffs. It had been shifted by the earthquake, so that the vertical well leading down to the bottom level tilted at something like seventy degrees, but the steel ladder was still in place. It was unlikely that anyone from the camp would go there, and it was dark at the bottom, but he fixed up a rough screen of old brushwood as an extra precaution. After that, as the opportunity offered, he took along the things he had decided he would need for his journey.

This was food for the most part, in as concentrated a form as he could find—chiefly bully beef and ham and beans. His biggest problem of course, was a supply of fresh water. Say, a hundred miles to Wight at fifteen miles a day—that meant a week's travelling. He had found, in the crumpled boot of a car, a plastic jerrican which held a gallon. A pint of water a day—not unreasonable in this climate and there must, by now, be rainwater pools among the rocks. And Alderney, of course. There were freshwater springs there where he could replenish his supply. That cut a quarter off the distance. Seventy-five miles: he should do it comfortably in five days.

He would wear the boots he had been keeping, and take his strongest pair of shoes as well. A couple of guernseys, and extra socks, for night wear; he would manage without a blanket. The mackintosh he had hidden up at the Val de Terres went into store and the box of cartridges which had been wrapped in it. He left the shotgun in his tent to prevent any suspicion of his intentions arising. It was one of a number of things which he would have to take at the last minute.

His preparations, since they had to be made without attracting attention, occupied the better part of two weeks. There was another spell of bad weather towards the end, but they all crowded into the main tents which stood up effectively, even to a fairly substantial earth tremor which occurred at the height of the storm. The tent poles went askew and one of them broke but it happened during the day and the men were able to put things right without much difficulty. There was a palpable sense of communal triumph over this which contrasted markedly with the misery of the earlier time.

Something else of importance happened, whether because of this, or the experience of mass living, or for some more obscure reason, Matthew did not know. But when the skies cleared and the small tents were put back in order, Irene did not go with Hilda but took her place in Miller's tent. He seemed a little dazed by this, but took it with boisterous good humour. Matthew thought that the others paid more respect to Irene as a result. She would run things well—coldly and efficiently and without much imagination. He wondered whether she would favour her sons or her daughters as her successors. Was that how patterns of society were formed, from the Ur-context of particular people at a particular moment of crisis ? The speculation held him only briefly. It was more important that Miller, in his new happiness, was relaxed and unwary. Matthew spent more time away from the camp, organizing his departure.

He was awakened by an earth tremor in the night. It was a common occurrence; they had grown sufficiently used to them to be able to turn over and go back to sleep. This time Matthew stayed awake. He had no idea of the time but there was the first faint glimmer of daybreak in the sky. He waited what seemed a long time—perhaps ten minutes—and then, as quietly as possible, slipped on his clothes. To check, he whispered: 'Billy ?' but there was no answer. He could just see the outline of the boy's figure under the blankets. He picked up the shotgun from beside his mattress and went out into the night. There was no sign of anyone else stirring.

It was difficult at first, picking his way over rough ground towards the bunker, but his eyes grew accustomed to the dimness which itself brightened as night shaded into day. He had brought with him a tiny pocket torch, which was too weak to be of any help in the open but provided a glimmer in the blacker depths of the bunker. The rucksack was already packed and he had filled the jerrican with water. He got them both out into the open, fastened the can securely across the straps of the rucksack, and the shotgun transversely above that, and hauled the whole thing on to his back. It was heavy, but the weight was well distributed, and he himself was tougher than he had been in the old days. He was confident he could manage it easily enough.

His most direct route to the sea bed, since he was travelling north, would lie in cutting across the base of Jerbourg and heading for Fermain Bay. But that meant traversing the nauseously familiar wreckage of St Martin's, and he headed for the Divette instead. The Monument, broken off a little below halfway, jutted at a crazy angle across the lightening sky. The Divette had been scoured by the tidal wave: there was not even a stump left of what had been grandiloquently called the Pine Forest. But the headland had collapsed outwards to some extent, and it was not too hard to pick a way down. Matthew reached the bottom, looked back briefly, and walked on into the valley which had once been the bed of the Russell.

It was, as Le Perré had said, the sense of unease which was worst. Matthew had walked out occasionally, on an ormering tide, and been conscious of the strangeness, the altogether alien quality, of the underwater world exposed to the harsh light of day. This was much more disturbing. In the grey pre-dawn light, reefs and shoulders of rock stood up, improbable in shade and contour. Here, for long centuries, the sea had rolled; and its presence lingered, in the pervading rotting smell, in the pools trapped among the rocks, occasionally in the dead shells of crab or lobster. It seemed incredible that it should not come rushing back. He found himself listening for the tiny distant roar which would swell into a thunder of returning vengeful waves.

In the greater lucency, the outlines changed, the sombre mystery of the rocks giving place to a jagged richness of silhouette and colour, with outcroppings of pink and yellow granite and dazzling streaks of marble across the grey. His disquiet remained; it was an even stranger land and he walked through it as a trespasser. He began to find familiar objects, part of the debris spilled as the town was carried away in the embrace of the retreating waters—broken china, part of a chair, a twisted bicycle frame, a canvas which might have been a work of art but was now a rotting smear of cloth and paint. These did not reassure him; on the contrary, they made things worse. Their incongruity pointed up his own. Where the shattered tower of Brehon dominated the skyline on his right, he found a gas cooker, apparently having suffered no damage other than through being wrenched from its pipes and brackets, standing impeccably upright on a sand bank. The sight of it sent a prickle of fear along his skin.

He was at the narrowest point of the Russell, the channel between Bordeaux and Shell Beach on Herm, when he first heard a cry. It was thin and distant but, he was sure, human. The sun was up—its rays warmed him as he climbed a spur of rock and looked back the way he had come. There was only the waste of rock and sand, mud flats and puddled water; but he heard the cry again. A child's voice and, surely, familiar . . . Matthew cupped his hands round his mouth and called in reply:

'I'm here!'

His voice echoed round him: 'Here . . . here . . . here . . .', diminishing to nothing.

Billy was gasping for breath when he came up with him, and had been sobbing; his face was stained with dirt and the tracks of tears. He looked at Matthew, full of guilt and trust.

Matthew asked him: 'What are you doing here, Billy? You followed me. Why?'

'I want to come with you.'

Matthew shook his head. 'It's too far, and a bit too hard. You'd better go back.'

Billy said: 'I knew you would go, after you'd said you would. And then this morning you went out of the tent, and I saw you had the gun with you, so I knew it was today. I kept as far behind as I could, and then I lost sight of you and I didn't know what to do. But I went up on the cliffs and watched, and I saw you moving, a long way off. So I ran down and tried to follow you. But I couldn't tell where I was going, and I got lost. That's when I yelled out.' He looked guilty again. 'I didn't want to, in case Miller and the others heard, but I was lost.'

Matthew sat down on a ledge of rock, easing the pack from his back, and Billy sat beside him. Matthew said:

'I must go alone, Billy, and you must go back to the camp. They can look after you, and I can't. You must see that's sensible.'

'I don't want to, Mr Cotter.'

'Who's going to look after Cobweb, if you come away?'

'She belongs to them, anyway. They make her work all the time.'

Matthew pointed to the rucksack. 'I've got my rations in there. For one, not two.'

'I wouldn't want to eat much.' He fumbled in the pockets of his jacket and produced a couple of slabs of chocolate, grubby-looking but intact. 'I saved these up.'

Matthew looked at him silently. There were so many objections, but none of them, he knew, would convince the boy. The only way was to be stern: to put on an angry face and order him to go back. By the time he reached the camp, it would be too late for Miller to do anything except, perhaps, beat him for not raising the alarm when he saw Matthew going. And he could not get lost on the way back; the island bulked large enough.

All this was sensible. It was impossible to tell what dangers or hardships lay ahead. He had allowed a good margin in food and water and could hope to find more on Alderney; but it was not a chance to risk a boy's life on. He had only the clothes he was wearing, a single pair of shoes which the rocks might cut to ribbons before they were halfway across the Channel.

But he knew he could not send him back alone through this scarred and savage landscape.

He said: 'All right, Billy. We'll see how it goes. Perhaps we'll both turn back, if it gets too difficult.'

SEVEN

THERE was cloud in the middle of the day, but in the afternoon the sun came out again, stronger than before. The home islands of the bailiwick were hazy hills behind them, Alderney a shimmering cliff-hung fortress ahead. Matthew was very glad of the company of the boy, of the chatter to which he could reply or not as he fancied. He had still not made up his mind whether they should turn back or not. So far the going had been very good, with long stretches on which they could keep up a fair walking pace. They had only one extensive detour, round a long pool of water hemmed in by jagged weed-incrusted rocks. The water in the pool was very clear and blue, and they saw fish swimming far down; it was at least twenty or thirty feet deep, Matthew calculated.

Since there was no particular urgency, they rested from time to time. Late in the afternoon they halted by a rocky formation which held dozens of small pools, ranging from a foot to ten or twenty yards across. Billy clambered over the reef like any child at the seaside. He would tire himself, Matthew thought, and called to him to come and sit down.

Billy shouted back: 'I will, in a minute. But I've got . . .'

'What?'

Billy held it up in triumphant demonstration—a lobster, about nine inches in length, its tail snapping furiously.

'That's a fine one,' Matthew said, 'but you'd better put him back before I start feeling hungry.'

Billy jumped down, his right hand firmly grasping the lobster behind the head.

'That's what I thought, Mr Cotter! We could have him for supper.'

'Even then, I don't think I could tackle raw lobster. And I don't know any way of cooking it.'

'There's dry wood.'

This was true: they were still in the area of scatter from the wave that had ripped off the east coast of the island. Within sight at the moment there were bricks, a huge chunk of shaped granite, the hose of a vacuum cleaner, a piece of a kitchen sink, and various bits of wood—a chair-back, a smashed window frame, and the twisted frame of a bed. Not very much further back, hidden fortunately by a crest of rock, there had been two twined and naked bodies which might have been connected with the bed frame: he had not looked at them very closely.

He said: 'I didn't bring any matches. Even if I had done, I doubt if we could have got a fire going. And nothing to cook it in.'

'There's my glass.'

Feeling awkwardly with his free hand—the arm had knit and the splints and sling had been abandoned but he still had difficulty with it—Billy brought from his pocket the magnifying glass which Matthew had picked up undamaged in the ruins of the chemist's shop and brought back to the boy as a kind of toy.

'I could make a fire with this, Mr Cotter. And can't we just roast it in the embers ? That's what they do in the South Seas, isn't it ?'

Matthew looked at him with respect. He said:

'Billy, the greatest chef in the world that used to be never had a bigger stroke of genius than that.'

Billy looked happy at what he recognized as a compliment.

'What's the best way of killing him ?' he asked. 'Can you break his neck, do you think ?'

They gathered wood and Matthew broke it up into as convenient pieces as he could. They produced a rough attempt at a field kitchen with a couple of bricks and an outcrop of rock, and piled the wood on to it. Then Billy squatted beside it and focused the sun's rays through the glass. The light dazzled pure white against the weathered surface of the wood, and then the spot of brilliance began to smoke. It was a moment of shared excitement. The smoke spread into a whorl and then, with a little quick dance, flame had caught and moved hungrily across the wood.

They put the dead lobster in while the fire was still blazing;

it hissed and crackled with the heat. As the fire died into embers it was encrusted with ash and looked unappetizing; but the smell was delicious. The embers glowed pale in the last rays of the sun. They waited with anxious greed for them to cool.

Matthew had thought that they would take the lobster with them and eat it cold when they stopped for their evening meal, but it was not humanly possible to resist temptation so long. He broke it open, burning his fingers on the hot shell, and split it down the middle with a knife. They sat side by side and ate it; Matthew had to hold himself back from gobbling the sweet white meat. When they had eaten the body meat, they cracked the claws on the rock and sucked them. Matthew remembered dusk on a summer evening, the window overlooking the harbour thronged with bobbing boats . . . Thermidor, washed down with Montrachet . . . or cold, with a delicate mayonnaise, thin brown bread and butter, a bottle of Chablis . . . The occasions were unreal, the experiences, he was sure, inferior.

They made a few more miles before they halted for the night. Uneasiness, which had retreated during the spreading normality of the day, came back with the evening shadows, which, softening the harsh outlines of the rocks, only emphasized the utter strangeness of the terrain through which they were passing. He stopped while it was still light enough to see the distant hills that were Herm and Jethou and Guernsey, and would have wished himself back there if there were any point in wishing. When they lay down, in a patch of loose yellow sand still holding a little of the sun's warmth, he thought he could hear, like listening to a shell, the far-away roar of the ocean, and was afraid again. He should have taken the boy back. In the morning . . .

They slept close together, and uneasily. There were a couple of minor tremors during the night and just before daylight the wind freshened. They rose to a grey cloudy dawn, feeling stiff and uncomfortable. Matthew had thought, the night before, that they might be able to cook some sort of breakfast, but one look at the sky was enough to banish the idea. Clouds moved fast and low over it, and he felt a spot or two of rain. As he opened a tin of corned beef, he said to Billy:

'What about it? Shall we turn back?'

'Why, Mr Cotter?'

'Perhaps this isn't very sensible. What happens if it rains? We've only got one mack between us.'

'I don't mind rain.' He added, with an almost adult thoughtfulness: 'After all, it is summer.'

'We don't know where we're going. Or why. Probably be better to go back.'

'We're nearer Alderney than Guernsey now.' Billy pointed towards the cliffs straddling the northern horizon. 'We might as well go that far, at any rate.'

He looked at the boy, and laughed. 'I suppose we might. Have you ever been to Alderney?'

'No.'

'Nor have I. We'll go and see what it's like. We might find people alive there. If there was a survivor on Sark . . . there were a lot more living on Alderney.'

They did not see the fault until they were within a mile of the island: it ran south-east and north-west and was not easily apparent from the line on which they were approaching. Matthew saw that the cliffs were torn by a jagged cleft and that the cleft ran away from them, a huge rip in the sea bed. As they got nearer, he could see that the same chasm ran inland, splitting the island, which, behind the seeming security of the southern heights, was riven in two unequal parts. He had been hopeful of finding someone alive because Alderney, like Sark, was a raised plateau—St Anne would not have been swept away by the wave as St Peter Port had been. But now, seeing the island torn in two, the hope went. It was difficult to imagine that any living thing could have survived the violence as the earth heaved and divided itself.

Nevertheless, having come so far, he felt that he had to make sure. They climbed the slope of the harbour bed—built in the flush of Victorian power to house the Grand Fleet—and went on up the hill. The rubble seemed to be even more finely pulverized than that which he had seen in Guernsey, but perhaps the impression was derived from the yawning gap to the north.

It was as though a gigantic meat-axe had slammed down across the island; the eye shuddered from it but continually returned. It would have looked better, he thought, if the sea had still been there. The waves would have covered the raw nakedness of the lower part of the cleft.

They hunted around the larger half of the divided island, and went to the edge of the ravine and stared across to the north, but there was no sign nor sound of humanity. They saw one dog—a yellow cur which barked and ran off—and quite a number of rabbits. Otherwise there was only death—the gleam of bones through rotted flesh, the residual stench, all the features of that horror's head which they knew so well. But they had one stroke of good fortune: they found a store of tinned foods that barely required digging for—some of the tins were actually at the surface. It was an oddly luxurious selection, including truffled pâté, artichoke hearts, sliced smoked salmon, and turkey and pheasant in exotic wine sauces.

While the sun shone briefly in the late afternoon, Billy managed to get a fire going. They found plenty of wood and built up quite a blaze. It would attract attention, Matthew said, if there were anyone alive on the island, but he was sure there could not be. Nevertheless, it was comforting to see the fire burning fiercely, smoke streaming away in the still strong wind. He punched holes in the top of the tin of turkey and set it upright in a low part of the fire. Juice bubbled out of the holes, hissed over the depressed top of the tin, ran steaming down the sides. The smell mingled with the smell of wood smoke. Idly, in the temporary comfort and pleasure of it, Matthew opened a small tin which had lost its label. It was in a class with the others: smoked quails in some kind of oil. The two small carcases were pale and naked-looking. He had a sudden wave of nausea as he stared at them. Billy was busy with something on the other side of the fire. He threw the tin away from him, as far as he could down the slope. With hopeless misery, he thought: if only death could put on its disguise again.

They slept better for the security of height, the awareness of being away from the sea bed. In the morning the wind was blustery, but there was sunshine as well as cloud. Matthew found a stream at which they washed—Billy perfunctorily but Matthew himself more thoroughly. Billy wandered away during this, and disappeared. Matthew was not worried. There was no danger here, and scarcely enough room for anyone to get lost. He dried himself partly on the small towel he carried in the pack and let the sun and wind do the rest. After that he put on his clothes and walked up the hill to the place where they had camped.

Billy came towards him, brandishing a black leather bag. It was a bicycle saddle-bag. He said:

'Look what I found, Mr Cotter! It will do for me carrying things, won't it?'

'On your back? You'd need a harness as well.'

'I found these, too.' He held up a pair of braces. They looked as though they had been expensive: broad silk elastic, midnight blue with a scarlet motif, the heavy clips having the dull sheen of what might be gold-plate. 'I thought we could make something out of them.'

'It probably isn't worth it, if we're going back. I can carry more than enough food.'

'Are we going back?' There was disappointment in the boy's face. 'Do we have to?'

'You'd rather go on?'

'Oh, yes!'

For the boy's sake, he ought to go back. To the south, less than two day's journey, lay the safety and comparative security of Miller's little band. To the north, all was unknown—sixty miles of sea bed to cross even on the most direct route, and with no knowing what obstacles or forced detours might present themselves. There could well be other faults like the one which had shattered Alderney; perhaps bigger. And he hadn't even got a compass. He would have to rely on the sun for his direction. What would happen if there were days, a whole week, of heavy cloud?

The idea, he saw, was foolhardy—now that he had the boy with him, irresponsible. It had been inspired by a wild hope and he had thought—seeing the fantastic destruction here—that the hope was dead. He had been prepared, he thought, to go back, to live out his life with the few others who had survived on Guernsey. But the hope was not dead, and nothing else mattered beside it. He looked at the boy: nothing, and nobody.

'Well,' he said, 'we'd better see about getting ourselves organized.'

EIGHT

THEY set out again late in the morning. Matthew had replenished the water from a stream well away from any of the polluted ruins; there might be contamination in the spring itself below ground but that had been true in Guernsey, too, and no harm seemed to have come. He had rigged up a harness for Billy's haversack and filled it with tinned food, and also filled up the spaces in his own. They walked off through grass that stood high and luxuriant and wasted; it was more than ready for the first cutting of the summer.

For some time they were forced to follow the cleft on its southern bank. It was forty or fifty feet deep, the sides precipitous. They were walking parallel with the line, eight miles away, of the French coast. After about an hour, though, they came to a place where the cleft, going through sand and mud, had fallen in on itself. They were able to scramble down and, with a good deal of sliding back, to clamber up the opposite side and set their course for the north. There was still a strong breeze, but it was a help now. The sky was almost cloudless and without the wind it would have been too hot for comfort.

The strangeness of the landscape wore off more quickly this time, and Matthew became increasingly conscious of its monotony. Rock, sand and drying stretches of mud alternated with patches of water. On the whole, the ground sloped down towards the north, but here and there they had to climb. There were reefs and individual rocks which rose quite high, one so much so that he thought its tip must have been above water in the old days. The sun moved down the sky, and he kept it behind his left shoulder. They were making at least a couple of miles an hour, he thought, perhaps more.

The first wreck they encountered provided a corrective shock. Billy glimpsed it first, away on their right, and they altered course to look at it. It was the drowned hulk of a cargo boat, or rather most of it. It lay on its side, decks pointing west, encrusted with weed and barnacles. It had not been a very big ship—less than a thousand tons—and Matthew judged that it must have been under water ten years at least, and possibly a good deal more. Around the stern there had been lettering, but RO was all that could be made out now. Matthew felt the fear he had felt earlier, the awareness of alienism and somehow of menace. They were in the deeps of the country whose horror touched all seafaring peoples: the land of drowned sailors. Billy did not seem affected by it. He raced round the wreck, peering at it from all angles, and wanted to climb up on it. Matthew told him no, and he came away reluctantly.

'There's nothing there but rust and rotting weed, Billy,' he told him. 'And we don't want to waste any time. We ought to get on.'

There was no material for making a fire, so they carried on until the stars were beginning to come out before stopping for the night. Matthew had made sure the boy rested at intervals, but all the same he was dog tired. They opened tins of Spam and ate them, and Matthew had a wave of hunger for starches. His stomach was full, but his appetite still clamant. Billy broke a few squares off his bar of chocolate, and offered Matthew them. He hesitated, and said:

'I'll take one, Billy. You eat the rest.'

He kept the chocolate in his mouth, sucking it until it dissolved. Billy was still eating the rest, and he looked away, unable to bear the sight.

They came on another wreck not long after they set out the next day. It was far more crumpled and dilapidated than the first, built of rotting slimy wood which gaped in places. It was, or had been, high pooped, and there were rows of holes beneath the bulwarks whose regular spacing showed them to be gunports. From one, in fact, a rusty, weed-hung muzzle projected, as it had done since it fired its last shot and the ship rolled in the waters and sank. How long since? Nearly four hundred years? Had it been one of the ships of the great Armada, harried by Drake and the storm through the cold grey waters of the Channel? Or a British vessel, more than two hundred years later, lost on its way home from Trafalgar? There was no way of telling, and it was of no importance.

Billy said: 'It's very old, isn't it, Mr Cotter?'

'Yes. Very old.'

'Do you think there might be treasure in it?'

'I suppose there might. It wouldn't do us much good if there were.'

'Can I look?'

There were two aspects to treasure, of course. The world's markets were all closed, and doubloons would buy nothing, not an egg nor a steak nor a crust of bread. But they were doubloons still. Magic and mystery remained, in a child's eye. Matthew seated himself on a flat rock, easing off the heavy pack.

'No harm to look,' he said. 'But we'd better go carefully. I wouldn't trust those timbers to bear any weight.'

She lay on her port side, and they found a place just aft of the stem where a hole was big enough to admit Matthew stooping. It was very dark inside after the bright sunlight, and he made Billy stand until their eyes grew more used to the dimness. He had been afraid of timbers that would give way, even under the boy's light weight; but he realized, as they began to move around, that the fears had been groundless. Although the general outline of the ship's exterior shape remained, her insides had dissolved. Bulkheads and fittings had fallen and lay, mixed with sand and mud, forming an uneven but firm floor. There was nothing but a dark shell and a smell of rot.

As Matthew stood there, thinking about the boy's disappointment, he felt the ground shiver and heard the wooden walls groan around them. His movement was almost instinctive: he grabbed Billy roughly and plunged for the open air, holding him. They came out into the hot sunlight and he felt a surge of relief which left him weak. He let Billy go, and breathed in deeply.

Billy said: 'It wasn't a very big one, was it?'

He was frightened, too, and trying not to show it. Matthew said:

'No, not a big one.' He paused, still collecting himself. 'And since she stood up to the very big ones, she wouldn't be likely to cave in now. Wood is better than bricks and stone—less rigid.'

It was true. The hulk was not the death-trap a house would have been. But he did not want to go back in there, leave the wide safety of the open. He said:

'There wasn't anything to see, was there? Nothing interesting.'

Billy shook his head. 'Not really.'

'Then we'll go on, I think. Or do you want to rest?'

'No. I'd rather go on, Mr Cotter.'

There were other small tremors in the next hour, but they did not worry them. Matthew, as he walked, thought of the wreck and of what he had said about it. It had come through the cataclysm—the heaving of the sea bed, the sucking outrush of the waters—and stayed more or less in one piece. Chance, he realized, must have had a lot to do with it. But if those rotting timbers could survive . . . He thought of Jane again, of the old house on high ground. The wooden roof could have protected her, and she would have been at the top of the house.

He looked back at the battered hull of the ship. A sign, perhaps. A renewal of hope, at any rate. He started whistling, and saw Billy look at him, curious but smiling.

They came to the place Billy called the Giant Steps. There was a whole series of faults, from ten to fifty yards apart, between which the sandy ground was flat and featureless. At each fault there was a sharp drop of some inches, in one case as much as four feet. It was like the terracing Matthew remembered seeing on agricultural land in hilly places; there was an impression both of artificiality and incompleteness. Some giant gardener would return, perhaps, for the sowing. The Steps went on a long way, more than a mile, and ended only where the sand gave way to rock.

At this point there were more pools, and fish swimming in them. In one quite small one a mackerel a foot long threshed exhaustedly. The pool was not more than three times its length and less than a foot deep. The fish could not have survived in so tiny a space since the waters went, and Matthew could see what must have happened. The small pool was separated from a much larger one by a ridge of rock, raised a few inches above the level of the water. The mackerel must have been in the larger pool, and leapt from there, blindly seeking the deep sea which it had lost. It had landed instead in this puddle, by now deoxygenated and stripped of nutrient. Here, quite soon, it would die.

Billy leaned over the rock pool and plunged his arms in the water. Droplets sparkled in the sun and the fish twisted slackly away from his fingers. He said:

'Shall I get him, Mr Cotter? I could catch him easily.'

'We've no fuel to start a fire.'

'We could take him with us. We might find some wood later on.'

Matthew shook his head. 'It's not worth it.' He felt a great compassion for the fish, for the urge towards life which had caused it to jump the ridge and for its present helplessness. 'If you can catch it, I should pop it back in the other pool.'

The fish had more reserve of strength than had seemed likely. It squirmed out of the boy's grasp, and in the end Matthew lent him a hand. Together they lifted the mackerel through the air and let it drop on the far side of the barrier. It swam down into the depths—this pool was more than twenty feet long and the sun's rays did not show its bottom.

Billy said: 'It will be all right now, won't it?'

'Yes, I should think so.'

It would last a little longer, a few more days, weeks, maybe months. But these pools were all drying out, withering, away from the sea's refreshment. In the end, it made no difference.

They went on more slowly. There were a lot of rocks, many sharp-edged, over which they had to climb. Once when they stopped to rest, Matthew examined Billy's shoes. The soles were getting thin, showing cuts and cracks across the leather. They would have to last until they reached the mainland and he could forage for more. He warned him to avoid rough ground as much as possible, but it was not the sort of advice one could expect a young boy to take notice of.

After the rocks came mud flats. The going was fairly firm to begin with, but as they advanced they found the mud soft beneath its outer crust. Their feet sank in, at first no more than an inch or so and then more deeply. When Matthew felt it sucking so much that it was an effort to raise his foot again, he decided that they must try to get round instead of keeping on their direct path. The flats stretched far out in front of them, but the firmer ground ran north east so Matthew turned that way. They walked with the sun at their backs, sinking towards a horizon which, for the first time that day, had some cloud. There was a dullness to the scene; on their right the grey rocks, ridge after ridge, on their left the barren blackness of the mud. Billy's lightheartedness left him, and he stopped chattering. They plodded on silently together. Matthew asked Billy if he wanted to rest, but he shook his head. It was depressing to think of halting in this desolation.

In the end, as the sun sank and darkness gathered over a scene that showed no intrinsic change, they had to halt. They had covered, Matthew calculated, something like twelve to fifteen miles the day before, rather more than that today. But the last five miles at least on a course carrying them as much east as north. The only encouraging thing was that the weather had held so far, and looking at the dull red afterglow in the sky behind them, he wondered how long that would last. The wind was stronger again, howling among the rocks.

They opened tins and had their evening meal. Quite apart from the question of heating food, a fire would have been a comfort; but even if the sun had not gone down there was nothing here that would burn. Matthew wrapped as much clothing as possible round the boy, and they lay down on the mud together, in each other's arms. The earlier mood of hope was all gone. He was conscious only of their wretchedness, their vulnerability.

The rain woke them before morning light, a swift violent shower that lashed against them and soaked them through. Matthew rearranged the mackintosh to give Billy as much protection as he could, and set himself to endure it. It did not last long, but left them wet and shivering with cold. They sat huddled together, waiting for the sky to brighten.

Day broke slowly and reluctantly, to the accompaniment of another heavy shower of rain. They were already so wet that this made little difference. Matthew opened a tin of concentrated soup and they wolfed it between them. It tasted unpleasant, but presumably it was nourishing. Then they set off again. The rain had softened the mud, forcing them to take to the rocks to find firm footing. The going was difficult and exhausting, particularly for Billy. Matthew was obliged to call halts frequently so that he could rest.

They went on in this way for what seemed like hours. There was no trace of the sun behind the scudding monochrome of the clouds; the day remained grey and dark. Rain eased off at intervals, only to return. They had been wet and tired and cold when they started, and became more so. They opened another tin—of sausage and beans—and spooned them out in turn.

At last the ground changed, the mud giving way to firm sand and shingle, interspersed with boulders and massive rock formations. Matthew had no idea how far they had travelled to the east, but he decided it would be sensible to turn off at something less than a right-angle to the line they had been following. Without the sun, he could only make an approximate guess at the direction in which they were heading. If this weather continued, he realized, they might easily find themselves going round in circles. And it had a depressingly permanent look to it. There had been no rain for over an hour, but the sky remained as threatening as before.

When he first saw the ship, he did not believe it. A mirage, he thought confusedly—but surely mirages required hot dry air, and brightness? Or an hallucination . . . Only the stem and twenty or thirty feet behind were visible, the rest being hidden by a ridge of rock. The element of fantasy lay in the fact that the ship seemed to be completely undamaged, her bows white and unscarred though oddly lacking in elevation. She rested on even keel in the sand, in an incredible act of balance.

Billy, clutching his arm, said: 'Look! What sort is she, Mr Cotter?'

'I'm not sure,' he said. 'We'd better go and take a closer look.'

As they came round the ridge, the trick of balance explained itself; so did the lowness of her bows. The ship rested amidships on a reef. It was nothing very much but it held her firmly upright. As to the puzzling nature of the stem section, that was made clear in the shock of seeing her full length. This was a tanker, one of the modern giants. She must, Matthew calculated, be eight hundred feet or more in length, getting on for a hundred thousand tonner. Her lines ran back, very low and straight, to a single squat tower at the stern. She might have buckled somewhat at the point of impact, but from where they stood there was no sign of damage at all.

Billy said: 'Isn't she terrific! Do you think we can go on board?'

She lay there, superbly erect on the dry sea bed, all grace and power and purity, a majestic artefact of the vanished world. She had ridden the departing waves, and dropped here like a bird. He said:

'We'll have a try, Billy.'

NINE

THE rain came down as they walked towards the tanker, not violently this time but with a drenching persistence. It beat against the white bulwarks which, low as they were, towered above their heads, and they sought shelter under the broad curve of her bottom. It occurred to Matthew that going aboard might be more easily proposed than achieved. There had been no sign of life on board as they approached. Although from the outside the ship looked undamaged, he supposed her crew could have been swept overboard or killed by the shock of impact. He did not see how he and the boy could scale these smooth sides without help, quite apart from the overhang.

At least they could make a survey of the ship from outside, though what it amounted to so far was a close-up view of the red underbelly of the monster. And monster she was. The arch of steel stretched ahead of them as an almost endless arcade. Looking along it, and upwards, Matthew had a renewed fear of being enclosed, roofed in. It was irrational; if the big quakes had not toppled her it was improbable that any of the still occurring smaller ones would. All the same, he moved out, into the driving rain, and Billy, without question, followed him.

They could see a little more now, but not much. They were approaching the tower at the stern of the ship. Matthew paused, cupped his hands, and called up. His voice rang hollowly, and there was no reply. There was only the wind, and the swish of rain.

Later, as they were rounding the stern, Matthew thought he heard a cry. He saw what might have caused it a moment later: a bedraggled-looking seagull walking across the sand. Apart from worms and fishes, it was the first life they had encountered since the dog and the rabbits on Alderney. Billy shouted at the sight and the gull took to the air, flapped a dozen yards or so, and resumed its original clumsy progress. Matthew wondered about it. Had the dim memory of past feastings brought it to the ship, or did it find some present nourishment here? He called up to the ship a second time, and his voice seemed to echo in the silence.

Immediately after that he caught sight of the ladder.

It was steel and nylon and hung from the bulwark, forward of the stern on the starboard side. It reached the ground, and more—the extra lay in a tangled untidy heap on the sand. Matthew went to it and tugged, at first gently and then with all his strength. It was firmly secured at the top. He looked at Billy, and said:

'What about it? Shall we go up? Do you think you can climb a rope ladder? It's pretty high.'

'I'm sure I can! Honest.'

'You go first.'

The boy went up easily. Matthew let him get a few yards' lead and started up himself. The ladder swung and bucked under their combined weights and he had a wave of height nausea. He halted, clinging tightly to the steel rungs, and the deep earthquake fear superimposed itself on the vertigo, petrifying him. If a big shock came, and this steel wall tilted and slid towards them . . . He tried to tell himself how absurd it was, but reason was overwhelmed by terror. Shaking, he heard Billy call down something. His first response was a meaningless croak. Clearing his throat, coughing, he forced himself into speech.

'What's that?'

'I said I'm nearly up! But it's harder. The ladder bangs against the side.'

'Rest a while,' he called.

'No, I don't need to.'

Gradually the fear diminished into something which, although it chilled him still, could be controlled. He moved one foot up, reached with his hand for a higher rung. He began to climb steadily, not letting himself think of anything but the mechanical process, the alternation of hands and feet. He heard a cry of triumph which told him Billy had got to the top, but did not reply. Now he had to be careful because incautious movements swung him and the ladder against the white-painted steel. He was nearly there, surely, but he did not look up. Suddenly the rail was in front of his eyes, with Billy's legs behind it.

It was funny that the fear left him as soon as he had swung on board—the earthquake fear as well as the height fear. He was on the raised deck surrounding the tower; below and forward the tanks ran in long line towards the fantastically distant bows. He was impressed by the size and strength of it all. It no longer seemed strange that the ship should have come through the cataclysm unscathed. Or relatively unscathed—part of the rail had broken away on the port side, and there might be damage due to buckling in the far distance: it was difficult to be sure.

And then he became aware of something else. He had an idea he had been conscious of it for a time, without realizing or understanding what it was. Now it nagged at his senses, impossible to ignore or deny . . . the very faint throb in the metal under his feet, the muted hum from somewhere in the ship. He stared incredulously at the squat tower in front of him. There was still no sign of life, but somewhere in there a generator was running.

Matthew shouted again: 'Hello, there! Anybody home?' He called: 'Hello . . . hello . . . hello . . .' and Billy took it up, calling with him. The rain came down harder and swept across the decks over the side. There was a swimming pool set in the deck, and the rain hissed off the surface of the water. A couple of reclining chairs, made of tubular steel and brightly coloured plastic, stood near the spring-board at this end of the pool. It was as though people had been swimming and sun-bathing there until the rain drove them indoors for shelter.

'There's no one,' Billy said. 'Unless they can't hear us from inside.'

'It might be that. We'd better go and look.'

They trudged across the deck to the tower. Matthew found a door and turned a handle to open it. He had another shock when he did so. He had been expecting a dark interior and found a corridor lit by electric light. Billy exclaimed beside him.

'There must be people on board,' Matthew explained. 'They've managed to keep the generators going—they'll be oil-fuelled, I suppose.'

'Shall we call them again?'

'No, I don't think so. We'll go on till we find them.'

The place was a warren of passages and companionways. Matthew opened doors at random and found cabins, washrooms, what appeared to be a chart-room. There was something odd which it took him a while to formulate, but which was epitomized in a cabin with two built-in bunks. The bunks were neatly made up with sheets and blankets, and everything in the cabin was in order. Matthew realized that the same neatness obtained throughout. Whatever chaos had been caused by the shaking the ship had had when the catastrophe happened had been tidied up to an almost fanatical degree.

What did it amount to? A ship's company finding themselves stranded on a drained sea bed, taking refuge—in some weird mass psychosis perhaps—in scrubbing and tidying? Or doing it under the commands of a lunatic captain, a Bligh of the Breakdown? One was as unlikely as the other, and surely in any case a ship's company, going however punctiliously about their duties, would leave some signs of their presence? But there was nothing, and no one. Their footsteps echoed in the corridors, and they opened doors into empty rooms.

One of these was a galley. The table tops were scrubbed and bare, cooking utensils laid out in rows. They had not found the generators, but there was a separate hum of power from a huge refrigerator. Matthew opened it and saw that it held a couple of roast chickens, a ham, butter, maybe a dozen cans of beer. Hunger twisted his stomach as he looked at them. But they were intruders, and the officers and crew had to be somewhere. He closed the door, with reluctance.

Billy, who had been looking round the galley on his own, called to him:

'Mr Cotter! Look here.'

He had found and opened a cupboard. There were shelves inside, a kind of larder. And they stood in a neat symmetrical row on the second shelf, not perfectly formed, perhaps, but staggering in their mouth-watering beauty. Three loaves of white crusty bread.

On the shelf below there was a butterdish, jars of preserves and pickles, and a cheeseboard under a transparent cover. A wedge of Dutch, a hunk of blue that looked like Gorgonzola, a piece of crumbling Cheddar. Matthew saw the look on Billy's face, and could not endure it. He took one of the loaves and said:

'Get me a knife. There's one over there will do.'

'Can we?'

But he was already on his way to get the knife. Matthew controlled an urge to tear at the crust with his teeth, and waited till the boy came back. Sawing at the bread, he said:

'We'll have to take a chance on their generosity. Anyway, I think I'd cut their throats if they said no. Here you are. Spread your own butter, and help yourself to whatever you want with it.'

He had cut thick slices for both of them. Billy put strawberry jam on his. Matthew's hand hovered before the various pieces of cheese. The Dutch was the biggest. He cut about half of it, noticed that he had left a stain of butter where he had cut, and cut another piece to remove the mark. Then he bit into the hunk of bread and crammed some of the cheese into his mouth with it. His teeth champed automatically and he found himself swallowing gobbets of food before he wanted to; hunger warred with the desire that this taste, this sensation, should go on for ever.

He jerked round as the door behind them opened. He was holding the piece of bread and found himself, like a guilty child, putting it behind his back. The man who had come into the galley smiled.

'That's O.K. You go right ahead. I guess you're kinda hungry?'

He spoke American English with a Mediterranean accent. Not Italian, Matthew thought. Greek? He looked as though he could be a Greek. He was a short fat swarthy man. He was wearing an immaculate white drill suit and a gold-braided peaked cap. He had shaved that day; although dark blue his chin was smooth. There was more than a whiff of lotion.

Matthew said: 'We were hungry. Very hungry. And we haven't seen bread since it happened.'

He made an expansive waving gesture of dismissal. 'You don't have to worry. I got lots of food, drink. You like a beer, maybe?' He went to the refrigerator and brought a can over. 'And the boy? A coke?' He smiled, showing white teeth and the glint of gold. 'I guess you could drink a coke, eh?'

They thanked him but he shook his head. 'I got plenty. My name's Skiopos, Captain Skiopos. You can call me Nick.'

Matthew introduced himself and Billy. Skiopos said:

'So he's not your son, then, the boy?' He flashed another smile. 'You just travelling around together?'

Matthew told him something of what had happened. Skiopos listened, without seeming to pay much attention. He said finally: 'It's pretty bad on land, eh?'

'As far as the Channel Islands are concerned, it is.' Matthew had finished his bread and cheese. He found himself looking at the loaf, and Skiopos said: 'Go ahead. Cut yourself some more. I made too much bread last time. It needs eating.'

Cutting it, Matthew said: 'You've been here all the time, then? By yourself?'

'They all went,' Skiopos said. 'I told them they were crazy, but they went. I told them, anything that dries up the Channel, that makes a pretty big mess of everything. You won't find no land of milk and honey out there, I told them. But they were shaken up, you know? What a night that was! A ship like this, tossing about like a matchstick. Someone pulled the plug out of the big bath. But we landed right way up and with only a bit of a shaking. An' I told them—we've been lucky. But they wouldn't listen. They took some food and headed north.'

'How long ago?'

Skiopos shrugged. 'Who knows? The day after we stuck here. But I don't keep no log no more. Who cares?'

The bread and cheese tasted better all the time, if that were possible. And the sharp bite of beer in his throat added an ecstatic dimension. He said:

'Lucky hardly seems the right word. You seem to have had scarcely any damage at all.'

'Enough damage so that if the tide comes in again, she won't float. But I reckon the tide's gone out for good and all. Would you like to take a bath, you and the boy?'

'Hot water?'

'Sure, hot water! I wouldn't ask you to take a cold tub. Plenty of soap, towels and all that. I got some bath oil if you want that, too.'

He led them from the galley along a passage and up a companionway to another part of the ship. Opening a door, he showed Matthew a luxuriously appointed bathroom.

'Here you are,' he said, 'and one for the boy next door. I think maybe I'll go and freshen up some, too. Now I've got visitors. You ring the bell when you're through, Matthew, and I'll come and get you. You'll maybe lose your way if I don't show you.'

Matthew ran the water and stepped into it as hot as his skin would bear. He gasped with the heat, and lay back, relaxing. On the other side of the bulkhead, he could hear Billy splashing about. He felt hazy, concerned only with the immediate sensuous pleasure.

Skiopos was back before they finished their baths. He called:

'You had a good wash, Matthew? I brought some clothes I think maybe will fit you. Is it O.K. for me to come right in with them?'

He looked even cleaner than before. He carried a neat pile of clothes, which he put down on a locker top.

'I think these are round about your size,' he said. 'I brought you pants, vest, socks, shirt, trousers. No shoes, but you don't need shoes on board. And I brought some things for the boy. They're too big, but I've got a scissors—we can cut them down, maybe.'

Matthew got out of the bath and wrapped the towel round himself. He started to thank Skiopos, but was cut short.

'I'll go, take these to the boy. You'll feel better after a bath, in clean clothes. Soon as you're dressed, I'll show you round.'

It was a relief not to have to put his old clothes back on. They lay in a spoiled heap on the floor. The clean linen smelt good, and was incredibly soft against his skin. When he had dressed, Matthew went through to see how Billy was getting on. Skiopos was dressing him, or rather, standing back and surveying him with benevolent interest. He said to Matthew:

'He has a good body, but little.' Billy smiled uncertainly. 'You are not a tailor, I guess, Matthew ? Come then, we try again.'

Billy, when Skiopos had finished, had a comical but a clean look. The shirt and trousers were much too big for him, the latter being kept up by a pair of gaudy blue and gold braces. Skiopos patted him on the shoulder and ran his plump stubby fingers through the boy's damp hair.

'So, at least you look better than you did. Now I'll show you something.'

The room to which he led them had comfortable seats set out in rows. Skiopos went to the facing wall and pressed a button. A screen rolled down and Matthew realized this was a ship's cinema: there was a hole in the wall behind the seats from which the film was presumably projected.

'You sit down,' Skiopos said. 'You make yourselves easy. I'll fix everything.'

Since they had come on board, events had had an unreal, dream-like quality, but none so much as this. Matthew and Billy sat down, and Skiopos went out. A moment or two later, his voice came to them through the hole in the wall.

'All ready ? Right! So we'll get this show on the road.'

The lights went off. There was blackness and, for a moment, the claustrophobic fear; but the screen came to life and the fear retreated. It was a cartoon, a Tom and Jerry. Looking sideways, Matthew saw Billy's face, relaxed into lines of ordinary childish pleasure.

Skiopos ran two more cartoons through and then stopped the projector and put the lights on in the room. He called to them through the aperture:

'I guess we'll have the intermission now. Stay where you are, folks. I'll be with you in a minute.'

When he came, he carried a tray. He said:

'As it's the intermission, we have ice cream and candy. How about that, Billy ? And you'll have a cigarette, Matthew ? Or a cigar ?'

He gave ice cream and a bar of chocolate to Billy, lit a cigarette for Matthew and a small cigar for himself. He sat with them and talked. Matthew listened to him, wondering whether he was mad or sane. He showed no sign of madness; he seemed to be entirely amiable and matter-of-fact. But the situation was crazy and his acceptance of their arrival too casual. He should have been more pleased to see a human face, or else resentful because they were using up his precious stores. Because they were limited, and what would he do once they were gone?

The pattern of past events became more clear as he talked. He had neither sought to persuade the ship's company to stay with him nor paid any attention when they urged him to go as well. Left to himself, he had fiddled with the generator until he got it going. They had been on their way south from London, carrying water ballast in their tanks rather than oil, and he had managed to rig a connection to feed it into the cooling system. Mad or not, he was obviously a very capable little man. After that, he had set about cleaning up the ship, which he had done with the thoroughness Matthew had noticed. He cooked for himself on the big electric cooker which ran off the generator, played gramophone records, ran the dozen or so films through the projector over and over again.

He said: 'You know, I thought maybe I'd be kinda lonely? But when you've got voices to talk to you, faces . . . there's one picture with Sinatra, Ava Gardner. They're kinda like friends. You know?'

Matthew was smoking the cigarette slowly, savouring it. He asked:

'What about wireless?'

'Radio? Aw, that's dead.'

'You can't fix it?'

Skiopos shrugged. 'I don't know too much about radio.'

'If you could get it going—there might be stations broadcasting from somewhere that you could pick up.' Skiopos looked at him with bland lack of interest. 'We know western Europe's been largely knocked out, and I suppose something of the sort must have happened to America. But it may not have been quite as bad elsewhere—Russia, China, New Zealand.'

'I don't know a lot about radio,' Skiopos repeated.

He did not, Matthew realized, want contact with the world outside. He was content to be the centre of this small world. Then why had he been so friendly towards them? Perhaps because they had come to him and he could show them his powers and wonders.

Matthew said: 'What about oil?'

'Oil? I got plenty of oil.'

'How much?'

Skiopos' face became restless, and he looked away. He said insistently:

'Plenty of oil, I tell you.'

'But when it runs out? When the generator goes dead? What will you do then?'

'I tell you, there's nothing to worry about. Nothing at all. You have to excuse me now, Matthew. I got to go and see to things. You go and walk about—amuse yourselves. I'll see you around.'

When they found Skiopos again, he was in the galley, cooking. He greeted them as cheerfully as before.

'When I don't have guests, I make do with a cold snack in the middle of the day, but I thought maybe you'd like something hot.'

'Don't bother about us,' Matthew said. 'More bread and cheese will do fine.'

But the smell was intoxicating: thick slices of gammon frying in oil.

'Nothing special,' Skiopos said. 'Just ham and tomatoes, a few fried potatoes. Give me another ten minutes, O.K.?'

While they ate, he told them something of his routine. He had an alarm clock to wake him at six-thirty. He got up then, bathed, sometimes shaved, and went to the galley to make himself breakfast: coffee, toast and preserves. Then he inspected ship, did what cleaning up was necessary, and went on shore for his daily constitutional. He did this whatever the weather, and had been engaged on it at the time that Matthew found the ladder and came on board.

In the early days of being on his own, he had worked in the afternoons as well, tidying up after the shock. Now this was unnecessary and he spent his afternoons by the pool or, in bad weather, with gramophone records and films. There was a ship's library but he was not, Matthew gathered, a reading man.

On this particular afternoon, he took Matthew and Billy on a tour of the ship. He was cheerful in manner, factual in description. It was as though they were official visitors, friends of a friend, and the tanker herself tied up in the Port of London, resting between voyages. He pointed out the damage she had suffered but spoke of it briskly; his voice carried the implication of ship-repairing gangs in the offing. They went up on the bridge, whose wings reached out on either side of the tower. They were well over a hundred feet above the sea bed here, with the radar and signal mast high above them again. The tanker's great length stretched away into the distance. The rain had stopped and visibility was better: they could see mile after mile of mud flats, shingle beds and rocks. A desolate enough sight, Matthew thought, to drive a man mad.

Skiopos stared ahead, as though he could still see the furrowed grey acres of the Channel. He said, in a quiet voice:

'She's a beauty, huh?

Matthew said: 'Very impressive.'

'Sure. My first command.'

'Was she?'

'I'm thirty-eight,' Skiopos said. 'On this line, you don't have a command by the time you're thirty-five, you maybe don't get one ever. I knew one guy five years younger than me who was skippering a tanker. Then this one came up, this beauty. Commissioned less than eighteen months. The guy who had her got something wrong with his kidneys—I don't know what, but bad enough to put him in hospital for months maybe. I was due leave. We get good leave, sometimes four, five months. They said did I want her, or would I rather take my leave. Isn't that crazy? I said yes on the telephone, and then I drove into the office to make sure they'd heard me right. I was to take her down to the Gulf two days after that. I was still on my first watch when the wave hit.'

'Tough luck.'

Skiopos looked at him in an abstracted, slightly puzzled way. He looked away again, along the vast length of his ship.

'She's a beauty. Finest tanker in the line. Come on. I'll show you the control room.'

Billy was tired. The hard going had worn him out, and there had been the cold wet wretchedness of the previous night. Matthew mentioned this to Skiopos, and they got him to bed early after a supper of tinned fruit and hot chocolate and biscuits. Matthew settled him into one of the bunks. He lay back, dazed, sleepy and happy, in clean sheets, on a foam-rubber mattress. The rest would do him good. So would the food Skiopos was providing. Matthew thought about that. There was no long-term future here, but there was no reason why they shouldn't stay for a time, and recharge batteries.

Skiopos insisted on preparing an elaborate meal for Matthew and himself. He served an hors d'œuvre first, with salami and sardines, pickled eggs, olives and potato salad. The main course was chicken in a fragrant sauce, on a bed of saffron rice. He produced with this a bottle of Retsina, chilled from the refrigerator. Afterwards they had coffee and brandy and cigars in the officers' lounge. Matthew complimented his host on the meal. Skiopos accepted his praise with the casual absent air Matthew had noticed before. Matthew went on talking, about the past and the possibilities of the future, but Skiopos scarcely paid attention. He said suddenly, breaking across Matthew's words:

'You'd like I should run you a film maybe?'

'It's a bit late,' Matthew said. 'You must be tired. I know I'm pretty tired.'

'I always run a film at night, sometimes two.' He stood up from his easy chair. 'We've got one with this English girl, Kathy Kirby. You like her, Matthew? Come on, I'll run it for you. Bring a drink with you if you want.'

It was more an order than a suggestion. Matthew poured himself another brandy and, after a moment's hesitation, picked up the bottle as well. Skiopos had gone ahead without waiting, and

Matthew followed him to the cinema. There was no pre-amble this time, no settling him into a seat. Skiopos went into the projection room without another word, started the film running and doused the lights. Then he came back into the room and sat down himself, leaving the projector running on its own.

It was a British musical comedy and rather better than Matthew had expected—he had never been a keen cinema-goer and in recent years had almost completely abandoned the habit. But Skiopos' reactions were more interesting than the film. He kept up a running commentary, but one directed to himself rather than the person sitting in the room with him. Nor was it entirely or exactly a commentary. What he was doing, Matthew realized, was talking to the film, to the characters in it. He made little jokes, and roared with unself-conscious laughter at them—there was an impression that both joke and laughter had occurred before, that the whole thing was, in a sense, ritualistic.

Skiopos went back for the change of reels and subsequently returned to his seat. Matthew was tired, and the combination of cinema and brandy made him sleepy, but he stuck it out to the end of the film. Feeling some comment was called for, he said:

'That was very good. I think I'll get off to bed now.'

Skiopos had already headed for the projection room, and made no answer. Matthew waited, expecting him to switch off and come back. The light did go on in the projection room, but not in the cinema itself. Then the machine began whirring again, and a title flashed on the screen. LIKE CRAZY. Skiopos returned to his seat. He was laughing before he sat down.

Matthew gave it five minutes. Then he said again that he was going to bed, and again got no reply. He had to pass in front of Skiopos to get out of the room. Skiopos shifted irritably in his chair as he did so, but a moment later was making a feeble joke to the comic on the screen. He did not turn round as Matthew went out.

He looked in on the boy, who was sleeping peacefully, and made his way to the next cabin. He wondered how long Skiopos would go on with his private film show but without much interest. He felt very tired; all he could think of was the clean softness of the bed.

Billy woke him the following morning, and seeing the boy standing in the doorway of the cabin, seeing the polished wood and metal, the brightness of artificial light, Matthew had an instant of forgetting all that had happened, of imagining himself somewhere back in the pre-breakdown world, and wondering where. It did not last more than a moment, and with the realization he thought of Jane, and the pain was sharp again, as sharp as it had ever been. Hiding this, he smiled at Billy.

'Hello, then. What time is it?'

'I don't know. I've been awake quite a bit.'

Matthew glanced at the port-hole. 'Sun's up. I suppose we ought to see about getting ourselves some breakfast. Do you fancy that?'

Billy nodded. 'I saw the captain.'

'Did you?'

'I said good morning, but he didn't answer me.'

'He was probably thinking about something at the time. Throw me that shirt over, will you?'

He washed and dressed, and together they headed for the galley. There was a sound of activity from inside, and opening the door Matthew saw that Skiopos was down on his knees, scrubbing the floor. He called: 'Good morning, captain,' but Skiopos did not even look up. He went on with his scrubbing as though he were quite alone. The white drill trousers were looking grubby and above the waist he was wearing a string vest through which fat bulged. There was a bald spot, Matthew noticed, just behind the crown of his head.

As he had guessed, the man was a psychotic, probably predisposed to insanity anyway, the actual illness triggered off by the earthquake and the wave. That was why he had stayed when the ship's company left, why he spent so much of his time tidying and cleaning. As for his earlier friendly reception of them, it could have been that he was in a manic phase then, a depressive one now. Or that he was capable of welcoming intrusions from the outside, but closed his mind when they threatened to disturb the fantasy by which he lived. The thing which made him generous with his supplies was the same as forbade any mention, any thought, of their running out.

Mad, then, but apparently harmless. If he did not notice them when they spoke to him, presumably other activities would be non-existent, too. Billy was looking puzzled and a bit scared. Matthew patted him on the shoulder, and said:

'We'll make ourselves some breakfast. Are you any good at frying bacon, Billy?'

The found bacon in the refrigerator and fried it along with slices of bread. Skiopos gave no sign of awareness of their presence. While they were eating, he finished scrubbing the floor, took his bucket and brushes to the sink to wash them, put them away in a cupboard, and went out. When the door had closed behind him, Billy said:

'What's wrong with the captain, Mr Cotter?'

'His mind's sick.'

'Like Mother Lutron?'

'Something like that.'

'But he didn't even see us,' Billy said. 'He looked at us as though we weren't there.'

'Yes.'

The mania did not basically affect the situation—there had never been any question of their staying here long. But he had thought they might stay a few days, to rest and feed up. The idea did not seem as attractive as it had done. And he felt a twinge of unease again at being enclosed.

Skiopos, he presumed, had gone off on his morning walk. Matthew wondered what would happen when reality broke in on this self-contained and cosy universe. When the generator died, and the lights went out? Would Skiopos stay on, making do, staring perhaps at an empty screen in a dark room and peopling it with phantoms? Until the food went, too, and he began to starve. Even then, Matthew doubted if he would leave the ship. Preserving the fantasy mattered more, probably, than preserving life.

He and Billy made things tidy in the galley. Even if they did not exist for Skiopos now, he felt this was the minimum return for hospitality.

Billy said: 'Are we going?'

He seemed eager to be off now. Matthew said:

'As soon as we're ready. I thought we'd pack a few things extra. Some of that bread, and butter.'

'The captain won't mind, will he?'

'I shouldn't think so. He doesn't seem to mind our eating it here, and it's cheaper than keeping us on as non-paying guests.'

'Do you think he'd mind if I had some ice cream, too? Before we go, I mean.'

Matthew grinned. 'It will have to be before we go. You can't take it with you, or not far.'

Skiopos was in the middle of his bread-making operations. He had mixed the dough and set it out in tins to rise: the actual baking was probably scheduled to take place on his return from his walk. There was a full loaf and a little over half of one in the larder, and Matthew, after some thought, took the former. He cut pieces off the ham, also, and took a wedge of cheese, half a dozen wrapped chocolate biscuits, and a small pot of strawberry jam. It would see them through a couple of days as an extension to their usual depressing diet, three with some care.

They tidied up the cabins in which they had slept, though doubtless Skiopos would go over them again more thoroughly. Matthew took his pack and Billy's to the galley. The fresh provisions went in, and there was room for more. Matthew went to the refrigerator again. The two roast chickens were still there, and presumably Skiopos had others in his deep-freeze. In the end he cut a carcase in halves with a kitchen knife, put one half in his pack and the other back in the refrigerator.

He said to Billy: 'O.K., then. We're ready.'

At least, it was not raining. As they came out on deck, Matthew saw that the sky was a pearly grey, with a patch of light golden haze which showed where the sun was. The air was mild and damp and the breeze had almost entirely dropped. The water in the swimming pool was still and dark blue, unrippled. This looked like being one of the afternoons on which Skiopos sat out and took the sun, now and then diving into the placid waters to cool himself. With a can of beer, probably, at his elbow. A lotus-eating life, while it lasted. And how long would it last? Another month—two?

Matthew was anxious to be off the ship and on their way, now that they had made a start. He had an idea that Billy felt the same; he was quieter than usual and seemed nervous. His boots clanged on the steel deck and a seagull—probably the one they had seen the previous day—rose from the rail and flapped away mewling across the sky. He came to the rail, and looked down. The view of the sea bed from this height made him giddy. It would get no better with looking. He was preparing to swing himself over the side when he saw something moving among the rocks. Skiopos. He was marching towards the foot of the ladder, looking neither to left nor right.

He was still twenty or thirty yards away which meant that Matthew could be on the ladder before he was. Matthew decided, nevertheless, not to claim his right of way—if Skiopos was still blanking them out of his universe an awkward situation might arise on the way down. He motioned to Billy, and they stood by the rail, watching. Skiopos came up in a steady even climb. Eventually he reached the deck level and pulled himself inboard. He was breathing heavily and sweating to some extent. He did not look at Matthew and the boy, although they were only standing a few feet from him.

Matthew said: 'We're going, captain. Thank you for the hospitality. We've left the place as tidy as we could.'

Skiopos walked away from them, across the deck in the direction of the tower. He gave no sign of having heard anything. Matthew called after him, in a slightly louder voice:

'We've taken a few things—I hope that's all right.'

Skiopos stopped abruptly and turned round; his movements had the jerkiness of a doll running down. He stared at Matthew, his eyes peering, as though trying to see something just beyond the range of vision.

Matthew said: 'Nothing very much. A loaf of bread, a bit of cheese and ham and so on. And half a chicken.'

Skiopos took a step forward, and halted. He said:

'You must put them back. All. You understand? All.'

Matthew said: 'Be reasonable. If we'd stayed on here, we'd have eaten a lot more than that.'

Skiopos had begun to shake with emotion—rage or distress or both. He said in a strained voice:

'Ship's supplies . . . do you understand? They are not to be taken away. You got to give them back. You're a bloody thief. Come on now—you got to give them back.'

The shotgun was strapped on top of the pack on Matthew's back, but only loosely. He could quite easily reach a hand round behind him and pull it out. Skiopos, whether or not he had weapons on the ship, had none with him at the moment. There was no way in which he could enforce his lunacy.

Matthew put his hand back and touched the stock of the gun, but did not withdraw it. If Skiopos allowed himself to be intimidated, and backed down—what then? They had a fifty foot climb down a swaying rope ladder to face, with the mad man up here on deck. It was too much of a risk. Even if he forced Skiopos to go down first, a risk still existed. He might pick up a loose rock at the bottom: one could not cover a man with a gun and descend a rope ladder at the same time.

And it was possible that Skiopos was mad enough not to be intimidated, anyway. If he attacked, forced Matthew to pull the trigger . . . He thought about what a gunshot wound, at close range, would look like. If he and the boy were starving, it would be different; but their stomachs were filled and they had food in their packs. It made no sense.

Matthew eased the pack off his shoulders. Skiopos, watching him, was still shaking, but came no nearer and said nothing. Matthew opened the pack and brought out the small packages. As he laid them on the deck, Skiopos came forward. He squatted, opening and examining them. When he was satisfied, he picked them up, bundling them in his arms, and walked away towards the tower. Halfway there, he dropped one of the packages and scrabbled to retrieve it. He did not look back and a few seconds later disappeared through the door into the ship's interior.

Matthew did his pack up again, and put it on. He said to Billy: 'I'll go first. You come after me. O.K.?'

On the way down, he had a few bad moments. Apart from the ordinary fears, it occurred to him that there was nothing to stop Skiopos returning, and shooting at them or throwing things down on them. Ship's supplies must not leave the ship, and they were carrying some away in their stomachs. The clothes, too. He was very relieved to step on to firm ground and to see the boy follow him.

They walked away at a good pace and saw the great stranded ark diminish behind them. But they were heading downhill again, and a couple of hours later it still bulked larged on the horizon.

Matthew said: 'Time for a break, I think.'

Billy had been silent at first, but was cheerful now, chattering as usual. But he had not said anything about Skiopos, or the ship.

Matthew said: 'Like something to eat?'

He shook his head. 'I'm not hungry.'

Matthew fished in his pack. He brought out one of the chocolate biscuits, and saw Billy's face widen with surprise and pleasure. He had kept them back from the rest. It had been worth the bad moments on the swaying ladder, he thought.

TEN

THE sun came out and scorched through the afternoon. They went on across sand and rock, heading roughly north, and camped for the night on a patch of sand surrounded by an oddly symmetrical circle of boulders. The discomfort was the more unpleasant after the bunks on the tanker, and they slept fitfully and woke up cramped and a bit miserable. But the night had not been too cold, and the sun came up and warmed them. They opened a tin of corned beef, and Matthew tried not to let his mind dwell on bread.

It was very hot again, and about mid-day they encountered more mud flats, at first broken up by bars of shingle but later continuous, a grey-brown plain stretching on and on, almost completely featureless. Unlike the earlier mud, this had dried hard—there were occasional soft spots but they were no more than inches deep. They could walk on it easily; more easily, in fact, than had been possible at any other time since they left the old land level. What was disturbing was the impression of endlessness. The horizon of sand and shingle and rocky spurs was lost behind them in the interminable dark waste, which ran, it seemed, forever, ahead and on either side. The place depressed with its suggestion of infinity. Their feet kicked up spurts of brown dust, which hung in the air. Matthew found himself sweating hard, and Billy was hot and exhausted. He gave him water from the plastic container, which he had refilled on the tanker. It had a cleaner, slightly sweeter taste than the water they had found on Alderney. Matthew drank some himself. If Skiopos had known they had taken it, he would probably have insisted on them putting that back, too.

They travelled on. Matthew had the notion that they were stopping to rest more often, but for shorter periods. Although their progress was enervating, the halts—sitting or lying on the baked mud—were not refreshing. After quite a short time the predominant feeling was restlessness, a need to get on even though nothing changed.

Any features that did stand out above the flatness were that much more conspicuous: the eye saw them a long way off and travelled to them. There were not many. An occasional length of timber, the shattered mud-caked wreck of a small coaster, once a tangle of rusty girders whose origin Matthew could not guess at. The last thing that day was the submarine. It was half buried by the tail, its bows pointing at an oblique angle towards the sky. It lay west of them and the sun was going down behind it; it was outlined in the golden-reddish light. It looked too crude and small to be recent. A relic of the First War, Matthew thought. Their course took them within a hundred yards of it, but they did not bother to investigate more closely. They were both tired and it was important, Matthew felt, to press on as far as they could while the light lasted.

Despite the sense of being defenceless, in the open without shelter, they slept better that night. The stars were very bright in a clear sky and later on the moon came up, in its first quarter. Matthew woke at one point and lay awake for perhaps half an hour, staring up at the heavens. In the past he had thought the night sky a meaningless jumble of points of light, immensity dwarfed by incomprehensibility. Now it had significance, the allusion of familiarity if nothing else. All the world had changed, but not the constellations. He fell asleep again, contemplating them.

All the next day and part of the day after they were on the flats. Cloud came up from the south, covering the sun, but there was no rain. Once birds flew overhead, a wedge of wild duck. It was the wrong time of year for them; they should have completed their migration long before the breakdown. Perhaps all the changes that had taken place had thrown them out of their pattern. Or perhaps the seasons themselves might be changing? But that was silly, Matthew told himself. This was summer, all right, a typical, rather better than average summer over the British Isles. But isles no longer.

They came to the end of the flats at last, and their spirits rose with the change of scene. There was a lot of shingle, occasional rocks, outcrops of chalk. There was also a dead whale, its carcase largely rotted—the stink heralded its presence for half a mile before they caught sight of it. Living creatures were feeding on it: two or three gulls and a carrion crow. Seeing the last gave Matthew hope of not being too far from the sight of land.

Which they achieved at last. On the fourth afternoon after leaving the tanker, Billy pointed towards the horizon.

'Mr Cotter! I don't think it's a cloud. Is it land, do you think?'

There had been some sun in the morning, nothing but heavy cloud for the last few hours. But there had been few detours necessary, and he had been confident that they were on course. And yet only rocks and shingle showed in front of them; the higher smudge in the sky which Billy had pointed out was away on their left—west of them, he would have said.

He studied it for a long time. Fieldglasses would have resolved the question right away, of course. One might as well, he thought wrily, wish for a good stretch of road and a Jaguar. He could not be sure, but Billy's eyes were younger and probably saw things more clearly. He said:

'Do you think it's land?'

'I think so. I'm not sure.'

'We'll have a go at it, then.'

They altered course, and plodded on. At one spot they found two walls of a beach-hut, tossed here and still standing. A sign along the front said: TEAS, PICNIC BASKETS, ICE CR—. Swept out by the wave, Matthew supposed. He looked up again, and in a moment of clarity saw that there was no doubt about it. The outline was sharper, more positive. They were heading for land.

The explanation of its position came as they got nearer and the land took on a shape that he recognized. There had been a flowing tide when he had last seen it, a spanking wind filling a sail above his head, and the smell of sausages coming up from the tiny galley of the friend's boat on which Felicity and he were spending the weekend. All that was gone, but he knew he was looking at the entrance to Poole Harbour. Their first course had been correct, and if they had not turned from it they would now have been in sight of Bournemouth. Or the place where Bournemouth had been.

It was getting late. The sky was darkening and it would not be long before they had to stop for the night. If they carried on as they were, they had a good chance of getting off the sea bed that day. The thought was tempting. There was more chance of there being some kind of shelter there, and the first thing in the morning, if the sun were out, they might find wood and make a fire. The smell of the sausages out of the past haunted him again.

But to head west was to head away from Jane, and he could not do it knowingly. He told Billy they were going the wrong way, and they turned again towards the north. They saw land there eventually but by that time the light was draining from the sky and, a little while later, they were forced to halt. They slept in sand again, and during the night it rained. Not much, but enough to awaken them and to soak them. It seemed a long time till morning.

They came up from the sea bed, Matthew calculated, at roughly the point where Bournemouth would have been. There was no trace of it now; the great wave had scoured as fiercely here as in the Channel Isles, ripping away all the marks of man. What was left was the basic contour of the land. Were these bare hills, he wondered, the ridges which had supported hotels and boarding-houses and rows of shops? In the early morning light there was a faint air of familiarity about them. But nothing moved, nothing lived here. They climbed over scree, slipping and struggling for a footing. It was a discouraging landfall.

The rain was holding off, but the sky was cloudy. At the moment, though, the coastline gave them bearings. They headed in a generally north-western direction, which should take them to the somewhat higher ground of the New Forest. Their clothes were still damp from their drenching and the morning did not seem to bring much warmth. Even walking they were cold, and when they stopped to rest they found themselves shivering. It was surprising, Matthew thought, that they had escaped illness; but one could be wretched enough without being ill. He looked at Billy with compassion. He himself had a purpose, at least, an end in view. The boy struggled on through a wrecked and meaningless world with no objective.

The high-water mark ran clear along the side of a hill; above it, abruptly, there were grass, bushes, a few trees. The sight was wonderful after the days of nothing but barrenness. Automatically they sat down in the grass, touching and touched by its soft dampness. Matthew caught blades in his fingers, pulled them out, crushed them for the smell. Now at last he was back in England. The scents of summer were intoxicating. Further up there was a cluster of high-stemmed marguerite daisies, with a pair of red and brown butterflies dancing above them. And in the distance he heard a blackbird calling.

He gave Billy one of the two remaining chocolate biscuits, and they set off again, up the slope. From the crest of the hill they looked down at a land superficially scarred but intrinsically unchanged—trees were down in places and a brown weal showed where there had been an earth slip, but in essence it was an ordinary rural scene. Except, of course, for the lack of husbandry. The shapes of fields and hedges were there, but the fields were overgrown and untended. Matthew saw wheat below them and, over to the right, something that was very much worth a detour: potatoes.

They found the first signs of men at the potato field. The whole of one corner had been taken up, the plants thrown down between the furrows. Matthew pulled up the next couple along the row. The potatoes were small still, the biggest no more than a couple of inches long. But there were quite a lot on each plant. They brushed as much of the dirt off as possible, and ate them raw.

Before moving on, they pulled up several more plants and filled the spaces in their packs with potatoes. In a clump of trees nearby they found twigs and branches which could have been broken to make fuel for a fire, but there was no sign of the sun coming out to enable the glass to be used. Matthew was annoyed by his own lack of forethought. He could have taken matches from Miller's store, or found matches or something similar on the tanker. His attention had been concentrated on the crossing of the sea bed, with too little thought of what would come after.

A few hundred yards from the potato field, they had a sight of human habitation, or the remains of it. The jumble of bricks and wood had presumably been a farmhouse; outlying rubble followed a pattern of farm buildings. There was the usual smell of death, though it was less pervading than it had been. Time was passing, flesh rotting down into the purifying earth.

Something else had happened here, too. The rubble had been turned over by human hands; the evidence for it was unmistakable. Rescue work? Or foraging? The latter, presumably—the disturbances had a recent look. A band of nomads wandering through the country, picking up what they could—potatoes, or a few tins from the ruins of the farmer's larder. It was depressing, and something of a shock, to have to think in those terms. He had had no clear idea of what might have happened to survivors in the wider reaches of England, but he had taken for granted that there would be organization at least on a level comparable with that which they had left behind in Guernsey. Now he saw that this might be quite wide of the mark. Where confines were narrow, discipline was stricter, and the chance of order emerging so much greater. Like string quartets or the Elizabethan sonnet. Chaos could be more complete here, and longer lasting.

The last indications of humanity that day were the most welcome. They passed from agricultural to common land—the wooded spaces of the New Forest itself—and reached a main road which Matthew guessed was either the A.31 or the A.35: travelling with neither sun nor compass it was impossible to know how far they had strayed from their original course. It made sense, he decided, to follow the road, which was buckled and tree-strewn, beginning to be encroached on by grass, but more passable than the land around it; though only if one knew which road it was. To turn right along the A.31 would take them to Southampton, but a similar manœuvre on the A.35 would return them the way they had come. The day was declining, but the cloud cover was so thick that he could not even guess at the west. The only safe thing, he decided, was an early halt, in the hope that the sky might be clearer in the morning. He felt tired enough, and Billy looked dead beat.

But Billy, to his surprise, begged that they should go on for a little. He said:

'Why? Aren't you tired? And I'm not sure which is our right way.'

'I thought I saw . . .'

'What?'

'Smoke.'

'Where?'

He pointed up the road—west, if it were the A.31.

'Past those trees.'

Matthew looked, but could see nothing. But Billy had seen land first, and the chance was worth taking. He nodded.

'All right. We'll go and look round the bend.'

Round the bend there were the ruins of houses, these too showing signs of having recently been worked over. Matthew looked round for people and saw no one. But the smoke was there. A few stones had been put together by the side of the road and it rose from them. Charred wood smouldered, and a few embers glowed.

Matthew put his hands to his mouth, hallooed, and listened for a reply. None came. He tried twice more, with the same result. The fire might have been abandoned hours ago. They had not bothered to douse it and might well have left it fully blazing.

The important thing was that it was still alight, though only just. Some wood—broken laths from the houses—was scattered a couple of yards away. He and Billy collected them and he set them carefully above the charred pieces and, bending down over them, blew gently and steadily. It took time, but at last the glow brightened into small tongues of flame and the new wood caught. Billy, meanwhile, had brought in more wood. The fire blazed up and soon they were sitting on either side of it, warming their hands.

They had a good supper that night. They grilled sardines in the tin, in their oil, and shared them, and after that heated up a concoction of wild boar with mushrooms and olives—one of the tins they had picked up on Alderney. But the best was last:

potatoes roasted in the embers as the fire died down again. They had their fill of these, and settled for the night, after Matthew had banked up the fire with thick pieces of wood and covered it over with clods.

They were doing well, he thought. Their bellies were full, the ground they were lying on was the solid and ancient earth of England, and with luck the fire would still be renewable in the morning. It was a pity they had met no one yet, but they obviously would, quite soon.

Billy woke him, clutching his arm and saying:

'Look!'

Matthew moved his cramped body, and did as he was bid. It was early morning, light enough to see fifty yards or so. And they stood at the very edge of vision—wraith-like, almost melting into the shadows. But clear enough to see. Two at first and then, as one of them moved, he saw a third grazing behind it. New Forest ponies. A brown, a dun, and a smaller sorrel. Matthew thought, with delight: they survived the motorists who massacred them summer after summer on the unfenced roads of the Forest, and now the motor-cars are gone and they still crop the grass as they did in the days of William Rufus. It was a wonderful sight.

That was the first thought; the second was acquisitive. They were not pack-animals in the way that donkeys or mules were, but they could carry some goods, and they could carry a boy. He motioned to Billy to be silent, rose quietly to his feet, and walked towards them. As he approached he talked to them easily, in a low voice. One of them looked up, seemingly saw no danger, and put its head down again to the grass. They waited until he was a few feet from them before jerking round and cantering away. Their hooves drummed the earth, more and more faintly, as they disappeared among the trees.

Billy, as he came back, said: 'Bad luck, Mr Cotter. I think they were pretty wild, though.'

He said: 'I'd forgotten that. They're probably unbroken, and I believe they take some breaking in. Even if I'd been able to get one, it wouldn't have done us much good.'

'It was nice seeing them.'

'Yes,' he said. 'It was nice.'

Matthew succeeded in coaxing the fire back to life, and they started the day with warmed-up corned beef and the rest of the potatoes. Stores were beginning to get low, and would need replenishing. He wondered how many people there were ransacking the ruins of the houses by the roadside. The point was, of course, that survival was more probable in the country districts, and so was the exhaustion of supplies of tinned foods. Towns and cities would offer much more scope in that respect. If they could reach Southampton . . . The estuary should have protected it from the full effects of the tidal wave.

He looked up at the sky. There was cloud still, but it was broken, and a patch of brightness showed the east. Which meant that this was the A.31, after all. They had their direction now, and could follow the road.

They saw people about an hour after they had started on their way. They were some distance from the road. Their clothes were the usual assortment of bits and pieces, and their general appearance unkempt. Matthew could only tell from the lack of beards that they were women, one in her twenties, one a good deal older. They had not seen him, and he called to them:

'Hello, there!'

Their reaction was immediate. They stared at him for a moment, and began to run away. The older one stumbled, and the other paused to help her. Matthew called after them again, trying to be reassuring, but they ran on. There was a thicket a couple of hundred yards away. They went in, not looking back, and disappeared among the bushes.

Billy said: 'Were they frightened?'

'It seems like it.'

'Why, Mr Cotter?'

The women's fear communicated to him as an apprehension. Could this be the pattern of things—small isolated groups of two or three people, grubbing for food in the fields and the ruins, running from the sight of their fellow men? Surely there must be some who could impose order, as Miller had done?

He said: 'I don't know, Billy.' He began to walk on. 'People do funny things these days.'

The encounter in the afternoon was very different.

They had been travelling across the open land of the New Forest, where apart from occasional bucklings of the road and fissures in the ground, and fallen trees, there was little to mark the change that had taken place. The sun was shining, and they had been able to build a fire at mid-day. They were making good progress, and Matthew was cheered by seeing quite a lot of birds: thrushes, a wren, a robin, and a pair of magpies, as bright and noisy as ever. They had also seen, in the distance, another pony. He and Billy were talking about this as they approached a mound of rubble which signified what had once been a village. He looked up, his attention caught by a slight movement at the corner of his vision, and saw the woman watching them.

She was standing by a large tree, at the edge of the mound and perhaps twenty yards from the road. She was dressed in brown—slacks and a jersey—which helped her to blend with the background. And she was standing still, watching their approach. She continued to do so in silence after Matthew had caught sight of her. Billy, sensing the distraction, looked and saw her also.

He said: 'She isn't running away, Mr Cotter.'

'No,' Matthew said. 'Not so far.'

He studied her as they approached. She was in her middle thirties, he judged, of medium height and with a good figure. She was, by present standards, well groomed. Brown hair, cut fairly short, was drawn back from a face that had—his first thought told him—intelligence and courage, but not beauty. It was lined about the mouth and eyes. She looked as though she had been through a good deal.

Matthew stopped, a few feet away from her. He said quietly: 'Hello. Billy was just saying that you weren't running away.'

She smiled, and it was a transforming act. To the other qualities it added warmth, in such measure that he was inclined to revise his opinion about beauty, too. She said:

'No. I didn't think you looked all that dangerous. Where are you from?'

'Guernsey.' She looked blank. 'The Channel Isles.'

'I mean, since the Bust.'

'So do I.'

'How did you get here?'

'We walked it.'

'So the sea's gone altogether?' Matthew nodded. 'What's it like out there?'

'Pretty much the same as here, as far as I can see.'

'Survivors?'

'A few. Eleven or twelve, apart from us.'

'Decent people?'

'Averagely, I should think.'

'Then why?' The question was pitched with an almost ferocious intensity. 'Why come here? What did you expect to find?'

Matthew said quietly: 'I don't know. My daughter was here. In Sussex, that is. I wanted to try to find her.'

She gave a short unhappy laugh. 'My God, you're greedy!'

'Greedy?'

'I had three children. And a husband I was quite fond of. If I'd been left with one of them, I would have been contented. I wouldn't have dragged a child on this sort of wild goose chase.'

'Coming was his idea,' Matthew said. 'I was out on the sea bed when he caught up with me. I could hardly send him back.'

'Hardly!'

Belatedly, he caught her meaning. He said:

'Billy's not my son. I dug him out. As I say, he followed me without my knowing, until it was too late to do much about it. Jane was my only one.'

He was conscious of the tense he had used, and thought that the woman was, too. There was a pause, before she said:

'I see. I'm sorry. I'm April. I had a second name, but ——' She shrugged.

'Matthew,' he said. 'Matthew Cotter, but I agree it doesn't matter. And this is Billy.'

The warmth he had noticed before came back to her face. She said:

'Come on. You might as well meet the others.'

'You're not alone, then?'

'Who can afford to be?'

'What were you watching for?'

'Trouble,' she said. 'What else?'

From the road a path led round the edge of the rubble; others, presumably, had made the detour. There were the marks of various foraging incursions into the ruins, and as they went on Matthew could hear voices and sounds of activity. They found eventually a small group of people engaged in digging. There were five in all. They broke off at the sight of April and the others.

April said: 'Just the two of them, and I think they're decent.' She had used the expression before, Matthew remembered; presumably it signified a necessary classification. 'Sybil, go and take my post, will you?'

Sybil was about twenty-eight, a cowed-looking, not very attractive girl, hiding a thin figure behind badly fitting blue overall trousers and a man's checked shirt. She nodded silently, and went back the way they had come.

April said: 'Have you found anything worthwhile?'

There were three men. One, his hair and beard so light in colour that they looked white in the sunlight, seemed to be in his early twenties; and there was a runtish red-haired man of about forty. The third was still older—over fifty, Matthew guessed. He was large-framed and gave the impression of having been overweight before being hardened by privation and hard work. He wore a blue shirt and dark grey trousers, and like April seemed to have been making an effort to keep up appearances. His hair was combed and his beard, black tinged with grey and white, was not as untidy as those of the two other men. When he spoke it was, like April, in an educated voice. He said:

'Not much so far. Some food.' He pointed to a small pile of tins on the grass. 'And we've reached a wardrobe which looks as though it might be worth digging out properly.' He looked at Matthew and Billy. 'Are they travelling through?'

'I think so.' She smiled. 'They've come a long way. From Guernsey.'

There was general surprise, and the last member of the group, a girl not much older than Billy, said excitedly:

'We went to Guernsey on holiday last year! We was going to go again.'

April said: 'I think we could knock off for a cup of tea. The kettle should be just about boiling.'

Matthew noticed then that beyond the pile of tins and various bags and items of clothing, a small fire was burning between bricks, on the top of which a battered silver kettle was balanced. He said:

'You have tea?'

'We have tea,' the older man said, climbing down from the rubble. 'We have a fair supply of sugar, thanks to finding a sack of the stuff protected from the elements. We have a little tinned milk, but we would dearly like to stumble on some more. My name's Lawrence, by the way.'

He held his hand out, and Matthew noticed that he had managed to keep his nails short and clean. They looked capable hands, the fingers long and sensitive. A musician, possibly? Not that it was relevant.

April and the girl went to see to the kettle. Lawrence introduced Matthew to the others. The young man was George, the red-headed one Archie.

'You've met April,' Lawrence said. 'That's Cathie with her. And Charley is look-out on the other side.'

'These look-outs,' Matthew said. 'Against what?'

Lawrence asked: 'Since you got across—are we the first you've met?'

'We saw two women, but they ran off before I could talk to them.'

'It was a rhetorical question,' Lawrence said. 'You still have your packs and they look as though they have something in them. And that shotgun. Any cartridges for it, by the way?'

'A couple of dozen.'

'That's a considerable armament. The point is, my dear Matthew, that some dig, but some do not. Some prefer to have their digging done for them. Hence the look-outs. It is infinitely depressing to labour amongst muck and dust and corpses only to have the fruits of your labour taken from you. And not gently, either.'

'There are bigger groups than yours about?'

'Much bigger. There's one, in particular, that's getting on for thirty strong, and something like two-thirds of them men in their prime.'

'They're not actually murderous?'

'No. Why should they be? At this stage, at least. As I say, they like to have their digging done for them.'

Matthew looked at the mound in front of them.

'This place—I should have thought it would have been worked over already. Since it's on a main road.'

'It has been. But not thoroughly, of course. None of them are, particularly in view of the hazards. And for the same reason, we switch around as much as possible. It's not a good thing to get fixed in patterns of behaviour.'

'I suppose not.'

'You don't sound convinced. I was out in Africa when I was a young man. The buck used to go down to the water-hole, and the lion went after the buck, and we went after the lion. These are our water-holes. Another attractive thing about this particular one is that you have a goodish view in the two most likely directions—along the road. Ah, that looks like the tea at last.'

Matthew gleaned a little more about the general situation while they were drinking tea, for the most part out of heavy plastic red cups which had apparently been obtained from a picnic set. As far as this group was concerned, Lawrence appeared to be the titular head, April the major influence. This was, in general, reminiscent of Miller and the girl Irene, but the personalities concerned were vastly different. Lawrence was a more intelligent, more cultured and weaker man than Miller had been, and the strength in April was not the cold negative strength of Irene, but something more positive and more emotional.

How far the link between them was sexual, Matthew was not sure. She showed little in that respect; Lawrence, in the way he looked at her, was more revealing. Their shared middle-class background would throw them together. The others in the group, with the possible exception of the absent Charley, to whom the girl Cathie had taken a cup of tea, had clearly been working-class. The distinctions had only to be made for their absurdity to be recognized, but in desperation people were likely to cling to absurdities. For a while. Eventually they would settle for what they had.

Apart from April, who stayed fairly silent, they plied him with questions—chiefly about crossing the sea bed. They found the idea bizarre and exciting, but there was more to their interest than that. He realized that what appealed to them was the very thing which he had found disquieting: the isolation, the knowledge of being alone in an empty land. It was part of the wistfulness of the preyed upon and hunted, which was still foreign to him.

Lawrence asked: 'What about water?'

'We had enough.' He pointed to the plastic container, tied to the pack.

'But did you find any fresh water, on your way over? There should be springs, surely.'

'There were a couple of streams. They were both brackish.'

'Residual salts, I suppose. Anyway, one couldn't live out there, could one? Even your friend the captain's time is limited. We could only carry enough food to last us a week, and there would be no way of getting more.'

'You've got a store of food?' Matthew asked.

'Yes. We're trying to build it up.'

For a time, he supposed, it might be possible to build up, but as the mounds were ransacked over and over again, the aspect would change. There would be the running down, the desperate hunt for the few remaining tins, finally starvation. And the winter to come. He said:

'Hasn't there been any attempt to organize things?'

'Organize?' Lawrence asked.

'On a long-term basis.'

'We found a goose,' Lawrence said. 'A live and kicking goose. We clipped her wings and penned her. Who knows—we might have found a gander. Or traded something with someone who had one.' He shrugged. 'The yobbos got her. They had roast goose that night—a few mouthfuls each, I suppose.'

'But can't they see how stupid that is?' Matthew said.

April said, as though driven into speech by impatience:

'What was your idea of what's happened? Who do you think survived? Just the teachers and bank clerks and local government officers, with some nice honest policemen, and perhaps the chief constable of the county as president? That's the way it ought to have been. But things weren't done as neatly as that. What did you expect, for God's sake? The orderly people, the people who could plan more than a few days ahead, have always been in a minority.'

'Can't a minority do something?'

'Yes,' she said, 'they can practise their running. They can pit their wits against the others, and learn how to keep out of their way.'

'There must be some who are still civilized,' Matthew said. 'Other groups, like your own. You could team up with them, couldn't you?'

April looked at him with the same fierceness, but did not answer. Lawrence said:

'What good would it do? It would only make it harder to hide, and offer a more tempting target to them.'

'You might find you outnumbered them.'

'One particular gang, perhaps, but they can combine, too. They would if there were good pickings. It might only be on a temporary basis, but long enough to strip us of everything.'

'It seems like a bleak outlook,' Matthew said.

There was a pause, before Lawrence said: 'We won't argue about that. Can you show us the way to a better one?'

Jane, he thought, living this sort of life . . . The idea was unbearable. Lawrence said:

'I suppose you don't feel like throwing in with us? We could take you and the boy.'

April had not spoken to the others about their first conversation. She looked at him and then, indifferently, away. He said:

'If Billy wants to stay, and you'll have him . . .'

Billy said quickly: 'No, I don't want to.'

'I'm going on,' Matthew said.

'Right away?' Lawrence looked at the boy. 'I would prescribe a few day's rest for the boy. He's had a gruelling journey.'

Looking at Billy himself, Matthew saw how true that was. He looked peaked, and desperately tired. He would have been glad for the boy to stay, to be free to continue his journey on his own, but he saw the impossibility of that. He represented whatever stability and permanence remained for Billy in the exhausting and frightening world in which he now lived. And had a responsibility for him—limited, he told himself, but a responsibility. He said, trying to keep the grudgingness out of his voice:

'A day's break might be a good idea, if you can put up with us.'

'As long as you like.'

'We have our own food. We won't be using your stocks.'

'That's not important. Whatever does finally bring us down won't depend on a day or two's rations for a man and a boy.'

Already beginning to regret the delay, Matthew said:

'Where is your camp? We don't want to go back on our tracks.'

'Our base isn't far away. A few miles north.'

'I was hoping to get to Southampton tomorrow. I thought there would be plenty to forage for there.'

'There is,' Lawrence said. 'Plenty. And plenty of yobbos waiting to take the stuff off you as soon as you've got it out. Most of the gangs operate from the outskirts.'

The tea had been too hot but was now cool enough to drink. The taste, sweet and metallic, took him back to Army days, when he had thought the world was mad and desperate. He sipped the tea and remembered how safe and unimaginably secure it had all been.

ELEVEN

MATTHEW helped them with the digging. They broke up the wardrobe and ransacked it; there were a couple of men's suits, a heavy overcoat, a hacking jacket, a cardigan and three pairs of shoes in good condition. Not far away they found a broken wooden chest with blankets in it. The ones on top were damp and evil-smelling, full of mould, but the bottom layers were not too bad. All were brought out and added to the pile of things. Before abandoning work for the day, they found another stock of food, including two tins of coffee and an unbroken glass jar, a foot high, of plums. Lawrence was particularly delighted with the coffee.

'The first we've found,' he told Matthew. 'We got tea in the early days, stacks of it. It's better than nothing, but coffee's always been my drink. I used to have one of those automatic coffee-makers beside my bed. It was damned good. I used to switch it on as soon as I had a night call, and by the time I was dressed it was just about ready. I think I miss that more than anything. Material things, that is.'

'Night call?'

'I was a doctor.' He stared at the tins of coffee. 'How long will these last? A dozen brews—perhaps a few more if not everyone likes coffee. But they'll drink it now, if they never did before. One doesn't pass up a novelty these days. I found myself eating pilchards last week. And liking them.'

'A doctor,' Matthew said. 'I should have thought that would —well, carry some weight still.'

'Weight? With whom? The yobbos? You're still overrating them.'

'The more primitive people are, the more impressionable, surely. And dependent on the mysteries of authority.'

Lawrence shook his head. 'It's a question of scale. There was a paper in *The Lancet* not long before it happened. A study of the psychological effects of the South Island quake, linking up with previous catastrophe reports—the Skopje earthquake, the bombings at Dresden and Hiroshima. Much the same results. Something like three-quarters of the population that survived showed mild mental disturbances of various kinds, about one in ten more seriously ill but little lasting psychosis, and what there was occurring among people apparently predisposed to it. The effects of the Bust seem to have been a bit different. I could do a nice little paper on it myself. In fact, I dreamt the other night that I had done it and that it was published in the *B.M.J.* Funny thing, I can remember the papers immediately before and after it, too. One on a new technique for nephrectomy and the other on strangulated piles. I'd called mine "The Ant-hill Syndrome". Rather a neat title, I thought.'

'Why ant-hill?'

'Because I read somewhere once about the way ants behave when the ant-hill's taken a beating. Up to a certain level of damage, the pattern's not unlike the one reported in *The Lancet*: initial disturbance and confusion but fairly rapid recovery as the survivors—or the more enterprising ones amongst them—get over the shock and set about putting things to rights. But it's quite different when the damage exceeds the level. Then, as far as the survivors are concerned, there's no recovery. Their behaviour becomes more and more pointless and erratic and destructive.'

'Because the queen's dead, I imagine.'

'I have an idea that wasn't the operative condition, though I can't be sure. But isn't our queen dead, too? I don't mean the person—the guiding force in our society, the source of purpose and identity. It's an interesting speculation. The point is that we're behaving like the second category of ants. There's a mass psychosis, which it would be absurd to try to influence. I suppose there may have been a few relatively sane ants, too. It made no difference. They died with the rest.'

'Don't you think you might be generalizing on the basis of special local conditions? It wasn't like this back on the island. One or two individuals were off their heads, but the rest got together and were doing things.'

Lawrence smiled. 'My dear man, you'd better do a paper, too! It could well be different in a small isolated community, in fact one would expect it to be. A few survivors in a tiny place surrounded by sea—or by sea bed, anyway—can re-establish identity. I hope they'll prosper. Perhaps our salvation will come out of the islands and the Highlands. By our, I mean human, of course. In a generation or two, perhaps.'

They headed north as the sun went down, burdened with their spoils of the day. They had a variety of bags and haversacks, and a number of net-like arrangements, woven of thick twine, which could be slung over the shoulder and used as carryalls. The country they went through was partly wooded, partly open, with relatively few ruins. Billy, who had rested during the afternoon, was very cheerful, and chattered as he walked beside Matthew. In pairs ahead were Charley and Cathie and George and Sybil, the latter two showing signs of close physical intimacy. Lawrence and April brought up the rear, and little Archie trotted along in front. He carried a bag full of tins in one hand, and with the other held a net, containing blankets and clothes, on his back. It was a heavy weight, and badly distributed, but he made no complaint.

Matthew had been expecting to see a camp something like the one they had left on Guernsey. He was surprised when they stopped in grounds which, though badly overgrown, retained the outlines of a large and fairly elaborate garden. It would have needed a couple of gardeners to keep it in anything like shape. In front of them was the rubble of the house to which the garden had belonged, but nothing else. The others put their burdens down, and he did the same with his.

He said to Lawrence: 'Is this a break for a rest?'

'No, we're here. As I've said, we have to take precautions. You'll see.'

The men of the party began shifting timbers from the ruins. They worked quickly, as though they were familiar with the routine, but it was something like ten minutes before they cleared them away to show a big oak refectory table lying upside down, most of its underpart shattered but the table top seemingly intact. The men got together and heaved at this. It was clearly very heavy, and they had to strain to lift it. Beneath it there were wooden stairs, leading, presumably to a cellar.

The sight of it brought up the familiar fear of confinement. He would not do it, he decided. He would sleep in the open. But April went down, and the others followed, carrying the various items they had brought back. Lawrence touched his arm.

'Come and see Ali Baba's cave. It wasn't his cave, though, was it? He only found it. Do you know, I meant to take my grandchildren to a pantomime last winter. I hadn't been since I was a boy myself. In the end, I was too busy with the practice. I thought next year would do. Mind your head, as you go.'

He was afraid of showing his fear, and followed. There were two candles lit, and April was using the second to light a third. It had been a big cellar, about twenty feet square, but one corner had filled with debris where the roof had collapsed. The floor was flagged, uneven in places where the stones had been forced up. The candles stood on two trestle tables in the centre of the room, and the food and clothing were put down on the tables in a jumbled heap. The bare brick walls carried some shelving—diverse and crudely made stuff which had clearly been put up recently. Things were laid out on the shelves and on the floor beneath them: food in one part, blankets, clothing and so on in another, and in a third section various pieces of equipment. He saw coils of rope, saws, hammers, nails, a high-focus battery torch, lengths of galvanized iron, a roll of roofing felt, shears and heavy scissors, a metal ladder, and a whole assembly of other things. They were very neatly ranged. The most conspicuous item was the back-axle unit of a small motor-car, with wheels attached. Lawrence, seeing his eye on it, said:

'I thought we might rig up some sort of hand-cart with that. But we're none of us very mechanically-minded. And it would be difficult to hide it. It's probably too big a project for us, anyway—too purposeful.'

April and the others were sorting out the things they had

134

brought in. She gave them quick decisive instructions, and they took them away to the places she indicated. The order that existed was of her making, Matthew realized. He noticed a door, in the wall on the left. Pointing to it, he said:

'Do you sleep in there?'

'Sleep? My God, no! Not below ground. That's only a cubby-hole, anyway. It was the wine-cellar. We had a lot of glass to clean out, and surprisingly a few bottles survived. A Beaujolais, a Mateus Rosé, a Musigny, and a Château Léoville Poyferré, '34. No whites, I'm afraid, which is a pity because I preferred white. But then, we have no means of chilling. We're keeping them for occasions which call for celebration—so far there haven't been any. Oh, yes, and one bottle of brandy came through. A Biscuit Grande Champagne. I'm keeping *that* for medicinal purposes which shows to what criminal depths a man can descend. I keep the rest of my medical stuff in there, too.'

Matthew said: 'It's an impressive collection. Do you think you ought to have shown it to me?'

'You don't think it goes with our excessive caution in other things? Well, of course, you're right. In part, I suppose it's due to simple recognition of someone who talks the same language. But in part it's sheer carelessness, a failure in consistency. Our own little contribution to the ant-hill syndrome. Still and all, I don't *see* you betraying our secret to the Southampton hordes and leading them here to plunder.' He looked at Matthew, his face, in the candle light, amiable and weak. 'You're going to find the road ahead something of a tricky one. Are you sure we shan't be able to persuade you to settle here?'

The others were occupied in sorting and stacking. Matthew told Lawrence briefly about Jane. Lawrence said:

'You know what the chances are, I imagine? Against her having survived, in the first place, and then against your finding her even if she has? But of course you do. You're a man of intelligence.'

'Not in this,' Matthew said. 'I realize that.'

'No, not in this. But we're none of us entirely rational any longer, as you've just pointed out.' He smiled. 'We're all waiting for a miracle. Yours is just that bit more miraculous, and at least you're going out to look for it.'

Matthew had noticed a roll of canvas next to the wheel assembly. When the distribution had been completed, George and the red-haired Archie got hold of this and carried it upstairs into the open. The others took bundles from the clothes section—they were tied with rope, some of them wrapped in a groundsheet. They carried these out, as well. April said:

'You and Billy help yourself to blankets. The pile on the right are the good ones—the others need washing and drying. We haven't got any spare groundsheets, I'm afraid.'

'We've been sleeping rough,' he said. 'But the blankets will help. You sleep out, too? In the open?'

'More or less.'

Along with the blanket rolls, items of food specified by April were brought outside, as was a large iron pot. Then the table top was replaced, and the jumble of timbers above it. Loose bricks and plaster were scattered on top, to give the whole an undisturbed disorganized look. Matthew asked:

'Do you have to go through this performance every day?'

'Every day and twice a day. And any day we may come back to find that some gang, picking over the ruins, have—as a whim, perhaps—shifted that table top and found the cellar. It gives life a spice of uncertainty, don't you think?'

They trekked from the house through the garden. There was a shrubbery and further on an overhanging rock face. It had been an ornamental grotto; niches held one or two figures, too badly weathered to be identified either as saints or demons. George and Archie unrolled the canvas they had brought and Matthew saw that there were poles inside. They set these up, with the canvas stretching from them to the rock face, where they tied the ends with rope to small upright spires of concrete through which reinforcing metal showed—part of the original adornment of the grotto. When they had finished they had an awning which covered the width of the grotto, about twenty feet, and, taking the overhang into account, gave some protection outwards for eight or nine feet. It was about the same distance from the ground.

'There you are,' Lawrence said. 'There's no place like it. Not entirely draught-free, but except when the wind is from the south you don't get wet.'

'And in the winter?' Matthew asked.

'Yes, we ought to give that some thought, oughtn't we? We will, Matthew. Tomorrow, or next week, or next month.'

Matthew shrugged. 'It's not my business, of course. But I would have thought you could be keeping your eyes open for winter quarters.' Or, at least, he thought, that April would be. Yet if she were, surely she would have organized them into it more thoroughly. With a quirk of curiosity, he added: 'How did you come to settle here, anyway? By accident?'

'Accident? Of a kind, I suppose. April lived here, before the Bust. Her husband and the children are buried on the other side of the house. She dug them out and buried them herself.'

She was supervising Sybil and Cathie, who were lighting a fire between bricks. There was strength in the way she stood and in the womanly firmness of her body. Matthew said:

'I'm surprised she wanted to stay here.'

'Are you? But surely she's allowed her little irrationality, too?'

'Yes,' Matthew said. 'I can't argue with that.'

For supper they had a stew, cooked in the big iron pot. Apart from the tinned meats, there were potatoes in it and other more or less fresh vegetables. It tasted good and was probably nourishing. They ate in relays since there were not enough suitable dishes. Billy was served with the first batch, but Matthew waited and had his with April and Lawrence. Afterwards, they smoked cigarettes and talked. The night air was fresh, but not cold.

Lawrence, Matthew learned, had been in practice in this district, having a house and surgery less than ten miles away. He and April had known each other in the old days, but not very well—it had been a matter of meeting occasionally at other people's drinks parties. Cathie was local, too, the only child of a policeman and his wife. George and Sybil were both from Ringwood, where he had been a jobbing printer's assistant and she had worked in Woolworth's. They were already together when they joined up with the others, but had not known each other before the Bust. Charley had lived in Cadnam and had been working in the docks at Southampton. The last acquisition had been Archie who had wandered in on them one day, and who talked vaguely about different places and different jobs.

Lawrence said: 'I thought at first that it was the effect of the Bust. I mean, we were all a bit unhinged at the start, and I thought in his case it might have become permanent. But I'm inclined to believe now that he's always been mentally a bit subnormal. But at least he's easy-going, and willing.'

'You have no other survivors round here?' Matthew asked.

'None that both lived and stayed,' April said.

'We got an old woman out, who died the following day,' Lawrence said, 'and a man who died the next week. Nothing I could do in either case. And there were two other chaps—one we dug out and one who joined on. They cleared off with the best part of our supplies one day. Fortunately that was when we were keeping things out in the open, before April thought of using the cellar.'

Matthew looked towards the awning where the other members of the party were sitting together. Billy was talking to Cathie. She was a lively child and he seemed to be getting on better with her than with Mandy on Guernsey. Following his gaze, April said.

'It would be a much bigger tragedy if the same thing happened now, of course. But I don't think it will.'

'No,' Matthew said. 'They're all on the timid side, aren't they? Who would protect them if you didn't?'

He looked at her, not at Lawrence. She said, in a suddenly tired voice:

'They're all right.'

Lawrence said: 'We aren't up to Indian Scout standards, I'm

138

afraid, for courage and enterprise. We couldn't even catch the bullock.'

'The bullock?'

'Something else that came through. It grazes in some fields. about a mile from here. We decided that a little fresh meat would be a nice change, and there's no question of saving the species after all. So we hunted it. We hunted it several times, in fact. But it's gone wild and wary and when it came to the point, none of us was keen on facing it. We tried digging a hole, and driving the beast into it. It charged us instead, and we scattered like chaff. Our fresh meat is still merrily on the hoof, and likely to stay that way.'

He was not paying a great deal attention to what Lawrence was saying, but while he was talking about the bullock charging and scattering them, Matthew's eyes happened on his pack, lying on the ground some yards away, with the shotgun still strapped to it. It was a vagrant idea at first, but it made more sense and became more attractive as he thought about it. Fresh meat . . . He and the boy could take some with them, and it offered a good way of repaying hospitality. They might not have much future, but they were nice people.

Matthew said: 'What about another hunt, in the morning?' He saw them look at him, to see if he were serious. 'Do you think we can get near enough to it for a shotgun to be any good?'

'We might,' Lawrence said. 'By God, I think we could! Just imagine it, April. Steak and chips!'

She asked Matthew: 'Are you a good shot?'

'Not good. Fair average, I would say. I've shot duck and snipe, never livestock.'

'We could salt it,' she said. 'We've got plenty of salt.'

'We could eat it,' Lawrence said. 'On and on, and wind up cracking the bones. Have you ever had marrow on toast, Matthew? Wonderful stuff, if we had any toast.'

'Let's kill him first,' Matthew said. It was night now, but in the distance, in the direction of the shrubbery, there was a flickering of light, a green glow. 'What's that?'

'The light?' April asked. 'Glow-worms.' She was silent for

a moment. 'They've always been here at this time of year, on this sort of night.'

They watched the lambency, concerned with their private thoughts, and then Lawrence stood up, yawning.

'Better turn in,' he said, 'if we're to make an early start.'

The start they made, however, was not a particularly early one. The sun was well up when Matthew woke and, looking along the line of huddled figures, he saw only one place where the blankets had been left empty. That was at the far end, where April slept with Lawrence next to her. He got up himself and went out from under the awning. The canvas was damp when he touched it, and the grass outside was heavy with dew. He walked through the garden, and heard a few birds somewhere, at their morning orisons. He had been shown the stream the evening before, the place where they drew water, and told that they washed further down. He found it and followed it. The cheerful sound of its running was pricked through by bird song. It was a moment out of the incredible past, an evocation of happiness.

He caught sight of her as he came past a line of rhododendrons and automatically stepped back. She was about twenty-five yards away. There was a place where the stream broadened and deepened and she was kneeling on the far side. She was facing him, but she gave no sign of having heard or seen his approach. She was naked to the waist, soaping the upper part of her body and her neck. Her breasts were round and full, the heavy nipples dark-aureoled. She arched herself, washing the back of her neck, and her breasts were pulled up by the movement, richer and more lovely than before.

He felt desire, the sharper for being unfamiliar, but what he was most conscious of was the awareness of beauty. A woman's body, kneeling by a stream in a garden, with birds calling from the distant trees . . . he had not imagined that there could be such a thing again. He watched with an ache of longing that was not physical. It was not a wish to pry on her nakedness, nor the fear of her or his own embarrassment if he went forward, that kept him standing motionless. It was the scene he did not want to lose. While he watched the past was alive, the new world nothing but a bad dream, a nightmare, from which he had awoken with a glad heart.

She bent lower, cupping water in her hands and splashing it over herself. Then she looked up, still kneeling. He knew that she could see him, that it was over. The present was real, and this had been the dream.

She said: 'Matthew.' Her voice was low but it carried easily across the distance between them. 'I didn't know . . .'

She broke off. He saw her smile first and only then become aware of her nakedness. She was surprised, confused perhaps, but not ashamed or embarrassed. There was an acknowledgement of vulnerability, but of safety also. She picked up a towel that was lying beside her, unhurriedly, and covered herself with it. She said: 'I won't be a moment,' and he nodded and turned away.

He turned back as he heard her walking towards him, her feet brushing through the grass. She was dressed now, in the brown jersey she had worn the day before. She said, smiling again:

'Hello, then.'

He said: 'I'm sorry for the intrusion.'

April shook her head. 'No, really. I usually have a good half hour before any of the others turn out. They're good sleepers, even Lawrence.'

Her simplicity and ease met a responding serenity in his own mind; the two fed on each other and grew with the feeding. The idyll was transmuted from fantasy into human terms. It was an episode into which each had stumbled and in which each, here and now, found contentment, for whatever private reasons. It was an escape, probably, but explanation did not alter it. They looked at each other, smiling, started to speak at the same time, stopped simultaneously, and laughed.

April said: 'I was saying I ought to start seeing to the breakfast.'

'And I'll go and have my wash.'

'You have soap and a towel?'

'Yes.' He showed her the towel. 'It's a bit grubby now.'

She took it from him. 'And damp. Use mine. It's a little cleaner and drier. I'll scrub this for you while you're out on your bullock hunt.'

'Thank you.'

Their eyes held for a little longer, calmly, without any kind of strain. It was this, the comfort and cheerfulness, of which he was most conscious. He had no feeling of regret as she walked away. He went down to the stream to wash, the towel over his shoulders. He held his head on one side and felt its softness against his face.

After breakfast, there were things to be packed up and stowed away in the cellar. Eventually, the party for the hunt was ready. Apart from Matthew and Billy, it consisted of Lawrence, George and Charley. Archie was staying behind with the women. Lawrence said:

'He gets upset easily, by loud noises or the sight of blood. Anyway, there should be enough of us.'

Matthew's first idea had been that Billy should stay behind as well, but he had begged to be allowed to come with them, and Matthew had relented. He was nearly eleven after all, and this was a world in which, once again, puberty would mark the beginning of manhood. Over-protection of the young was only possible in a complex society.

The morning was bright, the sunlight warm in open spaces through which they passed. There was a light-hearted feeling among them. It was a kind of game, with excitement whetted by appetite. They came to wooded country, enclosing a series of meadows, some adjoining, others separated by stretches of copse.

Lawrence said: 'This is his territory. He ranges round a bit, but within this area.'

As he spoke, there was the sound of a fairly heavy body moving in the undergrowth ahead and on their left. Matthew had both barrels loaded and cocked. He slipped off the safety-catch, hugging the gun under his arm.

He brought the gun up as the body crashed through into the open, fifteen or twenty yards away. It was a dog, very large and shaggy and black. A Labrador cross, Matthew thought, but it was hard to imagine the other side of its ancestry; it seemed to stand a lot higher than any Labrador he could remember. It had stopped abruptly, and held its stance, looking at them. There was an impression of recognition, or recollection. Lawrence called to it:

'Here, boy.' He whistled. 'Come here.'

It stayed still, and its tail moved slowly. Then it turned and ran, across the field and into the wood on the other side.

Lawrence said: 'It belonged to a local farmer. I used to see it round the lanes.' He shook his head, looking old and unhappy, the light-heartedness gone. 'It seems to be managing all right.'

They moved on. They found the bullock in the fourth field. It was grazing near a corner that was enclosed on either side by metal fencing with a wood beyond; as good a position, Matthew thought, as one could have hoped for. On the far edge of the field, he spoke to the others:

'I'll take the centre. George and Charley on my left; you, Lawrence, and Billy on my right. We'll walk up to him slowly, and I'll keep about five yards ahead of the rest of you. Whichever way he goes, I'll catch him from the flank as he comes past. I'll try to get him in the neck. If I miss, or only wound him, dodge out of the way and let him run through. Have you got that, Billy?'

They spread out, and walked across the field. The grass was tall—the animal was not likely to go short of grazing—and coloured with the yellow of buttercups, the mauve of clover. Wasn't clover bad for cattle, Matthew thought? This one looked in good shape. It raised its head once, surveyed the approaching figures, and put it down again. Perhaps it would be easier than had seemed likely. There were clumps of cow parsley near the centre of the field. He remembered seeing them as a child. They had been called Mother-Die then. Take them into the house and your mother will die. Then, too, the irrational had been given full rein, but there had always been an end to the day, a going home to a house, supper, a warm bed.

Matthew was about ten yards from the bullock when it looked up for the second time. Small eyes stared at him along the narrow powerful brown and white muzzle. The head gave two small nods, like an old man sourly conceding a point in debate. Then the front right hoof pawed briefly and the animal charged. It headed neither to left nor right, but directly for Matthew.

He brought the gun up quickly and fired. He did not have the butt seated properly and the recoil threw him to one side. He was dazed by this, by the explosion, and by the thudding charge of the bullock. It passed a foot or two from him, with an outraged bellow of pain. As Matthew got back to his feet, he saw that the others had scattered all right, and that the bullock was rushing on across the field. He lifted his gun for the second barrel, but at first George was in the fire-path, and after that the range was too great to be effective.

Lawrence, running across, said: 'You hit him, Matthew.'

'I didn't stop him, though.'

'He's losing blood. We'd better keep after him.'

'Yes.' He said to Billy sternly. 'But you keep back. Understand?' Billy nodded. 'He was wild enough before, and he's ten times worse now.'

The bullock had gone through into the next field, and by the time they reached the gap there was no sign of it. But the trail was not difficult to follow—great splashes of blood in the grass. The wound was obviously a severe one, and, losing blood in this way, the animal was bound to tire fairly quickly. They started after it in high confidence.

The confidence was somewhat diminished as time passed without their coming in sight of the bullock. The trail led through a copse—marked not only by blood but by bushes crushed and branches broken in a blind blundering progress —over open ground and a lane, across a field that was a tangle of untended pea plants, and still on. Twice they lost the trail altogether, and had to cast around to find it again. The second time, in a wood, they were all of ten minutes hunting it. When, at last, Charley cried out in triumph, and Matthew looked where he was pointing, he felt more surprise than anything else at seeing the animal.

This was a very small field, perhaps a paddock—there were

ruins of a big house nearby. The bullock was in the centre and on its knees. As Charley shouted, it struggled to its feet and ponderously turned about to face them. Blood dripped from a gaping hole below its right eye, and its jaw-bone glinted white in the sun. It gave a dull, moaning roar, and pawed the ground. It shuddered, and Matthew lifted the gun, ready for another attack. But it shuddered again, dropped back to its knees and, as they advanced cautiously towards it, rolled over on its right side.

They came to it in silence, still wary. But there was no doubt about its being dead; its eye stared lifelessly into the sun.

'Congratulations,' Lawrence said. 'The jaw, and then into the neck. He's done well to keep going so long.'

They all crowded close to look, even Billy. Matthew stood back. Despite all the signs and forms of death to which he had grown accustomed, he felt a little sick. This was his act, not God's. He turned away and checked the gun. He had reloaded before they started the pursuit. Everything was all right.

'He's a big 'un,' George said. 'How're we going to get him back? We'll never drag him.'

Lawrence was very cheerful. 'Don't worry. I've thought of that.'

He had brought tools of his old trade with him, in a small satchel on his back: a lancet and a bone-saw. With George, Charley and Billy helping him to manœuvre the carcase, he slit the hide and ripped it off. The flesh steamed, and there was the indescribable smell of blood, the rich stink of intestines. Matthew felt calmer and more settled, but not disposed to participate in this part of the proceedings; nor did he seem to be expected to. The successful hunter presumably did not have to be a butcher also. He sat down in the grass, a little way from them, and listened to the chatter of their voices, and the sound of the saw grating on bone.

Lawrence saying: 'I can see now why the vets did a longer training than we did. These probably won't be at all the right cuts. Never mind, as long as we get him portable.'

From nausea to calmness, from calmness to a kind of

satisfaction. It was something necessary to be done, and he had done it. He felt pride in that, and gratitude to the others for having provided the experience. They were, in April's words, decent people. A few successes, instead of failures and hardships, might make a lot of difference to their lives and this, undeniably, was a success. They would feast on fresh meat.

The sun was beginning to be hot. It was a good day. His mind ran back through to its beginning, and the stooping figure by the stream. He wondered again about Lawrence and April. An ant crawled on to his leg, and for a while he watched it, feeling the tickle of its progress over his flesh. He broke off a blade of grass and fished for it. The first time it evaded the probe; then it clung to it and he lifted it and transferred it to the flower of a thistle. He had a wave of confidence and contentment. In the middle of it, he thought of Jane. He did so with love and pain, but her image, instead of pressing close, was far away, insubstantial.

There was a cry from George: 'That's got him off!'

Billy's voice, deeply interested: 'It's terrific the way the joint fits together. Is that what human joints look like, Lawrence?'

Lawrence, he thought, but he still calls me Mr Cotter. Billy was happy with these people. Lawrence was talking to him, explaining something. The sun pressed down, still warmer. Matthew lay back and let it beat against his closed eyelids.

Lawrence managed to cut the carcase up into manageable sections. There was more than they could reasonably carry back—Lawrence calculated that they were three or four miles from their starting point—so they picked out the best sections and shared the load. The rest, on Matthew's suggestion, they wedged in the branches of a tree. They would come back for them as soon as they could, but the dog they had seen, or other dogs, would be likely to get here first.

Matthew had the shotgun in one hand, and a leg balanced on the other shoulder. The flesh was soft and sticky against his palm, and blood dripped down, staining the side of his shirt. They walked through fields and sun-lit glades, a happy and gory procession. A butcher's outing, he thought. No, something simpler and more primitive than that. The hunters going back to the kraal. It was their clothes that were wrong. Ill-fitting and ill-assorted as they were, they yet belonged to the days of hygienic cold stores and steaks wrapped in cellophane. They should be breech-cloths in the summer, furs and hides in the winter.

It was a long way back, and the burdens grew heavier, but their excitement and cheerfulness sustained them. They talked and laughed a lot. They were laughing at some joke Lawrence had made, when Charley said:

'What was that?'

Matthew had heard it, too. He had thought it was an animal, a rabbit somewhere near, perhaps, screaming at the sight of a stoat. But the second time he realized that it came from further off, and that the cry was human.

They stopped, falling quiet. Matthew said:

'We're nearly there, aren't we? Could it . . . ?'

'Yes,' Lawrence said softly, 'it could.' He put his hand up in a restraining gesture. 'There's no sense in rushing things. We need to see what's happening.'

The advice was good. Matthew nodded. 'You know the best line of approach.'

They put the bloody chunks of carcase in a thorn hedge, and Lawrence led them, as silently as possible, towards the garden and the grotto. They heard another scream, and Matthew was almost sure it came from a man. There was no sound from the women or the girl. As they got nearer, though, they could hear other male voices, one laughing, another, perhaps two others, indistinguishably shouting. Matthew checked the shotgun, as he had already done twice or three times. It was ready. The safety-catch was off.

They came through the bushes, and took their final cover, behind a hedge of hydrangea. Lawrence looked through first and turned away, sickened. Matthew moved forward, and peered through the gap between two plants. The grotto was in front of him, and about twenty yards away.

There seemed to be a lot of men there, but when he counted

them there were only five. Five, and Archie. They had tied his hands and feet and he was lying on the ground on his back. He still had his shirt on, but his trousers had been pulled down. His body looked small and pathetic, very white against the sunburnt arms of the men bending over him. One had what looked like a pair of pliers, the other a lighted taper. Nausea rose in Matthew's throat. From sadistic schoolboys to savages, the objectives were the same. The eyes and the genitals, especially the genitals.

He looked for the women, and Cathie. They were huddled against the rock face with two of the other men standing near them. The fifth stood roughly between the two groups. He was a big fellow, well-muscled, with long blond hair and a straw-coloured beard. He was wearing sandals, flannel trousers cut down to make shorts, and nothing above the waist. His skin, despite the fairness of his hair, was deeply bronzed. He said, in a loud cockney voice:

'Let's stop piddle-arsing about. You've got stuff here. You know bloody well you have. Even if there's only the four of you, you're bound to have some. And if you really have some boy friends round the corner, like you say, then you've probably got a lot of it. Don't think I'm soddin' stupid. You've been living here for weeks. There's a trail over there like the bleedin' M.1, and the ashes of a couple of dozen fires at least. So you've obviously got stuff. All we want to know is where it is.'

He stopped, waiting for an answer. Matthew could hear Cathie sobbing and, nearer at hand, Archie moaning softly. Nothing else. The man said:

'Right! Warm him up a bit, Stanny boy. See how long it takes a red-head to catch light.'

The hand moved the burning taper. Archie screamed again, and Matthew heard April's voice shouting something. He did not hear what it was. He was possessed by a blind hot fury, which admitted nothing to his senses but the squirming screaming body on the ground and the figures of the men around it. Lawrence said something and touched his shoulder, but he brushed him off. He burst into the open, yelling, the shotgun under his arm. They looked up from their victim, more in surprise than alarm. As the man with the taper started to rise to his feet, Matthew fired the first barrel. He saw one of the two stagger, the other spin to the ground. Then he swung round towards the blond leader.

The movement caught him off balance. He felt his ankle turn under him, knew himself to be falling. The man was moving towards him, beginning to run. Matthew pulled the trigger as he fell, with only the sketchiest attempt at aiming. But the man had run forward, almost on to the muzzle of the gun. The force lifted him up, and slammed him backwards; Matthew saw him fall, out of the corner of his eye, as his own body hit the ground. He lay there winded, gasping for breath, watching blood gout up from the body only a few feet from his eyes.

TWELVE

THE remaining two had gone crashing away and disappeared beyond the rhododendrons. Of those he had hit with his first barrel, one was sitting up, clutching his arm, the other lay on his face, showing a raw jagged wound down his shoulder and back. Matthew started to get up. It was easy until he put his weight on his right foot, and then pain jabbed sharply up his leg. He transferred his balance, and hobbled over to Archie.

Archie said: 'I didn't tell them anything. I didn't tell them where it was . . .'

His face was very white, dripping with tears and sweat.

Matthew said: 'I know. Take it easy.'

He found his knife, and began cutting the cords. The others were coming up, Lawrence leading. There were angry burn marks on Archie's flesh and some livid bruises. Matthew said to Lawrence:

'I think he's all right.'

Lawrence said: 'Yes.' He produced a jar of antiseptic cream from his satchel, scooped a little out, and put it on Archie's fingers. 'That will ease things. You rub it in. You know where it's tender.'

Archie turned his back, and rubbed the cream in. Then he hitched up his trousers. April had come to join them, with Cathie at her heels. Sybil, Matthew saw, had run to George and they stood hugging one another. April said:

'Did they hurt him badly?'

'Painfully,' Lawrence said, 'but not badly.'

She was drained of colour, her skin had a sallow look, but she was quite controlled. Her jersey, Matthew saw, was torn at the neck, showing her collar-bone on that side. She jerked her head.

'What about that lot?'

The one who had been hit in the arm was standing up. He clutched one elbow with the other hand, and blood dripped over it and puddled in the dust. Charley was standing guard over him. He had picked up the shotgun and was pointing it. The wounded man looked scared. Neither of them, probably, realized that the gun was not loaded. The spare cartridges were in Matthew's pocket.

Lawrence said: 'I suppose I'd better look at them.'

Cathy still hung behind April, but Matthew had the sensation that they were alone together. April looked at him, her gaze direct and serious.

'You did that very well, Matthew,' she said.

He said: 'I did it like a fool. It was a fluke that I hit him with that second barrel. If I'd missed . . . He would have had the gun. Three of them, against Lawrence, George and Charley. And Billy. I should have had more sense.'

'No, you did it well.' She smiled. 'I was proud of you.'

The jersey was torn, but the slacks she was wearing buttoned up the side, and none of the buttons was missing. He said:

'You were all right, anyway, you and Sybil.'

'Yes,' she said. Her voice was dry. 'We were all right. What happened on the hunt? You didn't find it?'

'Found it and killed it, and brought most of it back. We dropped it when we heard Archie yelling.'

'Poor Archie.'

Lawrence came back to them. 'The one you hit at close range is a bit of a mess, Matthew. The other two represent the problem.'

'Problem?'

'Only for me. Some kind of oath I took once, a long time ago. Not that it will make a lot of difference, probably. The one with the arm will live, providing he doesn't get too bad an infection. The other, I should think, will die anyway, since we have no facilities for the kind of nursing he needs.'

April said bitterly: 'I should have thought the only problem was whether we could afford to waste another couple of cartridges.' She looked at Matthew. 'Or whether Matthew could.'

He was surprised by her hardness, but, of course, it made

sense. They could not keep the men here, even if they had the means of nursing them. He said:

'The two that ran away—do you think there's any chance of their coming back?'

Lawrence shook his head. 'I don't think so. April?'

'If they were part of a bigger gang, they probably would. But I gather they weren't. From the way they were talking, there were just the five of them. Blondie was the one with initiative.' She looked at his body. Blood still flowed from the hole in the chest but more slowly; flies were beginning to settle on it. 'I don't think those two will stop running much before they reach the coast.'

Lawrence stared at the two men Charley was guarding with the empty gun. The second of them had struggled into a half-sitting position, resting on his elbow. He was beginning to moan with pain.

'So what does one do?' Lawrence asked. He looked at April in helpless appeal. 'What do you think?'

She did not answer him but went over to Charley. She put her hand out, and he surrendered the shotgun. The man who was holding his arm started saying something, but she cut him short.

'I'm not going to shoot you,' she said. 'We've got plenty of ammunition, but it's not worth using it on you. Get moving. You may catch up with your pals, if you're lucky.'

He opened his mouth again and, moving forward quickly, she slammed the barrel of the gun against his wounded arm. He cried out with pain, recoiled, and started walking away. After a few yards, he looked back over his shoulder. She jerked the gun up, and he began to run awkwardly.

April stood over the other man. He was moaning more loudly and bleeding fast. She said:

'You, too. Get going.'

He looked up at her. His face was rigid with pain.

'I can't . . .' he said. 'I'm hurt bad. I can't move.'

She said with grim satisfaction: 'You're going to die. But not here. We shall have enough to do burying one.'

The man groaned, but did not stir. She kicked him hard

with her sandalled foot, not far below the wound, and he cried out.

'You can move,' she said. 'Or would you like us to drag you out ?'

He braced his arm and levered himself up into a standing position. He was sweating, his lips set in a grin of pain. April stood back from him. There was blood, Matthew noticed, on her sandal.

'Bon voyage,' she said. 'Get as far as you can before you drop.'

Lawrence looked at Matthew's ankle. His fingers felt round it carefully.

'Just a sprain,' he said. 'It means you're going to have to lie up for a couple of days.'

'Cold compress ?' April asked.

'I think so.'

She nodded. 'I'll see to it.'

She went off in the direction of the stream. Lawrence said:

'So you'll have to continue to be our guest for a while.' He smiled, and then paused. 'We're very much in your debt, Matthew.'

'A gun is useful,' Matthew said, 'as long as the ammunition lasts.'

'Not only the gun.' He looked as though he were about to say something else, but thought better of it. 'April will fix you a bandage which should ease things. I'd better see about tidying the place up. I think we'll just drag him out of the way for the time being, and bury him later. Getting the meat back has a higher priority.'

George and Charley took an arm each and hauled the corpse away to the shrubbery, Lawrence following and directing them. Matthew lay back in the grass. His ankle throbbed and ached, but as long as he did not attempt to move his foot there was discomfort rather than actual pain. Cathie was crying, and Sybil was comforting her and talking to her in a low soothing voice. Archie stood staring vacantly after the body that was being removed. Billy crept up beside Matthew. He said:

'Your leg isn't broken, is it, Mr Cotter?'

'No. It's only a sprain. But I shan't be able to walk very easily for a day or two.'

'Are we staying here?'

'Till my foot's better.' Billy nodded. 'Would you like to stay on after that?'

'I wouldn't mind.' He added quickly: 'If you do, that is.'

He was saved from saying anything by April's return. She had brought water in a saucepan, and she soaked a bandage in this before tying it round the joint. She had good firm hands and she fixed it deftly. Matthew looked down at her brown hair as she bent over his foot. It had a slight wave in it and was soft and glossy, but with a few grey hairs. He thought of what her life would have been, but for the break-down. A house to run, a family to look after, a social round to attend to. She pulled the bandage very tight, and he winced involuntarily. She looked up at him.

'Sorry about that. But the tighter it is, the better.'

'I know. It's all right.'

'Does it feel any better?'

'A lot better. Have you been trained in nursing?'

'Not nursing. First Aid.' She sat back on her heels. 'You don't want a sock on, do you?'

'No. I'm quite comfortable.'

April nodded. 'I learned it the time there was all the C.N.D. fuss. I agreed with them—about the Bomb—but sitting down seemed such a useless response. So I learned First Aid instead. And how to cook a meal on an inverted plant-pot, with a candle underneath. Of course, the whole object was learning how to manage life confined to one small room, while the outer world was poisoned with radioactivity.'

Matthew said: 'Life does have its little ironies.'

'Doesn't it?' She looked at him curiously. 'What did you do, Matthew, before the Bust?'

'I was a grower. Tomatoes.'

'Of course, Guernsey Toms. Had you always been doing that?'

'No.'

She waited and, after a moment, he went on. He told her briefly about the break-up of his marriage and how he had left London for the island. She listened, and said:

'You're very lucky, aren't you?'

'Lucky?'

'You were already in retreat from things. You'd written the world off, hadn't you, apart from Jane? And you won't accept that Jane may be dead. So nothing has changed for you, really.' She saw him smile, and went on: 'Well, of course, the surroundings have changed. That's obvious. But in yourself. There's been no need to readjust.'

Matthew thought about it. 'In that sense, perhaps not. You think that makes me lucky?'

She hesitated, and said bitterly: 'The change has to be for the worse. The ugliness all round is bad enough, but the ugliness in oneself is the thing that really disgusts.'

She was talking, he thought, about her harshness to the two wounded men. He said:

'The moments of stress are more intense, and one does wilder, more violent things in them. We all do. It doesn't mean we've changed, really. And there's no point in brooding over them.'

She shook her head. 'No, it's different. I agree, though, that there's no point in brooding.' Lawrence returned, and she said: 'Where have you put him?'

'In among the laurels.' He held his hands out, and took April's. 'You're all right?'

'Yes. Fine.'

'How long had they been here?'

'I'm not sure. About half an hour.' She went on more quickly: 'I've been thinking about that. We made a mistake, you know, a stupid childish mistake.'

'What?'

'Keeping everything down in the cellar except the things we need for the day. That was what made them so sure there was a store somewhere.'

'What do you suggest? Having part of it up here? There's a good chance of finding it gone when we come back from foraging.'

'Better than losing the lot—as we would have done, but for Matthew. We could find a second hiding-place. Something that we could give up under pressure.'

'Any suggestions?'

April shrugged. 'No. We could keep our eyes open.'

Matthew said: 'You expect this sort of thing to happen again?'

'Well, of course. Quite apart from the possibility of one or more of this lot picking up with one of the big gangs and bringing them up here.'

'You could move away,' Matthew said.

She stared at him with sudden coldness. 'What would be the point in that? Nowhere is safe any more.'

There were a lot of arguments he could have used. The coming winter, in itself, represented one to which there could be no effective reply. Lawrence knelt down beside him and examined the bandaged ankle.

'Fair enough,' he said. 'You can stay here and rest, Matthew, while the boys and I go and bring the meat back. Fresh meat, April! That ought to cheer us all up.'

She relaxed and smiled. 'Yes. We need cheering up.'

They did not go out foraging that day. After the remains of the bullock had been brought home, the women cut up the carcase and salted that part which was not going to be consumed in the immediate future, while Lawrence led the men off to make a more final disposition of the body that had been left among the laurels. He came back to where Matthew was sitting in the sun with Billy.

'That's that,' he said. 'Not as far under as he might be, but deep enough to keep the dogs from digging him up again. A compromise between effort and hygiene.'

Matthew said: 'Aren't you a bit surprised, as a medical man, that there hasn't been more sickness—even plague?'

'The millions of unburied dead? I don't know. The kinds of sickness you get in war are not generally due to the dead, but the conditions. Dysentery at Gallipoli, for instance—it was the living that kept that going. And there may have been outbreaks, for all we know. It's still a communal life, but the communities are very small. We tend to dodge other groups of three or over, and the solitaries dodge us.'

'Are there a lot of solitaries, do you think?'

'Very possibly. But again, there's no way of knowing. One spots them now and then in the distance, but they sheer off pretty rapidly. One sees their point. How's that ankle of yours feeling?'

'All right.'

'The bandage will need re-applying from time to time. I'll do it, if you like, while April's busy.'

Matthew shook his head. 'It can wait.'

Lawrence looked across to where she was working with Sybil and Cathie. He said:

'I don't see how we could have managed without her. She has such courage.'

'Yes.'

'Not just in a crisis, but in the ordinary grind of life. What we call life these days. One has moments of weakness, despair. It's a great help to have April around. She will not let herself be beaten, and she makes one ashamed of giving in. I remember when we first met, after the Bust.'

He was silent, and Matthew waited for him to go on. He said:

'It was a long time before I managed to get myself free— evening of that first day. And I was tired. I lay out in the open, and slept. The following day I began to realize something of how big it was. I hunted around a bit in the ruins of my own house and those near but there was no one alive. So I dug into my surgery and found the supply of Nembutal. I knew how much I needed to put myself out for good, and it seemed the only sensible thing to do. But I heard someone calling, and called back. It was April.'

Lawrence paused. 'I behaved like a fool. I ranted about there being no point in anything, told her I was going to end things. She listened and said I could do what I liked, but first I must have something to eat. She made sandwiches for me—the bread was a bit stale, but I ate them. I hadn't eaten anything since it happened. After that, I felt better. I've had bad moments since, but she's always been there, to hang on to.'

Matthew said: 'Even knowing her so short a time, I can see she's a pretty remarkable person.'

Lawrence looked at him acutely. 'It's not a matter of a relationship—you understand? We're different generations. I'm twenty years older than she is. She needs someone nearer her own age, with a strength that she can lean on when things get a bit tricky.'

'As far as that's concerned,' Matthew said, 'I should have thought she might lean on the past. This house, the memory of her family.'

'It's not enough. To give, as she does, requires something else. So far she's been living on her reserves, but there's a limit to that.'

'Is there? I suppose so.'

Twenty yards away, April was cutting up meat, with Sybil and Cathie helping her. The two men watched her in silence.

For the mid-day meal they had a fry-up of offal—heart, liver and kidneys—but in the evening there were steaks. They were grilled over the open wood fire and served, as usual, in relays. As before, April had hers at the end, with Lawrence and Matthew. Along with the steak there were baked potatoes, and fresh greens. Matthew commented on these:

'They're very good. Where did you get them?'

'From the kitchen garden,' April said. 'There are still a few things in it.' She smiled. 'Some tomato plants, too, Matthew. They're growing-up through the ruins of the cold-frame.'

'Where is it?'

'Over beyond the shrubbery.'

'I'll take a look in the morning,' Matthew said. 'I can hobble that far.'

She said warningly: 'The more you rest your ankle, the sooner you'll be able to walk properly.'

Lawrence tipped the rest of the bottle of wine into the enamel mug, and looked at it.

'Not much more than a mouthful each,' he said. 'But one

small bottle of wine to this intolerable deal of people. We must roll it round our tongues and make it last. It's the occasion that counts. All the same, I'm glad I only opened the Beaujolais. It's nice to think the Léoville Poyferré still lies inviolate.'

'What occasion are you keeping that for?' April asked.

'I'm tempted to keep it for a private one. Self-consolation, when at a low ebb.' He looked at her, and smiled. 'Or for some really big celebration, perhaps, such as a wedding.'

Matthew said: 'How one forgets things. The taste of really good fresh steak.'

'Make it last,' April said. 'God knows when we shall enjoy it again. Probably not ever.'

'Two of the large animals survived on Guernsey,' Matthew said. 'At least two. A donkey, and a cow which, by a stroke of luck, appeared to be in calf. I suppose there's a fifty-fifty chance of it throwing a bull, and a reasonable chance, if it does, of the breed surviving. If that can happen on a small island, surely it's bound to happen here as well.'

'You're forgetting the ant-hill syndrome,' Lawrence said. 'We had a clear conscience about going after that beast because we told ourselves it was a bullock. But even if it had been fully-sexed—well, I think we should have been tempted. After all, we don't know that it would find a mate, or, if it did, that we should be likely to benefit from it. And we're the relatively civilized ones. We have scruples, or so we tell ourselves. Most of the others aren't going to bother about breeding stock.'

'The animals might survive anyway,' April said. 'The bullock did, until Matthew turned up with his shotgun.'

'*Now* they might survive,' Lawrence said. 'This summer, when the pressures are only those of idleness and appetite. Do you dig your own tins out, or do you get someone to do it for you? Do you make do with corned beef and stewed steak, or do you go out for a hunk of prime fresh fillet? There isn't much of an edge to that. But when the tins get more and more difficult to find—what happens then? By the middle of winter, they would have brought the bullock down with their bare hands, and eaten it raw. There may be entire beasts that have lived through it so far. The opposite sexes may even get together. But

I wouldn't put any money on their being a solitary bull or cow in these islands in a year's time.'

April said: 'You underestimate Nature, Lawrence.'

He smiled. 'I would say you do.'

'This is the soft country,' she said. 'I suppose animals are vulnerable here. But up in the hills, in the mountain valleys, it's bound to be different. They'll survive up there.'

Lawrence said: 'You could be right.'

'I'm sure I am.'

'And so might we. Up in the hills.'

There was a pause. April looked away, unresponsive, but Lawrence went on. It would be so much better for them in every way up in the hills: more food, more safety, the chance to farm eventually. They could live there, if not well at least with some sense of continuity and purpose. And the children could grow up there, forgetting the past, accepting a present that was bearable, looking to a future with some promise. He spoke doggedly and earnestly, and April said nothing. Finally his persistence failed before her silence. He turned to Matthew.

'What have you been thinking about? You're very quiet.'

He would not associate himself with the implied criticism of her that ran through what Lawrence had said. The argument, he was sure, was good, but it was not the way to do things. He said:

'How good a meal this is, principally.'

'Compliments to the cook,' Lawrence said. His tone was placating now; he smiled at April. 'I do agree.'

She looked at Matthew directly. 'And what else?'

'What Lawrence said earlier, about killing beasts with bare hands. There are twenty-two rounds left for the gun. After that, except in the unlikely event of finding more cartridges, it's useless. I was thinking about those light steel rods you have down in the cellar. What were they for, Lawrence?'

'I don't know. We picked them up in some ruin, and I thought they might come in handy for something. I've never worked out what.'

'If one could notch the ends,' Matthew said, 'and find something suitable to string them with—they might make bows.'

Lawrence said: 'I know where there's a wrecked grand piano. The wires might do. Arrows?'

'One could cut those. Perhaps find some way of tipping them with metal.'

'Yes,' Lawrence said. 'It could work. That's the wonder of the practical mind. Don't you agree, April? You and I discuss the theory of survival, while Matthew works out the essential details.'

'We were talking of the survival of species,' she said, 'not of our own. What are you going to shoot arrows at, if our fellow savages have dragged what few cattle there are down with their bare hands, and drunk their blood?'

'In the hills . . .' Lawrence shrugged. 'Anyway, it's not just hunting. There's self-defence as well.'

'Of course,' April said. 'Self-defence.' There was an edge to her voice. 'Bows and arrows. You must let us have what other ideas you think up, Matthew, before you leave us.'

Matthew thought of saying: perhaps I shan't leave; but the expressions on their faces stopped him. The different expectancies, the different shadows of regret. There might be a time, but not now.

He finished his steak, and April said:

'Pass your plate. There's another one ready.'

'I think I've had enough.'

'Nonsense.' She took the plate from him. 'This is an occasion for gluttony.'

Lawrence said: 'And drunkenness.' He peered into the depths of the enamel mug. 'Just about enough for a libation, if one believed in the gods. Finish it up, Matthew.'

THIRTEEN

THEY used an old well-shaft for a decoy store. The brick surround at the top had been destroyed by the earth tremors, and a good deal of the lining had fallen in, but a couple of feet down one of the iron spikes was still firmly in place and they were able to tie a rope to it, holding a net with a reasonable quantity of items from the cellar store. Then they put a few boards across the top of the well and made it look generally untidy. It provided a reasonable concealment against any solitary who might come that way while they were out foraging.

Though for the two days after the bullock killing, Matthew was there anyway. Billy and Cathie stayed with him, and he watched them playing about the grotto and the garden like ordinary carefree children. In the afternoon of the second day, there was a series of tremors, and they stopped playing and came to him, their faces shocked and remembering. They did not last long, and the earth did not move much, but these were the first since Billy and he had joined the group. For some time after all was over the children sat near him, talking little and quietly.

Matthew tried walking again before the others returned, and found that he could manage quite well. The sprain could not have been a bad one: there was some discomfort but he could limp along without much trouble. He went to the kitchen garden April had spoken of and examined it. A long line of rubble marked the wall which had separated it from the rest of the grounds, and broken branches of espalier apple and pear trees poked through. Some still had green leaves and in one place, incredibly, a small apple was growing—a Cox's Orange, he thought.

The garden was a mess. It had been raided haphazardly, and not looked after; there were more weeds now than plants. He discovered the tomato plants, and cleared some of the broken glass away to give them room to grow. But it was all too discouraging. It would take weeks of work to get it straight, and for what? He made his way back to the grotto, and watched the children playing.

But he was restless and wandered off again after a time. He explored the grounds of the house more thoroughly than he had been able to do before, and was surprised at how extensive they were. It was difficult to tell just where the boundaries had been, but they must have included several acres. He wondered what profession April's husband had followed—a pretty rewarding one, it seemed. He was thinking of this when he came to a rose-garden, full of brightly flowering bushes and standards, beginning to run wild but still neatly metal-tagged with their old identities. There was, he saw, a cross on the other side of the barrage of colour—crosses. He went round, and counted four of them. They bore no names. There was only one person to whom they could mean anything, and she would need no reminders.

He heard her calling him from a distance, and walked away from the graves, so that he was some way from them when they met. She was faintly flushed, and smiling. She said:

'The ankle seems to have improved a lot.'

Matthew nodded. 'I should think I could come out with you tomorrow. How did things go today?'

'Only moderately. We thought we were on to a good thing in the morning. Charley turned up several tins together, and then the remains of a shop counter. But someone had worked the vein before us. Our total haul was two of sardines, one processed peas, one sauerkraut, and five of rice pudding.'

'It could have been more interesting.'

'Yes, indeed. We picked up a few other things later on, but nothing to remark on.' She put a hand on his arm; he was very much aware of the contact, of her physical presence beside him altogether. 'Are you sure your foot isn't hurting?'

'Quite sure. I was taking a walk. I think the exercise does it good.'

She said: 'There are some lovely walks round here. I used

to like walking very much. Now one feels guilty about not doing useful things, like cooking or hunting for food.'

Matthew rested his other hand on hers for a moment. 'Forget the useful things for a while. Show me one of your walks.'

She said doubtfully: 'I left the others putting the stuff away.'

'They can manage for once. And it won't matter too much even if the rice pudding gets stacked with the pickles.'

'No, you're right. One can take the small details too seriously.'

They walked companionably together, at ease with each other and enjoying the benison of the evening. Late sunlight slanted through the trees, turning the green to pale lemony gold. The air was soft and carried a haunting smell, a recollection of past summers. There was the buzz of insects, and birds calling—more, Matthew thought, than there had been since the break-down. Not through natural increase, obviously. Had they taken refuge, perhaps, flying to lands further from the centre of the big shock, and were they now coming back to their old places? The mild tremors of the afternoon did not seem to have disturbed them. He spoke of this to April.

She said: 'To what lands? Do you think we were worse hit than most? Wouldn't other countries have sent some help, if that were so?'

'Yes,' he said, 'one comes back to that. Perhaps we were among the luckiest.'

'It depends what you mean by lucky.' Her voice was harsh suddenly, but after a pause she went on more gently: 'Lawrence found one of those long-range wireless sets, not long after it happened. Transistorized and battery-powered, with three or four short-wave bands. It seemed to be in working order. When he switched it on there was a live sound—you know, crackle and hiss. But no signals. He spent a long time going over the wave-bands, listening for a station. There was nothing at all.'

'Do you still have the set?'

'No. We left it there.' To his look of surprise, she added: 'It didn't seem to come into the category of genuinely useful articles.'

'Even if the air was dead then, stations might re-open.'

'The set would only last as long as the batteries.'

'Something might have come on within that time. In some part of the world that had only been lightly hit.'

'I suppose it might,' April said. There was a hedge, pink and white with dog-roses and convolvulus, and she stopped to stare at it. 'Would that do any good, do you think?'

'One would know—that some sort of organized society existed somewhere.'

She went on, without warning, and he had to walk quickly to catch her up. She said:

'No one is coming to save us. That's something that has to be understood. No aeroplanes dropping out of the sky with cargo. No great ships steaming in with meat and grain and bananas and avocados.' She turned to him, smiling unhappily. 'Well, you know that, don't you? There isn't even a sea for them to sail on. We are here, and we have no help outside ourselves.'

Matthew nodded. 'Yes. I know that.'

They walked in silence for a time. They were in open country and they went across a field of long grass towards a small wood. Before they reached it, there was an oak. It was of great size and girth, with centuries of growth behind it. It was alive still, but leaning over at an acute angle; on the opposite side, some of its huge roots were clear of the ground and snapped off.

Matthew said: 'The winter gales will finish it off.'

'Yes.'

April went up to the tree, and pressed herself for a moment against the bark. The gesture was incomprehensible, but sad. Matthew watched her, aware, as he had been that morning at the stream, of her beauty and her uniqueness. She turned to face him, and he wanted to say something, to explain a little of what he felt. But she spoke first.

'The children loved it. It was fairly easy to climb, even when they were little, and there was so much of it, so many branches, and the chance to be hidden in leaves. We used to walk out here, and they would climb up and I would see them higher and higher—just glimpses of them now and then, and hear their voices calling to me. And, of course, my heart would be in my mouth for them, with fear of their falling, but I knew I must not call them down.'

'Were they all boys?'

April nodded. Her eyes were steady on his.

'Five, and seven, and ten. That was Andy. Dan had wanted him to go away to school, but I prevented it. It was the only thing I remember us fighting about. We compromised, in the end. He was to stay at home till he was thirteen.'

He would have thought there might be awkwardness in listening to her talking about them, but there was none. Her mind was open to his, in trust, and in her voice there was valediction as well as love for those she had lost. He said:

'I saw their graves.'

'Yes. One goes through stages. There are bad moments still, but not so often, and not so bad, I think. And one knows there can never be anything as bad as filling the earth in over them.'

They began to walk back towards the grotto. April's hand was near his, and Matthew took it; their fingers linked in warmth and reassurance. She talked about the foraging—they would have to go rather further afield, she thought, to find anything worthwhile. Although she did not say so in words, he got the impression that she was ready, or almost ready, to accept the fact that it made no sense for them to go on living here. He said, keeping it in general terms:

'At the moment, we're scavenging on the past. That means there are better pickings where there have been more people. But more risk of the yobbos, of course, too. This is a kind of in-between territory, isn't it? Isolated enough to make foraging difficult, but not far enough off the beaten track to be free from occasional visitors.'

She shook her head. 'They don't matter.'

'I doubt if Archie would agree.'

'We were fools to have all our eggs in one basket, and then to hide the basket. I agree there. But we've cleared that up. There won't be any cause for heroics if it happens again. Archie can take them to the well.'

'It's not only that, is it?'

'What else?'

'If we'd got back later . . .'

'Well?'

Her obtuseness surprised him. He said: 'Two women, one of them at least very attractive. There's more to it than the question of losing supplies.'

She stopped and stared at him. There was incredulity in her ιace, and the beginnings of something else which he could not ιdentify. She said:

'You don't think you arrived just in time to prevent our being raped, do you?'

'I think that might well have happened.'

She gave a short gasping laugh. 'But didn't? What made you think . . .? Because we didn't talk about it? Or perhaps because they let us pull our trousers up? That was considerate, but by that time they had decided to amuse themselves with Archie.'

He heard her voice grow more bitter as she spoke, and knew that part of the bitterness at least came from what she read in him: bewilderment, the shock of realization and, although he fought against it, something of revulsion. He was horrified, not only by what had happened but by the way she spoke of it, casually and brutally. Not meeting her eyes, he said:

'I didn't know. I'm sorry.'

'You don't know anything,' she said, 'do you? But what did you expect happens nowadays when a gang of men find un-guarded women?'

He asked, unwillingly but compulsively: 'It's happened before?'

'Look at me!' Her face was angry. 'Do you want to know about the first time? The day after I found Lawrence, two days after I dug those graves. I saw them first. I called to them, be-cause I thought the most important thing was that those who were left should make contact. I suppose I thought that if people had been changed they would be more human, not less. I couldn't believe it when they got hold of me. I fought, of course. I hadn't learned how stupid it was to resist. That was the only time it was really painful.'

'And Lawrence?'

'We'd split up, covering as much ground as possible. He was within earshot, but even though I fought I didn't cry out. They were both strong and under thirty. He could only have got hurt, one way or another. When they left me, I crawled away and found him again. It creates quite a bond, you know, when a man comforts a woman after two other men have knocked her about and raped her.'

Matthew said: 'I've said I'm sorry. You don't have to talk about it.'

'Don't I? Are you sure? The point is, it wasn't just comfort. Lawrence could offer practical help. He had some of those foreign-body contraceptives in his surgery. We dug them out, and he fitted me. It's a coil of stainless steel and nylon, with a funny tail. A terribly cute little gadget. And he fitted Sybil and Cathie when they joined up with us.'

He was trying not to show anything, but she was watching him closely. She said:

'Yes, Cathie! Which was just as well, because it happened to her a couple of days later. There were eight that time, and two of them couldn't wait for me and Sybil to be free. That was one of the times the men had to watch. The good thing about the ones you saw was that they left Cathie alone. Three of them had me, and the other two Sybil. I'm generally popular. One of them took me with him once, as far as Southampton. I made the mistake of talking, and he liked my accent. I got away in the night, and came back here.'

Matthew said: 'If it helps . . .'

'All this,' she said, '—it isn't even the beginning. I haven't told you anything. That man I kicked—the one who was badly wounded—you remember?'

Matthew nodded. 'Yes.'

'He spat in my face while he was in me. Do you think you have the remotest idea how that makes you feel—about yourself, and about men?'

'No. I know I haven't.'

'There have been five times altogether. I don't know how many men—sometimes the same man more than once. The secret is to co-operate because then it's over quicker and less

... less hideous. As an extra precaution we have sponges as well as the gadgets. It's not a great deal worse than going to a dentist used to be, if you have the right mental attitude, and the odds are pretty high against conception. But there's always the possibility, of course. Have you thought what that would be like, Matthew? Pregnant, in these conditions, by a beast on two legs who's used you the way a dog uses a bitch? And the other little possibility—of V.D.? The odds are not so high there. So far we've been lucky. At least, I think we have. It's too early to know about the latest episode.'

He felt he must stem the flow of this wretchedness and misery which was pouring from her. He put his hand on hers, holding her, feeling the bone under the flesh.

'I didn't know,' he said. 'I ought to have done. It was stupid of me.'

She turned away. 'Not that. Your look when you realized.'

'It's happened. Bad things come to an end, as well as good. You'll forget about it in time. What you do counts, not what's done to you.'

She stared at him, her face full of pain.

'You still don't know anything. I had one man, my husband. I was proud of my body, because he loved it. Now . . . Lawrence wanted me, so I let him take me. It didn't mean as much as being raped, but it meant as little. I was sorry for him, and I despised him.'

Matthew said: 'That was generous.'

'Generous! My God! And Charley? A boy only a few years older than my son was. And knowing it was the sight of other men using me that had excited him? Do you call contempt generous?'

He was silent. His hand still held hers and, as though suddenly aware of this, she took it from him. She said, her voice lower but harsh:

'Sex and motherhood are the centres of being a woman. Now they mean nothing but disgust and fear. Little Archie . . . No, he hasn't had me, but only because he hasn't asked.' She glanced at him, and away. 'I'd learned fear of most men, contempt for all of them. Then, when I was washing at the pool, I looked up and saw you watching me. And I had the insane idea that there might still be strength and goodness—in a man, between man and woman. It was my illusion, and not your fault.'

'I don't think it is an illusion.'

She ignored the remark. 'I'm sorry about the outburst. You listened very patiently, Matthew.'

The anger and bitterness had gone, but he could almost have wished them back. She was a long way away.

'Listen,' he said. He sought her hand, but she moved from him. 'Surely you don't fear me?'

'No.' She sounded tired. 'I don't fear you. But I despise you. I despise you as a man. As a person, I think I envy you. What I said when I was bandaging your ankle—I didn't realize how true it was. Nothing has changed for you, except the scenery. For the rest of us it was God bringing our world crashing down about our ears, but for you it was—what? An epic in Cinemascope, Stereosound and 3-D. Jane is still alive, and you can amble your way towards her through the ruins. Do you know what? I think you'll find her. And she'll be dressed in white silk and orange-blossom, and it will be the morning of her wedding to a clean young man with wonderful manners, and you'll be just in time to give her away.'

He said: 'I want to stay here.'

April shook her head. 'You can't do that. I can tolerate the others, but not you.'

'In time, you could.'

'No. You remind me of everything that's finished. I would have to go myself, if you stayed. I don't think you would force me into that.'

There was a response, if he could find it, which would break through the meaningless tyranny of words, which would restore the early morning moment of recognition. But even if he found it, he wondered, could he afford what it would cost?

April walked away from him, towards the garden and the grotto. After a time he followed her, but he did not try to catch her up.

FOURTEEN

It was wiser, Matthew decided, not to risk the Southampton gangs. He thought of going north at first, until the better idea occured to him of heading south-east, towards the coast. By following the line of the tide, he could keep his bearings even without the sun; and the morning had started cloudy.

Lawrence had pressed him to take food from their store, but he had refused. For his part, he had offered them the gun, with the same result. The atmosphere was strained. Their reactions, when they realized he was serious about leaving, had been a mixture of regret and resentment—all except April, who if she showed anything beyond her usual serenity, showed indifference. When Lawrence, at the beginning, started to remonstrate with Matthew, she cut him short.

'He's made up his mind, Lawrence.'

'But the whole thing is lunatic.'

'Leave it at that.'

After a pause, Lawrence said: 'And Billy?'

Matthew said: 'I think it would be better for him to stay with you, if you're willing to have him.'

April said: 'Of course we'll have him.'

Billy said: 'No. I want to go with you, Mr Cotter.'

Matthew said: 'You should stay, Billy.'

He shook his head stubbornly. 'I don't want to.'

Lawrence said: 'I thought you were going to let me teach you medicine, Billy? What I remember of it, at any rate.'

The boy looked agonized and embarrassed. He started to speak but stumbled over the words, and was silent. April said:

'He will be as safe with Matthew as he will with us.' There was a hint of tiredness in her voice. 'Perhaps safer. There would be no point in his staying here against his will.'

That was the end of the discussion. They packed their things up and set off. At first Billy talked a good deal, with forced cheerfulness, but Matthew made little response and eventually he grew quiet. They came to the place where they had met April—a figure ran scurrying away from the ruins as they approached—and crossed the road, making their way across country.

Matthew found his mind shying away from the thought of April. It was impossible to dissociate her from her rejection the previous evening, whose bitterness and contempt became, in retrospect, the more harsh. In part he was aware that there was more to it than this—that he was, and had been, revolted by what she had put into words. He had found himself, afterwards, unable to look at Charley without disgust. But thinking about his own reaction was as unpleasant as contemplating the things that had happened to her, and that she had done.

He thought instead of Jane. The idea that she had survived had begun to dominate him again; he pictured the house, its isolation and the stoutness of its timbers. She would be there, waiting because she knew he would come to her eventually. There had been the time, he remembered, when she was only five and they had gone up to Hampstead Heath for the fair, and somehow he had got separated from her and lost her. He had hunted for over an hour through the crowds and had finally found her, anxious but dry-eyed, on the steps of the roundabout She had told him that she had known he would come for her; that was why she had not minded being alone.

He fleshed out the bones of his belief with other recollections. The house had a large cellar, and Mary had always kept good stocks of food, partly, he thought, because of her childhood in the war when her mother had been a great hoarder of rations, but ostensibly because of the risk they ran every winter of being cut off by snowdrifts. It had happened to them twice, since they had been in the house, the second time for nearly a week. She would have stayed at the house, he decided, and there was nothing near it that was likely to attract the yobbos.

Billy was saying something which he had missed. He said: 'What was that, Billy?'

'Someone's been camping.' He pointed. 'Over there.'

There were signs of occupancy, and the remains of a fire.

172

If there were any fuel, and it could be coaxed into life, they could stop and have their mid-day meal here, he decided. They went over to investigate. The fire was cold and dead. The remains of the feast lay near it—chicken bones, a chewed carcase, feathers. Further on, something gleamed in the grass. Matthew picked it up. It was a camera, a Pentax. It seemed to be undamaged. Just hold it in your hands, he thought. But what had made somebody take it in the first place?

They came to the wave-line early in the afternoon. It was the same as before, the great scouring line running away in the distance. Beyond it lay the dried mud of the Solent, and past that the shadowy plateau of Wight. Looking out there, Matthew saw a group of moving figures. They were too far away for him to tell how many, but he judged there were at least a dozen. They were heading towards the island. One of the gangs, probably, looking for fresh plunder.

Towards evening they crossed Southampton Water. There was a ship there, half buried in the mud. It had plainly been ransacked; there were empty tins and other objects strewn nearby. Matthew thought of camping for the night. They could see a long way and no one was in sight; and there had been a light shower of rain earlier which looked as though it might be the herald of more. The ship offered a possible shelter if it did rain again.

In the end though, he decided to go on. The uneasiness he had felt going down into the sea bed from Guernsey had returned; relief from that was more important than physical shelter. He said to Billy:

'Another mile or two won't kill us, will it?'

'No.'

His ankle had stood up to the journey well; he hardly noticed it any more. They climbed the long slope towards the dark barren horizon in the east. Where the cranes and chimneys of Portsmouth had been there was nothing but the same grey waste. From time to time there was evidence of the city's destruction and scattering—bricks, boards, odd articles. And human debris. But these were reduced, by time and possibly scavengers, almost to the anonymity of skeletons, with just a few rags of flesh adhering to the bones. They lay cold and odourless and insignificant in the dusk.

They found shelter after all, not far from the tide mark: a hut which had been swept from someone's back garden, on the very edge of the wave perhaps, and dropped here almost in one piece. The door had been wrenched off and there were a few boards missing, but apart from that it was in good shape. Inside there was a drift of soft sand and, as they found during the night, sand-fleas. They slept fitfully. Billy was tossing and turning a lot, and seemed to be having bad dreams. It did not rain much, but in the morning set in as a steady downpour. They had a cold breakfast from a tin, and stared out at the sopping grey sky.

After an hour or so it slackened, but it did not stop entirely. The light was not perceptibly better. They were both cold and bored, and Matthew decided it would be less unpleasant to go on than to stay. Billy had been given a small plastic mackintosh out of the stores which would keep him from getting too wet. He seemed to be shivering more than usual, but walking might be the best answer to that. There was no way of warming him here.

They kept in general to the tide line, and this in due course brought them to ruins which Matthew thought were probably Havant; looking south he could see a bulge of land, with the stumps of a few trees sticking out of it, that might have been Hayling Island. There were stretches of paved road, some of them running for twenty or thirty yards before they broke up in sand and shingle, and in one place a telegraph pole stood up, almost vertical, out of the flatness. It was not long after that that Matthew heard a voice calling, and looked inland. A man stood there, waving his arm to attract attention.

He was a tall man, Matthew saw, and powerfully built. He had some sort of fur across his back which, along with a beard of a much brighter red than Archie's and far more luxuriant, gave him a wild savage look. Matthew pulled the shotgun out of his pack, and checked that it was ready. The man bounded towards them over the rubble, tremendously agile and sure-footed for his size. He said:

'Where are you going, then?'

'East,' Matthew said laconically.

He nodded. At close quarters he looked more amiable, and there was nothing threatening in his manner. He pointed to the gun.

'That thing loaded?'

'Both barrels.'

'All they that take the sword shall perish with the sword. Matthew 26:52. You feel like some food, a drink maybe, before you go on east?'

Matthew lowered the gun, but kept a finger close to the trigger-guard. He said:

'That's very kind of you.'

'I like company. You can't honour God without delighting in God's creatures, and Man is the crown of His creation. So God created man in His own image, in the image of God created He him. The boy looks cold. He could do with a sit by the fire, to warm his hands.'

'Yes,' Matthew said. 'We both could do with that.'

'Come on, then. Follow after.'

He went off at a great pace, stopping occasionally to encourage them as they climbed and stumbled over the shattered bricks and mortar. The ruins had looked level, but as they went further in they found the contours less even; there were hillocks and depressions and small valleys which probably marked past thoroughfares. They were led for about ten minutes, and came to a hollow where the prevailing chaos had been partly thrust back. It was about twenty-five yards across. The floor had been paved, with bricks and pieces of flagstone, and in the centre there was a building.

It was of boards, crudely but effectively nailed together, about twelve feet by eight, and seven or eight feet high. There was a flat roof, sloping slightly from one side to the other, most of the way along, but at one end there was a pyramid which raised a wooden cross a few feet higher. The top section of the pyramid was covered with bits of broken glass which had been stuck on. At the nearer end, a rusting chimney projected from the roof, with smoke issuing from it. The red-bearded man went ahead of them and pulled open a door.

'Welcome, friends,' he said. 'Come right in.'

It was not as dark inside as Matthew had expected; although the wall they had first seen had been blank, that on the opposite side of the hut had a window in it. The frame had no glass but was covered with a more or less transparent heavy plastic material; it was closed at present, but looked as though it would open. There was a warm comfortable fug in the room and the acrid smell of wood smoke. This came from the sawn sections of timber which crackled on top of the fire, but the main fuel, Matthew saw, was coal. Coal was heaped in the corner near the door, with a pile of billets beside it. The fire-basket was of heavy iron—a garden-waste incinerator, distorted but retaining the chief part of its shape—and there was a metal plate underneath on which the ashes fell. Above, thinner metal had been beaten into a cowl, which was topped by the chimney. This, he saw, was made up of empty tins with both ends cut away, the ends having been made to fit together by careful crimping and stretching. It picked up quite a lot of the smoke from the fire, but by no means all.

There were shelves on the wall facing the window, one of them holding the tools which had presumably been used to make the cowl and chimney: pliers, pincers, a couple of hammers, nails and string and so on. And to make the furniture. This consisted of a low bed, a shaky-looking table, two chairs and, where the roof rose to form the inside of the pyramid, a couple of steps and an altar. The bed was a frame with a close-mesh wire mattress, lifted just off the ground by blocks of wood at the four corners, and with blankets, folded and squared Army-fashion, at the top. The altar was a very simple affair, but covered by a cloth which had scenes worked in scarlet and gold. A home-made lantern hung above it from a chain, with a piece of candle flickering behind fragments of red glass.

'Sit yourselves down,' he told them. 'I'll put the stew-pot on, and we'll have a bite to eat.' He took a piece of board off a big black pot, and lifted the pot on to the fire. After looking into it critically, he got some tins from a shelf—stewed steak and carrots and potatoes—opened them quickly, and emptied them in. He added water from a plastic watering-can.

'How do you manage for food?' Matthew asked him.

'Well enough. There's a place not far away that used to be a wholesaler's. I don't go short.'

'What about competition?'

'Competition?'

'From other foragers.'

He shook his red locks; his hair was long but well combed.

'It's a lonely part, this. I don't get many visitors. Those that come are welcome to what there is. I bring the food up as I want it. And the coal. I know a place where there's a regular mine of it. The old station goods yards. They had a load in when the Almighty called Time.'

'Water?'

'That, too. The Lord's provided very well for His servant. Not more than five minutes' away, just about where Woolworth's used to be, I found this stream gushing out of the earth. A good head of water, and it's still flowing.'

'Is it all right for drinking?'

'You're thinking about the bodies? I thought of that, too, but it was a weakness of faith. It is sown in corruption; it is raised in incorruption. I Corinthians 15:42. If the Lord God preserves a man, in the day of the pale horse, shall he fear any evil? That was in the beginning, of course. Now I boil water before I drink it. The Lord does His part, but He expects us to do ours.'

'So you lived here before,' Matthew said.

'Yes,' he said comfortably. 'I lived here—lived a little, and worked a little, and sinned a little. I had a wife until she left me. That was nearly a year ago. I came back from work sweating with the heat, and the house was cool and empty. She took the children with her. They went to her mother in Maidstone, and there, I suppose, the Lord took them all. Blessed are the dead which die in the Lord.'

'Do you know anything of what it's like further east?' Matthew asked.

'No, brother, nor want to know. Except that He will be coming from there.'

Matthew said unwarily: 'Who?'

'The risen Lord. For He comes out of the East, as the day after night. So I wait. I thought once of going out to meet Him, but I had a dream, and the Lord said: "Blessed are they that wait". For He is gathering up His flocks, and the sheep must bide the coming of the Shepherd.' He went across and looked at the stew-pot, stirring the stew with a tablespoon. 'This won't be very long, friend. But a stew must boil every time you put it on the fire. Otherwise you run the risk of food poisoning. Do you have faith, brother?'

'No,' Matthew said, 'I wouldn't say that I have.'

'The time is short. When the Shepherd has gathered his sheep, all will have been accomplished.' He went to where Billy was sitting on the edge of the bed, and sat beside him and took his hands. In a much more gentle voice, he said:

'What's your name, child?'

'Billy.'

He sounded puzzled, but not uneasy. There was something in the man, Matthew guessed, which he accepted and in which he had confidence. The man said:

'Well, now, Billy, do you believe in God?'

Billy looked at him and then, very slowly, nodded. The man said gaily:

'That's fine! Not fine for God, but fine for you. The time will come when we'll be wandering through the great heavenly meadows and in the distance there will be the mountain of crystal, and on top of the mountain the palace of gold, studded with rubies and emeralds and diamonds, and the Great King sitting on a silver throne. And all your old friends will be there, and the angels singing like nightingales, and the loveliest lady that ever walked the world.' He slapped the boy's cheek lightly, in affection. 'The time will come, and not far off. You look out for the Lord, on your travels, and when you see Him, run to Him and say: "Lord, here I am!" and when He lifts you up, say: "And this is my friend, who has no faith, but who looked after me when the pale horse rode by, and his name that sat on him was Death."'

He straightened up, and went back to the fire.

'Stew's about ready. A bit more pepper needed.' He brought

a tin of pepper from the shelf, and sprinkled it liberally. 'You need a right peppery stew on a wet day.'

He ladled stew into a couple of plastic dishes, bright red and bright yellow, and sat smiling at them while they ate.

'You should have bread, too,' he said. 'Thick white bread to mop up the gravy. You'll just have to drink it up. You, especially, Billy lad. You look as though you need nourishing.' He turned abruptly to Matthew. 'So you don't seek the Lord, friend? Then what do you seek?'

'My daughter,' Matthew said. 'She was in Sussex when it happened.'

He shook his head. 'Had you but asked and waited, the Lord would have brung her to you.'

He made them have second helpings of stew, and afterwards brought out a tin of toffees. Matthew had not eaten sweets for years, but he had some now, and the red-haired man filled Billy's pockets with them. He also insisted on putting food in their packs, entirely stripping his shelf. When Matthew demurred, he said:

'The earth is the Lord's, and the fulness thereof. And I can get plenty more, friend. There is only the labour of digging and bringing, and I have nothing to do with my time but work and watch and pray. If you are rested, and warmed and fed, I imagine you will want to be on your way. I will come with you to the place where we met.'

He talked rationally, of ordinary things, as they retraced their steps. Only when they came to the tide line did he break off and, after a pause, said abruptly:

'I'll pray for you, friend.'

Matthew said: 'Thank you. And thank you for the food.'

'Man does not live by bread alone.' He grinned suddenly. 'Or by tinned meats, dug out of the earth. I wish you good fortune.'

'And I you.'

'God guards.' He looked down over the fall and emptiness of the sea bed. 'For the first heaven and the first earth were passed away,' he said. 'And there was no more sea.'

FIFTEEN

THEY found no shelter that night, but the rain had died away and their clothes had dried on them. They lay with the blanket wrapped tightly round them, the boy's body in the hollow of Matthew's. Billy was shivering for some time, and later Matthew woke to find him shivering again. Although the night was dry, it was not particularly warm. He spoke softly but got no answer, and concluded that the boy was shivering in his sleep. When they found Jane, everything would be simpler. He could set about making some sort of permanent habitation, as the red-haired hermit had done. He was not a handyman, but he felt sure he could make a job of it. And Jane would be able to look after Billy properly: she had always been good with children. There would be problems, of course, but here, in the darkness, at the hour that was usually the time of uncertainty and despair, he felt a glow of confidence and optimism. They would find Jane, and everything would be all right. He thought of April, and there was a moment's coldness and sickness until he deliberately turned his mind away. They would find Jane, and all would be well. He fell asleep again in the security of this.

In the morning, Billy said he was not hungry when Matthew offered him food. It was not particularly appetizing—cold stewed steak—and Matthew said:

'Maybe later in the day we'll be able to get a fire going.' The clouds were high, and there were patches of clear sky directly overhead; there seemed a reasonable chance of sunshine during the morning. 'But we can't travel if you don't eat, Billy.'

He nodded. 'I'll try, then.'

The sun did come out towards the middle of the day, and there was a long period of brightness and warmth. Matthew found some driftwood and got a fire going. He made a stew of sorts, with meat and condensed soup; and instant coffee. Billy was not keen on eating, but had some at his urging. He stayed close to the fire, even though the sun was shining, holding his hands in front of the flames to warm them. He had probably got a slight chill, Matthew thought. What he needed was rest and warmth. He toyed with the notion of going back to the hermit's hut, but rejected it. They could not be more than forty miles from Battle. By tomorrow evening, the day after tomorrow at the latest, they should be there.

But the following morning the going became difficult. At first this was evidenced merely in a multiplication of the usual fissures and faults to which they had become accustomed, the minor bruises caused by the shocks. But there were more and more of them and they were bigger and more varied, interspersed with new raw hills of earth and rock, showing the twist and grind of fantastic pressures. At one spot, the rear end of a sports car pointed at the sky, the bonnet being wedged in the earth which had closed round it and held it rigidly. There were two ragged remnants of humanity slumped together over the dashboard, one in a rotting dinner jacket and the other with skeletal shoulders and skull, trailing yellow hair, above a stained and faded red silk evening dress. The car and its occupants had plainly been under water. Presumably the earthquake had trapped them first, and the great wave flooded over them afterwards.

There were other things wedged in the earth, so tightly embedded that the wave had been unable to carry them away. Stumps of wood, a section of iron railings, half of a metal garage door, a twisted television aerial, and a lettered plate: Shakespeare Road. Matthew guessed this was the site of a seaside town. Littlehampton? Or perhaps Worthing. It was not easy to judge the distance they had travelled. Billy plodded on beside him, but did not talk much. He looked tired and flushed, and Matthew had to call halts at more frequent intervals.

Eventually they came to a point of even greater upheaval. There was a ridge of scarred earth and stone which ran inland and out into the sea bed, seemingly endless. They could not go round, and had to climb it. It was heavy going even for Matthew and Billy was continually slipping and falling. At the top they were getting on for a hundred feet above their starting point, and could look back over the flat and desolate land through which they had come. There was a view out over the Channel bed, also, and in the distance a great hulk which looked to Matthew like one of the Queens.

He pointed it out to Billy, who nodded and gazed out with lack-lustre eyes. Matthew said:

'Have you got some of those toffees left?' Billy nodded. 'It might cheer you up to have one.'

'I don't feel like it.' He looked up. 'Would you like one, Mr Cotter?'

'No, thanks. How do you feel about going on?'

'I'm all right.'

Billy bent down to get hold of his pack and put it on, but Matthew stopped him.

'You have a rest from that. I'll carry it.'

'I can manage it quite easily.'

'Never mind.' He touched the boy's forehead and found it hot to his fingers. 'I think by tomorrow we'll be able to stop and rest properly.' He stared round at the scene of bareness and devastation. 'We can't stay here.'

There was an upward slope to the land after the ridge, not a very pronounced gradient but one which went on and on exhaustingly. The ground was extensively shattered, riven with cracks and fissures and littered with loose rocks, from cobble size to huge boulders taller than a man. Above the tide line, it was still all devastation; at one place there was a stretch of woodland in which not a single tree remained upright—the whole had been smashed to a level of undergrowth.

They had covered nowhere near as great a distance as he had hoped, but he had to call an early halt: the boy was too tired to go on. The sun was quite low in the west. Matthew tried to get a fire going but failed. He opened a tin of sardines but Billy would not eat anything. Matthew covered him in the blanket, and sat near him, talking of anything that came into his head, trying to cheer him up. After a time his breathing changed, and Matthew realized he was asleep.

Billy woke during the night with a sharp cry that wakened

Matthew also. He was shivering again, with greater violence than before. Matthew said:

'What is it, Billy?'

'I want to go home.' He was sobbing with deep gasping sobs; it was more an adult misery than a child's. 'I don't like the trees.'

He was feverish. Matthew said: 'There aren't any trees, Billy. It will be all right.'

'The trees all broken . . . I'm cold. My feet are cold.'

'We'll find you a warm place tomorrow, a warm comfortable place.' He hugged the small body to him. 'Try to get to sleep, Billy.'

In the end, the boy dozed off. Matthew lay awake for some time, thinking about the destruction by which they were surrounded. There were these belts, stretches of land where the shocks had caused greater damage than elsewhere. Alderney, for instance. They would be out of it tomorrow. The going was bound to get easier. They would reach Battle by evening, perhaps before. After that . . . He had not just been comforting the boy: after that, it would be all right.

He thought Billy seemed better in the morning; he spoke more cheerfully, and managed to eat some ham. But Matthew still would not let him put the pack on his back, carrying it himself by the straps. The going was easier, too, justifying his optimism. There were fewer fissures and land-slips, and they passed close by a copse in which most of the trees were standing. Not long after they started they had skirted the rubble of buildings which Matthew thought might be part of the hinterland of Brighton, and their course now took them through a valley with hills on either side that looked like what he remembered of the Downs. Far up on one of the slopes, he saw a moving dot of white, and recognized it as a sheep grazing. It gave him a lift of hope. Perhaps the good lands would lie beyond the bad.

Billy was faltering, and he cheered him up by telling him a story of what was going to happen—the land was getting better, and they would find this place up in the hills, with trees all round—not broken trees but trees you could climb—and they would build a hut, like the hermit's only bigger, and Jane would be there with them, and she would nurse Billy until he was well and after that she would look after them both, and they would go and hunt for food for the winter, and chop wood so that they could have warm fires. Billy said something, but he did not quite catch it.

'What was that, Billy?'

'Will it be long?'

'Not long. Keep at it, old chap. When we get there, you can rest as long as you like. Do you want to rest a bit now?'

'No.' He shook his head. 'I'd rather go on, Mr Cotter.'

The line of horizon grew nearer. They were going up towards the crest of this long long rise. Going down would be easier, and they should be able to see across the plain the hills which were their objective. It would not seem so bad once they were in sight. He said to Billy:

'We'll rest at the top there, and I'll point it out to you.'

The sun had come out and for the last two or three hundred yards they were bathed in sunshine. When Matthew saw beyond the crest, beyond the sharp crumbling drop, to what lay beyond, it was a dazzle of silver first, a great gleam which he did not understand. Understanding came as he stood there, and his gaze took it in fully.

This was the missing sea. Bright blue, polished by sunlight, it stretched on ahead of them, with no break or sign of land.

He stood, confused, half-seeing, half-remembering.

On such a summer's day, the first time they came to the island, they had gone to the cliffs, to Icart, and there had been that broadness, that silvered blueness, and they had been away from everything, alone together, the small golden-curled figure beside him in a scarlet windcheater with a bright blue lining, and she had gasped with wonder and pleasure, and he had known that what he had was peace, an end to all the irritations and bickering; and known that there was a term to happiness.

. . . He heard April's voice.

—I despise you as a man. As a person, I almost envy you. Nothing has changed for you, except the scenery.

He argued with her now, as he had been unable to do then:

—She was worth searching for, worth abandoning everything else for.

—You had lost her already, April's voice said. —You lost her when she went away, grown up, to live her own life. You were searching for a fantasy.

—For the living person, no fantasy. She might have survived. There was a chance.

—No chance, and you knew that. You chose the fantasy because you could not face life. You never could.

—It was different for you, he said.—You buried your dead.

—Yes. He heard the warmth and bitterness and strength in her voice. —I buried my dead.

He turned from her, from the accusation, from the experience of pain and ugliness, to the sea of the past. There had been rain in the night, he remembered—he had heard it beating against the hotel window—and the morning had been clean and fresh, diamond-bright, and the gorse flowers sharply golden against the sky. Jane had gone running ahead along the cliff walk, picking flowers, and he had followed her. They would come and live here, he thought, and he would have this for a few years, and then the recollection of it.

. . . April's voice. —You chose the fantasy. Even so long ago.

—Reality, not fantasy. I knew I had to lose her. I was prepared for that.

—And afterwards?

—Afterwards? Nothing. Nothing that matters.

—No, she said. —That's why I despise you.

The sea, he thought, the heart-easing beauty, the contentment. To stand and look out at something like infinity, with the small figure silent by one's side. Although her body lay far out under the calm water, the moment had been real and was real. If from staring he looked down quickly beside him . . .

He looked, and knew himself, and understood. Not Jane, but Billy, staring uncomprehendingly at the sea, still shivering in the warm sun. He had taken his fantasy to the bitter end and seen it drown. That was not important. But the boy was ill.

SIXTEEN

THE slope was downhill and the sun was warm in their faces, but they did not get very far on the return journey that day. Suddenly Billy was tired, complaining of pains in his legs. They stopped to rest at increasingly shorter intervals, and at last, as the sun went down, Matthew decided that he must have sleep. There was a fairly large mound of ruins nearby, and after he had settled Billy as comfortably as possible, he went foraging. The debris was very fragmented, but it looked as though it had not been turned over before.

The things one found, though, were less and less valuable with time and exposure to the elements. Blankets, with a Harrods label, but damp and musty, growing some kind of fungus in the folds. If they were washed and dried out they would still be all right; here and now they were useless. A stack of tins, but most of them blown and all of them rusted and with labels that the wetness had made indecipherable. The smell of death had largely given way to the dank smell of rot. Death was still in evidence, but showing the cleaner gleam of bone. A skeleton in stained and tattered red pyjamas, crushed in the ruins of a bed. Matthew was turning away when he saw the shine of metal; a lighter, clasped between fingers from which the flesh had gone.

At first he was disposed to leave it: the fuel would have evaporated, and the chances of finding a new supply were pretty small. But the arm moved, jolted slightly by the shift of his weight, and the lighter slipped from the bony fingers and fell. Matthew picked it up and saw that it was not an ordinary lighter but a butane one. He spun the wheel, and the flame jetted out. Quickly he cut if off; it was too valuable to waste.

After that he abandoned foraging and instead collected wood and built a fire close to the place where Billy was lying. The boy had been asleep but he awoke and stared at the leaping flames. Matthew went through the food that was left in his pack and found the tin of pheasant in wine sauce that he had picked up on Alderney. It was something, he thought, that might tempt the boy's appetite, and he set about warming it up. He talked to Billy while he did so, telling him that they would soon be at the hermit's hut where he could rest properly. And when he was well, they would go back to the grotto, to Lawrence and the others, and stay with them. He would like that, wouldn't he?

He nodded. The night was drawing in fast, and the firelight glowed on the whiteness of his face. He said:

'Jane is dead, isn't she, Mr Cotter?'

'Yes.'

'I'm sorry.'

And that was true: the boy was sorry for him. He felt ashamed, angry with himself. He said:

'Never mind. Supper's nearly ready. Let's see how much you can eat this time.'

That was not much, and only at Matthew's patient urging. Later he dozed off, to wake in nightmare. The earth was moving, the house falling down around him. He was trapped, and could not move. He called out for his mother, and Matthew held him in his arms to comfort him.

'Dad,' Billy said, 'Dad—is it all right, Dad?'

'It's all right. Go to sleep. There's nothing to worry about now.'

There was plenty of wood but most of it in unwieldy lengths. Matthew found enough that could be broken by hand, though, to keep the fire alive until the small hours of the night. Billy slept fitfully at first but later fell into a heavy slumber. Matthew dozed beside him. He awoke at first light and set about finding means of getting the fire going again. Billy slept on and the sun was well up before he wakened.

He was, Matthew knew, not really well enough to go on. On the other hand, there was no means of looking after him properly here, and no shelter. The weather had been kind again, but it was unlikely that that would last. If the rain returned . . . And they were not much more than a day's journey from the hermit. Billy could be left there while Matthew covered the final stretch to the grotto. And Lawrence not only had medical skill and experience, but some medical supplies. It was the only sensible thing to do.

Billy was listless and disinclined to move, but Matthew coaxed and jollied him into activity. Once they had started he seemed a little better, but he was very weak and Matthew gave him as much chance to rest as possible. He let him have quite a long rest in the middle of the day, when he got another fire going and warmed up soup. While it was warming, Billy said that it smelled good, but after a few sips he turned his head away. The high temperature had returned; his forehead burned to the touch.

They made poor time during the day, but they had luck with the evening stop. They were travelling above the tide line, and Matthew saw ruins on the far side of a field and rectangular blocks of yellow which intrigued him. He went closer to investigate, and called Billy to follow him. The ruin had been a farm, and nearby a Dutch barn had collapsed in splintered and shattered wood, scattering baled straw all round. Some of the bales were still wired, but many of them had broken open. It was a fairly easy matter to make a bed for Billy, and the straw also helped in starting a fire. After he had done that, Matthew went hunting round the neighbouring fields, and found potatoes. Foragers had been here before, but there had been little method or concentration in their ransacking, and he found quite a lot of potatoes in the ground. He came back and told Billy.

'We'll bake them. Do you think you'll like that?'

Billy nodded. 'I think so.'

'How do you feel now?'

He coughed. He had begun coughing during the day, a deep rasping which sounded painful, but he did not complain about it.

'Not so bad.'

He ate a couple of baked potatoes and a little meat, and Matthew thought he would settle. He found straw for himself, and went to sleep exhaustedly. Billy's coughing woke him, and he went to the boy to find him feverish and uneasy. He sat with him for a long time before he fell into deep sleep. Then he got back into the straw and woke to a day cloudy but bright. It must be at least an hour after sunrise.

Matthew had seen a stream beyond the potato field, and he went there now, to wash and to refill their water container. He took Billy's empty bag, also, and filled it with potatoes. Even though they were hampered by Billy's feebleness, he had good hopes of reaching the hermit's hut that day. The potatoes would be a small return for hospitality. He took his time, choosing the best tubers, and came back whistling to the place where he had left Billy. He stopped whistling as he came round the corner of the ruins of the barn. Billy was still there, but so were others. Half a dozen men, and two bedraggled women.

One of the men was holding the shotgun.

He was a dark shaggy man, an inch or two over six feet, wearing a black leather jacket. He gave the appearance of being in authority over the others; apart from holding the gun, a pair of fieldglasses were suspended from a strap round his neck and rested against his chest. There was a scar down one side of his face, only partly masked by his black beard. It looked a recent one, acquired either during the earthquakes or in fighting subsequently.

He said, in a thick north-country voice: 'So you've got back. Are there any others, or is it just you and the lad?'

There was no point in lying to him. Matthew said:

'Just us.'

'That's what it seemed like.' He lifted the gun and sighted along the barrel, drawing an imaginary bead on something in the distance. 'Quite a useful piece, this. Where did you get hold of it?'

'I picked it up.'

'And a box of cartridges. Very handy. Just the one box? No more tucked away somewhere?'

Matthew said: 'No. You can see we're travelling.'

'Aye, it looked like that.' He put down the gun, and stared at Billy, still lying in the straw. 'He's not a bad-favoured youngster.' He bent down and pushed a grimy fist against his cheek. 'What's thi name, then?'

'Billy.'

'Fair enough. How'd you like to come with us, Billy?'

Matthew said: 'He's sick. I'm taking him to some people who can look after him — a doctor.'

The man stood up and, almost without looking, cracked Matthew across the face with the back of his hand. He said:

'I'll tell you when to talk. I'm asking the boy, not you. You can do what you bloody well like.' He laughed. 'I couldn't fancy you much.' He turned back to Billy. 'How about coming with us, eh?'

Billy had a fit of coughing. When he had finished, he said weakly:

'No, thank you. I want to stay with Mr Cotter.'

The man had been smiling, but the smile faded. He said:

'And you will do as you're bloody well told, or you'll feel the edge of my strap. Get up!'

Matthew said: 'He's sick.'

He turned round slowly, and took a step towards Matthew. He said:

'I warned you, didn't I? You must be more bloody stupid than you look.'

'I don't know what it is,' Matthew said, 'but the other two died of it. There were four of us. There's this cough and after that blotches and sores.' He tried desperately to remember the symptoms of plague. 'And swellings in the groin.'

The rest of them had fallen back at his first sentence. The leader stuck it better. He stared at Matthew, and weighed the gun in his hands.

'Guns don't carry germs,' he said, 'or if they do, I reckon I'll take a chance on it. Tins don't, either.' He swing round to the others. 'Tip that bag out, and take the tinned stuff. Come on, jillo!'

They hung back, showing their reluctance. He studied them for a long moment, and then broke the gun and clipped the barrel back in place.

'Both loaded,' he said. 'I can spare one cartridge—two if I have to. So pick up that stuff, and we'll get moving.'

They scrambled to obey him this time. He must have shown in the past, Matthew thought, that his threats were not idle ones. And he was a powerful man: some of the other men and both the women showed marks that might have been those of violence. Matthew wondered about the gun. Clearly he saw it as increasing his power. But if one of the others got hold of it . . . And he would have to sleep.

As one of them picked up the box of cartridges, he said:

'I'll have that!' He took half a dozen cartridges and stuffed them in the breast pocket of his jacket, and then gave the box to one of the women. 'Mind you look after it. All right. We'll be on our way.'

They started to move off. The big man looked at Matthew and shook his head slightly.

'You may be lying,' he said, 'but it's not worth taking chances. And the kid's sick, all right. But just in case you are lying . . .'

He swung without warning, and with extraordinary power and skill. The punch caught Matthew on the side of the jaw, and he felt himself lifted and slammed down. The ground hit him hard. Lying there dazed, he worked it out that the man must have been a professional boxer at some time. He did not have much leisure to ponder this, though. A boot caught him savagely in the side, making him cry out with pain. He doubled up, feeling sick. He heard footsteps going away, and looked up. Billy was watching him, frightened.

He said, with difficulty: 'It's O.K. He didn't really hurt me.' He made an effort to smile. 'It helped, your being sick. We'd better think about moving, too.'

They had left the two bags, the blanket, and the extra clothes, the knife and the enamel mug. There was also the butane lighter, in Matthew's pocket. He put everything inside the big haversack and carried that by the straps. It was as easy as putting it on his back, and it enabled him to carry the boy pick-a-back when he was tired sometimes. Matthew was determined to get to the hermit's hut that day. Once there, knowing Billy was in good hands, he could press on and find the others. Lawrence would come back with him and treat the boy. In a couple of days he would be well again. It was a pity about the gun, but it did not matter essentially. It could only have had a limited usefulness. They could make those steel rods into bows, as he had suggested, and cut arrows to go with them. Brute strength might be the temporary answer to chaos, but intelligence and ingenuity were bound to come out on top in the long run.

This optimism and confidence helped him to keep going, and to make the effort to keep Billy's spirits up as well. They would go with Lawrence and the others up into the hills, where there were fewer people and probably more animals, and find a place where they could live undisturbed and in peace. He explained about the bows and arrows. They could use them to defend themselves if anyone did attack them; and to kill game. There were bound to be some pigs that had survived, because the short-legged animals were much less likely to be crippled by shocks, and in the wild state they would multiply very fast, having no natural enemies. Except man, of course.

Billy listened, not saying much but seeming to like hearing him talk. Matthew had a moment's uncertainty when he was reminded of the similarity between what he was saying now and what he had been saying on the outward journey, about Jane, and the house in the woods, and being safe. But there was a big difference, he reassured himself. The other had been fantasy, based on nothing but his own refusal to accept the virtual certainty of Jane's death. What he was talking about now was a practical proposition, involving real people, not phantoms. There might be obstacles, but the idea was sound.

He had thought, during the early part of the morning, that the sun might be coming through; the clouds were low and patchy. But they thickened instead of clearing, and a breeze freshened from the south-west. There was a hint of rain in the air. At mid-day he stopped and got a fire going. The yobbos had left them the potatoes, either because they thought they might have picked up germs from the bag or because they were not worth taking: there were plenty of potato fields about, pressumably, and the women could always be put to digging. Matthew baked some of the smaller ones. He could not spare the time to cook them properly, and the insides were hard. But Billy, in any case, would not eat anything. Matthew swallowed some to stay his hunger and keep up his strength, and they started off again. He needed all the strength he had; in less than half an hour Billy was faltering, and he had to carry him.

But unless something unexpected happened, they would reach the hut by nightfall. Matthew recognized landmarks—a coil of rusting wire, an oil-drum half buried in sand, finally a two-pronged rock a hundred yards off shore. That had been no more than an hour's trek from the hermit. The sun would be down, he thought—there was a glow behind the western clouds —but the light would last for a while. Billy, who had been walking, was beginning to lag again, and now stumbled.

Matthew bent his shoulders beside a shelf of rock.

'Come on,' he said. 'Up we come. We're on the last lap.'

The final stretch, across the rubble, was difficult, because it was now almost dark and the going was treacherous. Matthew thought he was lost, and was thinking of calling to the hermit when he saw, through the gloom, what looked like level ground. He went towards it and saw it was, in fact, the courtyard the hermit had built, surrounding the hut. Then the hut would be . . . He saw it, and stopped. The sight of the bright sea barring his way had been sudden, too, but the shock it carried had been the realization of his own delusion. There had been an awakening too, and the beginning of a different and better kind of hope.

This was an altogether savager blow. The hut had been fired; blackened timbers gaped roofless to the sky.

SEVENTEEN

IT had not happened that day: the charred wood was quite cold to the touch. There were signs of wanton damage inside, apart from the burning. The altar had been smashed first, he thought; the lantern lay shattered on the floor. The cowl had been battered in and the basket of the stove tipped over; presumably that had started the fire. But the fire had not entirely gutted the place. The wall with the window and the end wall behind the altar were still standing and supporting a section of roof. The fire had burnt out before consuming the lot, perhaps helped by a shower of rain.

Matthew looked for the hermit's body. There was no sign of it in the wreck of the hut or in the courtyard. Had he done this himself, he wondered, in a fit of religious mania, before setting off on some pilgrimage, God knew where? But he had smashed the altar. Then in revulsion against his God, an acknowledgement of despair and defeat? It was possible, he thought, but not likely. The damage had the look of ordinary human violence, not of perverted inspiration.

The bed was still there, against the relatively undamaged wall. It had been scorched by the heat which had also blown out the plastic covering of the window frame, but it was in quite good shape. Matthew stripped the blankets back, and found them all right apart from the smell of singed wool. Billy was beside him, quiet and fearful. Matthew said:

'We can get you to bed, anyway. I'll help you get undressed.'

Billy said: 'Was it those who took the gun?'

'It might have been. I don't know. They're not here now, that's certain. And tomorrow we will go and find Lawrence. What you need is sleep.'

He knelt beside the boy and removed his shoes. The soles were badly worn, in one place to paper thinness. That was something else that would need seeing to, once they were back at the grotto. He eased Billy between the blankets and tucked them in round him.

'How's that?'

'Like the bunk on the ship ... Where will you sleep, Mr Cotter?'

'I'll find a place.'

He was very tired, but he needed to get a fire going. Nothing edible had been left; the big black pot that the hermit had cooked the stew in was lying upside down in the courtyard. All he had was the potatoes he had brought as a gift. It was a question of making a fire or eating them raw. It helped that the tools had not been taken; part of the handle of the saw was burnt, but it was usable. Matthew ripped down some of the charred planks and awkwardly sawed them into manageable lengths.

Afterwards, he cut slivers of wood with his knife. It was even more laborious than the sawing but in the end he had a little pile of chips. He propped pieces of wood across the pile, and, after a couple of abortive attempts, set fire to it with the lighter. The flames rose, died down and then, when he was beginning to despair, caught the bigger pieces. When we have a settled place, he thought, we'll keep a fire going all the time, winter and summer. There were few sights more lovely, more comforting.

He sat watching the fire and warming himself until his head nodded and he had to check himself from falling towards the flames. The heat scorched his forehead and roused him. He took the twisted metal that had been the cowl and bent it round still further to form a distorted kind of Dutch oven. He put the potatoes inside, pushed it, open side out, against the fire, and built the fire up round it. Then he found some of the remaining planks and laid them side by side for a bed for himself. It would not be soft, but was preferable to lying on stone and bricks.

Matthew pulled the potatoes out when they were cooked, and replaced them with others. Billy was sleeping exhaustedly, and it did not seem worth waking him. He ate several potatoes and put the others by. Those in the Dutch oven he prodded with his knife; they were not quite ready. Another ten minutes, perhaps. He lay down on his planks and stared at the blaze.

The only sound was the crackle of wood, and Billy's quiet breathing. In the fiery darkness and loneliness, he spoke to April.

—You were right; but it was stupidity and ignorance, and one can change that. I am changed already and, learning from you, can change more. You understand a finer language but if I listen to you long enough, perhaps I will know it, too. And until then I can make signs to you, loving signs.

The rain in his face wakened him. It was coming down hard, hissing in the almost dead embers of the fire. The night was very black. He groped his way to Billy's bed. Part of it was dry, protected by what remained of the roof, but rain was pelting against the bottom half. He found both their mackintoshes and tucked them round the blankets as protection. Beside the head of the bed there was a place where one could sit and stay reasonably dry. Matthew huddled there, waiting for the night to pass. After a time, Billy began crying out in delirium. Matthew talked to him, but the boy scarcely seemed aware of him. He was talking about Captain—a pet dog, Matthew thought. Captain was lost, and he could not find him. Matthew told him Captain would come back, but he took no notice.

At last the rain slackened. Soon after that, the sky began to lighten with the approach of dawn.

Both the potatoes he had put by and those he had left in the Dutch oven were wet and sodden, the latter having been burnt to a crisp first. Even if he could spare the time, there was no hope of re-lighting the fire with wet wood. Billy was sleeping again, and Matthew went out to reconnoitre. The hermit had said that the source of his food supplies was not far away, so there might be a chance of finding it.

He found it quite easily: the hermit's body was a marker. He saw that first, but on coming closer realized there were two bodies. They lay together, the hermit's fingers clenched round the other's throat, his body showing various wounds, including what looked like an axe blow against the side of his skull. The general picture was clear, but there was no way of reconstructing the details. Perhaps they had found him in the hut and forced him to lead them to his cache; or perhaps they had stumbled on him here and fired the hut afterwards. What was certain was that he had turned to violence in the end, and strangled one of them while the others cut him down. He had been an immensely strong man.

The yobbos had taken what they could carry of the easily available stuff. Matthew did not have to dig far to find more. He took four tins of corned beef—more than enough for the day, and, with Billy as weak as he was, it was essential to travel light.

He looked at the bodies again. There was very little smell from them; it could not have happened more than a couple of days before. He saw something rucked under the body of the man who had been strangled, and recognized it: the altar cloth from the hut. That was probably what had cost him his life, a penalty for sacrilege.

Matthew tugged at the cloth, and it came free. He looked at it for a moment. There were three scenes, all of martyrs. Stephen under his shower of stones, Catharine on her wheel; in the centre, Sebastian with his arrows. Matthew draped the cloth over the hermit's head, and walked away.

Billy was awake, but delirious again. His skin seemed to be hotter even than it had been earlier. Matthew realized he could not leave him here—it was essential, anyway, to get him to Lawrence without delay—but on the other hand he could neither walk nor be relied on to maintain his hold if Matthew carried him on his back. In the end, Matthew tore one of the blankets into strips and, from the strips, rigged up something which would keep the boy in position on his back. It was not comfortable, for either of them, but he hoped it would do. Billy again refused to eat. Matthew wolfed down one of the tins of meat, along with a potato that was only partly wet and then, after managing to hoist him into place, set out for the west.

The boy was a weight, of whose heaviness and intractability

he became more aware with every yard they covered. He alternated between moaning or crying wakefulness and periods of lying slumped forward against Matthew's right shoulder, so leadenly and unresponsively that Matthew had moments of fear that he might be dead, and twisted his face round to feel the quiet breath on his cheek. He tried to settle into an automatism of walking, blotting out all considerations except the need to set one foot in front of the other, but although for a time he could believe he had achieved this, the strain accumulated and released itself at last in bursts of pain and weakness. Then there was nothing for it but to rest, to find as soft a stretch of ground as was possible, lower himself awkwardly to his knees, slide forward on his arms and so lie prone, the boy's weight even heavier on his back. He could not, either for the boy or himself, face the job of undoing the harness for what must be no more than a short break.

He did release him in the afternoon. They were crossing the dried mud of the Southampton estuary again. Matthew was conscious of his extreme weakness and decided that, although he did not feel hungry, he must eat. He opened one of the remaining tins and tried to get Billy to have some, but the boy was listless, almost comatose. He settled him as comfortably as possible, and ate the meat himself. The sun came out while he was eating, and afterwards he allowed himself to lie out, soaking in its warmth. For a few minutes, he thought, but his body betrayed him again. He had no idea how long he slept, but the sun seemed a lot lower in the sky. Billy was awake, watching him with empty heavy eyes. He coughed, and it racked his body.

Matthew got Billy back into position, and set off. His shame at his lapse made him try to walk faster, but that only brought the fatigue on more quickly. He had to rest, and go on at an easier pace. Time and distance had become distorted and out of phase: the bank of the further shore came no nearer but the sun seemed to be visibly slipping down the sky. He knew with a certainty that twisted like pain that they would not reach the grotto that day.

In this realization, it was more and more difficult to defy the tiredness which seemed now to be coursing with his blood into every remote part of his body. Each step he took required an act of separate concentration. Somehow he climbed the hill of the shore and, after resting a while, staggered on. There was grass, long and lush, and two butterflies waltzing over it. He wanted to lie down, to sink into the softness and freshness, but would not. That clump of trees—he would stop when he reached them. He got there, and summoned his strength again. That hedge . . . that bush . . . that heap of rubble . . . He went on, from point to point, from objective to objective.

As the sun fell below the horizon, the last of his stamina drained away. There was a dry ditch, with a thick thorn hedge over it. Matthew dropped to his knees and released the harness. He eased the boy to the ground and bent to look at him. His face was sweating, his mouth open and parched. Matthew took the water container which had also been tied to the harness, and put it to Billy's lips. He drank thirstily. Matthew drank himself and then lay down, holding Billy in his arms. They fell asleep while it was still light.

Matthew was awakened by Billy crying out and struggling. It was night, but there was a moon, quarter full. The air was fairly warm, and fresh; the sky was full of stars. He gave Billy another drink of water and talked to him, telling him it was nearly over: tomorrow, for sure, they would be there. After a time, he fell asleep again, and Matthew watched the moonlight on his sleeping face. There was a snorting groaning noise not far away and quite loud—a hedgehog's mating cry.

He felt hungry and opened one of the two remaining tins of meat, leaving half in case Billy would eat some in the morning. He drank some water, and heard the container gurgle emptily. It would need refilling when he found running water.

He thought of the stream, near the grotto, and of the sight of April kneeling there. He was conscious of a great loneliness, and of a sense of failure. There had been something offered which he had no right to expect or hope for, and he had rejected it. He had known that in doing so he had wounded her, but only now was he beginning to understand how deeply. And yet she had the strength and sanity to accept the wound, and to heal herself and him. He was sure of that, more sure than he could remember being of anything.

Billy was sleeping, apparently peacefully. Matthew lay down beside him and let his tiredness take over again. There was still the last stretch to do. But he felt confident once more.

They encountered a group of people not long after they set out the following day. There were three men and two women, all quite young and looking fairly clean. When Matthew became aware of them, they had already seen him; they were resting near a ruin which, from the objects laid out on the grass, they had been digging into. Something else about them was distinctive: they had a dog. It was an Alsatian, and it stood beside one of the men, in the unmistakable stance of a dog with its master. There was no point, Matthew thought, in altering course, and anyway the burden of Billy's weight made him reluctant to deviate from a straight line.

The man with the dog called out to him when he was a few yards away:

'What's wrong with the boy? Broken a leg, or something?'

Matthew stopped and stood, swaying a little from the involuntary spasm of his muscles. The dog bristled, and gave a low growl.

'He's sick,' he said.

They stared at him in silence and then turned away in dismissal. One of the women, a plump Jewish-looking girl with her hair in a net, said something, and the other one laughed. Only the dog continued to pay attention to Matthew and Billy; it kept its eyes on them and snarled softly. Among the tins on the grass were some of evaporated milk.

Matthew said: 'Do you think you could spare a tin of milk? Or a little out of it. I've only got meat, and he can't eat that. He might be able to manage milk.'

The woman who had spoken before said: 'Joe, don't you think we could . . .?'

The man with the dog cut her off. 'Shut up.' He turned to Matthew. 'Bugger off. We've got enough to do looking after ourselves, without sick kids.'

The dog, aware of the tone of disapproval, growled more loudly. Matthew started walking. For some time he could hear the growling, and the laughter. Billy said feebly:

'I didn't want any milk, Mr Cotter.'

'We'll soon be there,' he said. 'When we get to the grotto, Lawrence and April will look after you.'

'I could try walking again.'

'You stay where you are. We'll soon be there, Billy.'

He lost his way at one point, but the sun gave him a general direction and he arrived at last at what he was sure must be the A.31. But he was not sure whether he had reached it west or east of the place where he had met April and the others. The decision whether to go left or right was an agonizing one; the fatigue of the previous day had set in earlier, and the thought of travelling in the wrong direction was unbearable. Matthew lay in the grass at the edge of the road, on his side with Billy in the harness behind him. The sun was hot and he was sweating, and his muscles ached from the strain. To go on lying there was a physical imperative, but he knew he had to resist it. The grotto could not be more then three or four miles away. He struggled back to his feet and, with a gambler's fatalism, walked towards the west.

He reached the mound that had been the village about half an hour later. He had a great sense of achievement, a feeling that, though the grotto still lay a couple of miles to the north, he might at any moment see one of them. April, in particular, he visualized as part of each unfolding scene—across that field, past those trees . . . she would be there, and he would call to her and see her look, the quick recognition, her smile.

Billy said: 'I remember that pond.'

'So do I. Are you feeling better, Billy ?'

'A bit better.'

'We're nearly there.'

He said, to the April who might be on the far side of the copse:

—I was a fool. I've not learned wisdom, but I've learned that. I suppose it's a start. Help me. Help me.

The chatter of the stream was the same, and beyond it the sun gleamed on the glossy green of the rhododendrons. Matthew walked past them and saw the grotto. It was empty; there was no one there. The anticipation had been absurd, of course: during the day they would be, as usual, out foraging. They would come back towards sundown.

He freed Billy from the harness, and eased him down to lie in the grass. He was immensely tired, but no longer painfully so. He had made it, and all they had to do was wait.

EIGHTEEN

HEAT seemed to grow through the afternoon. Billy slept a good deal of the time. When Matthew had recovered some of his strength, he went down to the stream and stripped and washed himself. He had nothing to dry himself with, but he sat in a patch of sunlight until most of the dampness had evaporated. His clothes ought to be washed, too, but that would have to wait. There was a thickening of white clouds in the sky. The sun went in, but it was still hot and in the distance he heard the rumble of thunder. He hoped the storm, if it were to come, would not break before April and the others got back.

As the day ended, Billy woke up. He was sweating, peaked and querulous. He said:

'Where are they? Where's Lawrence?'

'They'll be here soon.'

'How soon?'

'Soon.'

Billy said restlessly: 'I'm so hot.'

'I'll get something to cool you.'

He tore a strip off the boy's shirt, rubbed it as clean as he could in the stream, and brought it back dripping. He mopped Billy's face and neck with it, and it seemed to ease him. But he had gone back again; he was once more running a high fever. When Lawrence came . . . Matthew strained his eyes to see through the bushes and the more distant trees. The sun was long gone and evening was shading into night. He knew they would not be coming back that day.

The explanation followed convincingly on the realization. They had been finding foraging more and more difficult in the area within reach. They must have gone so far afield that they could not return to the grotto the same day. They would come back tomorrow. He told Billy this, and the boy stared at him apathetically.

'We can manage on our own for another night, Billy, can't we?' He nodded slightly. 'How are you feeling, son?'

'All right.'

But the tone was flat, the voice a whisper. Matthew had a moment's anger with Lawrence for not being there, but saw the unreasonableness of that and checked himself. He thought of something else: the extra store of food in the old well. He told Billy to lie quiet, that he would not be gone long, and went over there. He felt apprehension, a sick anticipation of disappointment as he saw the boards that marked the place, indistinct in the dusk. Then he was there, and pulling them to one side. The well shaft gaped blackly. Matthew put his arm down and felt for the spike. The rope was there. As he hauled it up, the weight at the end of it was a relief.

He heaved out the net, selected one or two tins from it, and dropped the rest back. Then he returned to where Billy was. He was sitting up, looking anxiously for his return. Matthew said:

'I've found some milk. You'll have a little, won't you?'

'I thought you'd gone.'

'Not for long. I told you. Here you are. I've punched holes in the top.'

'You won't go, will you, Mr Cotter?'

Matthew shook his head. 'I won't go.'

The storm broke fairly early in the night, with drenching rain and thunder and lightning chasing each other across the sky. Matthew did his best to keep Billy dry, keeping him under the grotto's overhang and covering him with his own mackintosh. He himself got soaked at the beginning, but scarcely noticed his wetness in his concern for the boy. The fever raged in the small body as tumultuously as the storm; he threshed about restlessly, calling out for his parents and for the dog, Captain. Matthew sat beside him, talking to him and trying to comfort him. He felt a great despair at his inability to do anything. The boy was desperately ill, perhaps dying. It would be a bitter irony if, after the struggle to get him back here, he should die before Lawrence returned. He took the boy's hand, and held it.

'Hang on, Billy.' The fingers were dry and hot against his cold wet palm. 'You must hang on.'

Towards morning the thunder rolled away towards the west, the rain stopped and the air grew still. But the boy showed no sign of improving. The mental and physical agitation remained but the physical movements, Matthew thought, were weaker. His voice was weaker, too. He seemed to be speaking to Matthew sometimes, as well as to his parents; but in the same terms, Matthew felt—as though he were not there. Yet when Matthew took his hand away, he cried out pitifully until Matthew grasped him again.

Matthew stayed, cold and wet and cramped, while the sky brightened. It had been an ordinary summer storm, violent but short-lived, and the sky above the grotto changed from indigo to a clear clean blue. The blue was quite pale, the sunlight bright on the tops of the trees, before Billy fell asleep and Matthew was able to let go his hold. Asleep, Matthew thought, but no better. He had no idea when April and the others would be back; apart from anything else, the storm might have delayed them. Billy needed Lawrence's skill, but there might be something among the medical supplies which would help for the time being.

On the way to the cellar he went past the rose-garden. The four graves were there, with their wooden crosses, and on each grave a rose had been laid, blown now and battered by the rain. Matthew stood and looked at them for a moment before going on to the ruins of the house.

The early part—getting the covering rubbish away—was easy enough but time-consuming. He was out of sight of the grotto, but in earshot if Billy should call for him. He got down to the upturned table, and, with his fingertips under the edge, heaved to lift it. It did not budge.

Trying again, he remembered that this was a job normally done by three of them—George, Charley and Archie. If he could get more leverage, it would be a help, but he saw no way of doing that. He bent over, straining with all his might, and felt it lift, but not enough for him to be able to wedge something under it. He straightened up, wiping sweat from his brow. It might be necessary to leave it until the others came back.

As a last resort, he tried sliding the table. He cleared a space at one end of it, and then went back to the other. He braced himself against a tangle of beams and stone, dug his heels in against the table edge, and pushed out with his feet. The first time nothing happened. With his second effort, though, the table moved along an inch or two. Matthew readjusted his position and pushed again. This time it moved perhaps six inches and revealed a little of the stair well. Only the narrowest of gaps, but enough to encourage him to try once more.

Eventually he had to go and clear more debris from the far end, but by that time there was room to stand on the top stair and shove the slab of wood forward. It went relatively easily. Matthew did not bother getting it completely clear of the well. It was enough that he could squeeze through the space and force his way, lying on his back, down the stairs.

It was very dark, with only the tiny slit of light behind him. Matthew flicked on the butane lighter, and peered around.

At first, he thought that nothing had changed. The trestle tables were there, and the shelves, and, as he moved his arm, he saw tins and clothing and the metal ladder and the roll of roofing felt. It was true that the candles were not in their usual place on the tables, but that did not seem important. The stores, too, were not as neatly arranged as they had been, in places were in disorder. Perhaps April had been supervising things less closely. But he was more interested in the room beyond—the medical supplies, and the brandy. He went to the door, and pushed it open.

The little cellar, he saw at once, had been stripped. The shelves that had held Lawrence's medical supplies were empty, as was the rack with the few precious bottles of wine, and the brandy. There was nothing in the room but dust.

His immediate reaction was that, for some reason, they had moved everything out into the larger room. He went back to it and walked round with the lighter, checking everything. He did not find the brandy, but he discovered something else. There was more to it than disorder: a good deal of the stuff that had been here was missing, too. Had they made yet another cache, somewhere else, for the really important material? It was possible, but it was difficult to understand why. Or where. There could hardly be any other place within reach as well concealed and secure as this.

Unless ... He remembered the graves first, a thought apparently random but seen with a new significance. April had put no flowers on them before; perhaps because she had not felt she needed to, with the rose-garden blooming beside them. And now, the rose left on each grave. A token. Of goodbye?

Lawrence had wanted them to leave, to go up into the hills where they could defend themselves better, find animals, eventually start farming. It had been a sensible and obvious course. The reason they had not gone before was that April would not leave her dead, and the rest were helpless without her. If she had changed her mind ... And he saw all too clearly how it could have happened. Her contempt for his own obsessive fantasy, for his refusal to adapt to the realities of life, was something she might well have turned on herself. Her link with the past, like his, was a crippling one, both for her and others. Once she saw this, she would have rejected it. It only needed courage, and she had that in ample measure.

Matthew examined the stores again, trying to remember what had been there. The matches and candles had gone, he saw, the small hammer, the lightweight saw, the scissors ... all sorts of things that combined usefulness with portability. He had the impression that, as far as the tinned foods were concerned, it was the proteins that were in shorter supply now. They would have taken what they needed and could carry. The rest they had left here, sealing it up in case, perhaps, at some future time, they could come back for the other things.

Did that mean they had not gone far? He checked the quick dart of hope. They were looking for no particular place but a refuge, a defensible home. They would go on until they found it. And when they found it, they would stay there.

He was still walking round aimlessly, trying to cope with the realization, and he found himself in the small cellar again. The tiny light he was carrying gleamed on something lying on the corner of the shelf against the wall, and he reached up to get it. A small squat bottle, of aspirins. It must have been overlooked when the other things were taken. Well, it was something. A bottle of aspirins to treat a boy who was possibly dying.

He realized something else, then—that down here he would not be able to hear Billy if he called for him. He went quickly to the stairs and, lying on his back, heaved himself out into the open. Billy was not calling, but he headed for the grotto all the same. He had been away long enough.

Billy woke a short while later, in delirium. He tried to get up and, when Matthew restrained him, fought against him. He struggled with all the strength he could summon, but it was not very much. There was about half an hour of this before he relaxed, slumping back so heavily and helplessly that Matthew put his ear to the boy's chest to reassure himself that the heart was still beating. He crushed a couple of aspirins into the tinned milk, and fed it to him with a spoon. It was difficult getting it into his mouth, even more difficult persuading him to swallow. He was not sure that any went down, but at least it did not come out.

For the rest of the day, and the night that followed, the boy was alternately febrile and comatose. Matthew used the latter intervals to get various things from the cellar—blankets and clean clothes for him and eventually the poles and canvas which made up the awning. He came back from that trip to find Billy awake again, on his knees and crying. He forced him gently back and gave him some water with more crushed aspirin. This was in the afternoon, and he himself had had nothing but a tin of meat and some cold tinned tomatoes. He had no means, anyway, of starting a fire since there was no dry wood.

He got the awning up before dark, but in fact the night stayed clear. It was quite warm, and the stars were bright but very far away. Matthew watched them revolve through the long hours, in between nursing Billy and talking to him. Twice he fell asleep for short spells; the second time he was wakened by Billy feebly trying to climb over him to get away. He felt leaden, and his head and eyes were aching. What would happen to

Billy if he got it, too—whatever it was? He shook his head to clear it, despite the pain. He was not going to be ill.

Dawn came, and there was no change in the boy except that he seemed still weaker. His strength was draining away almost visibly, and when he cried out now it was in a voice so feeble that it was almost a whisper. Matthew himself was still feeling unwell and exhausted. He could not be bothered to eat anything. All he wanted to do was sleep, and he could not sleep while the boy needed him. The morning passed in a kind of nightmare. It was a clear day, hot at the outset and growing hotter. He went to bathe in the stream to refresh himself and, coming in sight of it, thought for a moment that he saw April again, kneeling there. The air seemed thick, oppressive, and he heard a cuckoo, its duotone beating mockingly against his ears. He washed, only half aware of what he was doing, and took back a wet cloth to cool Billy.

In the middle of the day there was another burst of fever. The boy's body arched against Matthew's restraining arms; his pulse hammered frighteningly fast. His mouth gaped and his tongue was swollen and white against dry cracked lips. At the same time, sweat was pouring off his body. Matthew managed to get a little more aspirin in water down his throat; apart from that there was nothing he could do but hold him, and wipe his face with the cloth. He was sure now that the boy was dying. He thought of the morning when he had first heard him call, from under the rubble of his home, and felt an enraging sense of futility. The boy was dying, the time and hardships between pointless.

The boy had followed him, he told himself, and there was nothing he could have done about that except what he had done. He had looked after him as well as he could. It would have been better if he had been willing to stay with Miller, or later with Lawrence and April, but that was nothing he could help.

Except by giving up his own fantasy. He stared at Billy's face, the skin drawn tight over sharp and delicate bone, and knew that the worst charge against him was that he had never even thought of doing so. He had given him some care. There had been no question of giving him love.

He held Billy's hand. The pulse was very fast still, and seemed to be irregular. A waste, and of his own doing. He lay down beside the boy, and gathered him in his arms.

. . . He was in Hyde Park, on a cold ragged day, and was looking for something. Not something, someone. Someone who mattered, whom he loved but had let down. The grass was yellow and scrubby from a long arid summer, and the autumn wind bent the branches of trees over and blew paper wrappers about. The terrible thing was that he did not know where to look; whichever way he turned, he was conscious of the great spaces behind him, the vistas which could hide the lonely missing figure. Then it came quite simply to him: the Serpentine. He could see its grey waters in the distance, and he went towards it, hurrying, almost running. But however fast he went, it was no nearer. Despite his anxiety and unhappiness, this struck him as ludicrous—Alice in Wonderland. And April, beside him, said: 'You've been going the wrong way. I despise you for that, Matthew.' He clutched at her arm. 'You can help me find her! You can, if you want to.' She shook her head. 'You can!' 'It's only a matter,' she told him, 'of facing reality. Look.' And they were by the lake, looking along it towards the bridge. The boat was there, in the distance, with one small figure at the oars. Going away, irretrievably going away. He shouted after it, against the wind: 'Jane! I'm here. Come back. Don't leave me, Jane.' But the boat, with Billy in it, went on, under the arch of the bridge, and was lost to him. And he turned to April, in his anguish, and she was no longer there.

When Matthew woke, he saw Billy's still figure and thought it must be over. He touched his face, expecting to find it cold, and to his surprise found the warmth of life. The ordinary warmth: the fever had gone and he was sleeping quietly and peacefully. He felt joy and thankfulness, muted at first and then ringing through his body, so clamorous that his head swam with it. He put his hand on the boy's brow, but gently so as not to wake him. The fever was gone completely.

It was late afternoon, with the sun throwing blocks of golden dust-specked air between the trees. Matthew found wood and built a fire. When he had got it going, he saw that Billy was awake and watching him. He went to him, and asked:

'How are you now, Billy ?'

'I'm all right, Mr Cotter.' The voice was very weak still, but clear. 'I've been asleep.'

'Yes. Do you think you could eat something ?'

Billy hesitated. 'Yes. I am a bit hungry.'

The big pot had been left down in the cellar; presumably they had thought it too heavy to take with them. Matthew made a stew, finding a few fresh vegetables in the kitchen garden, and fed Billy and then himself. Afterwards they sat together, looking into the fire.

Billy said: 'How did we get back here, Mr Cotter ? I don't remember.'

'I carried you a bit of the way.'

'I think I remember a dog. I'm not sure, though.' He glanced up at the awning under which they were sitting. 'What about Lawrence and everybody ? When are they coming back ?'

'They aren't coming back here, Billy. They've gone to find a better place. Somewhere that will be safer.'

'So we shan't see them again ?'

'I wouldn't say that. I should think they've gone up into the hills. When you've rested and got a bit stronger, we can go and look for them.'

'Do you think we could find them ?'

'I don't see why not.'

'It would be nice if we did.'

'It's only a matter of looking. There aren't that many people left. It may take us a while, but I think we should be able to find them in the end.'

'Lawrence said he would teach me how to be a doctor. Not a proper doctor, but some of it.'

'Yes. You'd better lie down now. If you're to get your strength back, you must rest as much as possible. Rest and eat, and we'll have you well in no time.'

Matthew's own headache and heaviness had gone, too. It had been worry, chiefly, he thought, and fatigue—most of all, the sense of futility. All that was ended. There was something to do, a purpose. Something to look forward to.

During Billy's convalescence, Matthew busied himself with preparations. There were no shoes of Billy's size among the things in the cellar, but there were larger ones, and he found a hammer and some tacks he hoped would do. He cut the larger shoes up and soled and heeled Billy's as best he could, using odd bits of metal and stone for lasts, and learning the job as he went along. In the end he produced something which Billy said was comfortable and which, he hoped, would stand up for a few weeks until they could find something better. He did a similar repair job on his own shoes, and washed and mended their clothes.

After that, he had a shot at making the bow he had spoken of to Lawrence. The steel rods had been left, and there was an odd length of nylon rope which could be unravelled to make strings. He got a bit of rough metal and tried filing notches at either end of one of the rods. But the steel was harder than he had thought, and after hours of work he had made very little impression. So he abandoned it and cut a straight length of ash. It made a reasonable bow, and he cut arrows and hardened their points in the fire. Later he practised shooting with them and Billy watched, applauding when he scored a hit on the target.

The last thing he did was to get supplies together for their journey. He had been tempted many times, during the two terrible days carrying Billy on his back, to abandon the haversack which had Billy's smaller bag inside it, but he had managed to hold on to it. Now he started packing the two bags again, choosing, of the things which the others had left, those that were most likely to be valuable. And on a fairly long-term basis. It would be a weary time before they could hope to find them—months, possibly years. They had to be ready for a long haul.

There was a spell of cold wet weather. For most of two days the rain beat against the canvas awning and dripped from the bushes in the garden. During the morning of the third day, the wind dropped and the sky began to clear. Billy was restless from having been cooped up and went running through the garden in an exhilaration of freedom. He was fit enough, Matthew decided, watching him. They would leave the next morning. There was no point in putting their departure off longer.

In the evening he left Billy making supper and went for a walk. The wind had blown the roses from the graves, all but one, of which only the stem and a couple of petals were left. Matthew broke off new blooms and laid them where the others had been. Walking on, he found himself taking the same path he had followed with April. He reached the oak. The winds which had blown the roses had not been strong enough to topple it. It hung at the same awkward unlikely angle over the long grass of the field. There was movement in the branches: a squirrel. Squirrels were edible, were they not? If only . . .

. . . April's voice.

—If only you had your bow and arrows with you!

—Well, why not? I'd probably miss, but it would be worth trying.

—Your bow of unseasoned wood, with its unflighted arrows?

—I know. But they will do for now. All these are makeshifts. Everything is a makeshift. It will be different when . . .

—When?

—When I find you.

Now her laughter was cruel, and edged with bitterness.

—So you still want to sacrifice him to your own illusions?

—No illusion. And he wants it, too. He wants you, and Lawrence.

—An illusion. The same illusion as before. What difference does it make that you have half-persuaded the boy to want it also? The same illusion, Matthew. That's why I despised you then, and why I despise you now.

—Your voice in my mind is the illusion. There is no reality until I find you.

—And how long will you search? One year? Two years? Until you die? And the boy? Is that the legacy you will bequeath him? If he survives the years of wandering and hardship.

The squirrel hopped to a lower branch and stood cleaning its face only a few feet from him.

—You ask me to give you up?

—Not me. You gave me up that evening. Your fantasy. But that's too much to ask. Isn't it, Matthew?

He had a restless night, and woke early. While Billy was still asleep, he got things ready for their departure and made up the fire for breakfast. It was the smell of cooking which awakened Billy. He got up, yawning, from his blankets.

'Are we going today, Mr Cotter?'

'When we've had breakfast, and cleaned up.'

'North, to the hills?'

'No. South.'

The boy looked at him, puzzled. Matthew said:

'Over the sea bed. We're going back to the islands.'

NINETEEN

BILLY pointed it out, on the eastern horizon, a couple of miles distant at least. Even so it looked huge, dwarfing the rocks in which it rested.

'Uncle Matthew, it's the tanker, isn't it?'

'Yes.'

'Is the captain still there, do you think?'

'I suppose he is.'

There was no smoke against the pale blue sky, and he tried to remember if there had been any last time. The weather had been bad then, of course, and a slight discharge of smoke would probably have been unnoticeable. It would only be slight, on a small stand-by generator. Perhaps one would not see it at all.

But if the oil had given out, was Skiopos still ruling his crumbling kingdom—still cleaning and tidying and polishing? What would he do in the long evenings, once the film projector stopped working? Peer out from the bridge, perhaps, searching for the sea which had abandoned him and his command. Matthew thought of April, as he still did sometimes, with a pang that carried, as well as unhappiness, the embers of hope. They flickered and glowed with the thought. Once he had taken Billy back to the island, and settled him in with Miller and the others . . . what was there to stop him going north again on his own? It was Billy's safety and future that counted.

Billy said: 'It's all right for us to be west of it, isn't it, Uncle Matthew? I mean, since we had to go off-course on the way over, with that first lot of mud.'

April's voice laughed in his mind, and he knew he would not do it. There were habits of thought which might persist, but one came to a recognition, an acceptance, and they no longer had power. Not being indulged, they would in time die altogether. And there was more than Billy's safety and future; since the illness there was Billy himself. He looked at the boy's face, serious of expression, still, after all that had happened, a child's, but reaching towards maturity. For the first time since the Bust, he was disposed to thank God for what he had.

'Yes,' he said, 'we're bearing west a little. There isn't a lot of point in stopping off at Alderney. It will save us a few miles if we aim direct for Guernsey.'

'It will be funny being back there.'

'It will be safe,' Matthew said. 'No yobbos.'

'What about from France?'

'Not even from there. No one's going to be tempted to cross the sea bed for what small pickings the islands might be able to offer.'

Matthew looked about him, at the dried mud and sand, the arid rocks. The sun gleamed on patches of caked salt. It had become land, but a barren inhospitable land. In a way, it offered more protection to the islands than the sea had ever done.

They found fewer pools than on the outward journey; many of them, probably had dried up. In one they did discover there were fish, but dead and floating belly-up in the warm stagnant water. Later they came on a stream, and traced it to its source, a spring bubbling strongly from between rocks. This water was fresh and cool, cold even. They refreshed their hot bodies with it, and emptied away the stale water from the container and refilled it.

They came on another wrecked ship not long after that. It was a cargo ship, of less than a thousand tons, and it lay on its side with its broken superstructure tilted north. The big wave had dropped it there, Matthew thought; it did not look as though it had been under water. They scrambled into it to investigate and found a skeleton, wearing a tattered blue jersey and trousers, wedged against one of the bulwarks. The bones glistened, cleaned by something sharper than putrescence. Matthew looked into the hold and saw a brown shape dart among the shadows. He wondered if some of the crew had survived and, like the crew of the tanker, had left the stranded ship. The rats, at any rate, had not. There was no immediate danger, and a food supply for the present: the rotting smell from the hold made him think the cargo had been an edible one.

Billy cried: 'Look!' and he turned quickly.

'What was it?'

'A kitten.'

He saw it himself a moment later, a tabby kitten, perhaps nine or ten weeks old, picking its way along the sloping deck. And another, a third. The rats live on the cargo, and the cats live on the rats. A balanced ecology, for the moment. But based on rapidly dwindling resources.

'Can we take one with us?' Billy asked.

Matthew smiled. 'If you can catch one, you can try taking it.'

He watched the boy chasing the kittens; it made a pleasant, slightly ridiculous scene. There was no question of his catching one, of course, and he would very likely have regretted it if he had. In thousands of years, the cat had never fully accepted domesticity and the reversion was swift and complete. These were jungle-wild.

The following day there was mist all round when they woke. It lifted to some extent as the sun got up, and Matthew thought it was going to lift altogether, but he was mistaken. Now and then the pale disk of the sun could be seen, hidden by drifting veils. It was enough to give them the barest confirmation of direction. They made good time, chiefly over mud flats which Matthew suspected were a westerly continuation of those around which they had been forced to detour on the outward journey. Here, too, there were places where the surface crust of mud broke under their feet, but these were rare. The weeks of drying-out had had their effect.

They camped on the mud that night and lay clasped together, shivering. At least, Matthew thought, it was nearly over. The following day, if his calculations were right and if the mist lifted, they should be in sight of Alderney.

And beyond Alderney, Guernsey. Miller would be pleased, he thought, both by their return and by the news they brought of the barbarism and desolation outside the confines of his kingdom. Matthew himself felt no anticipation, but a more willing resignation than he had expected. He listened inside his mind and heard April's voice again, small and far away now, but kinder, all bitterness gone. A place for Billy to grow up in, a kind of home. She approved of that. The voice, the memory, would fade, but he knew she would stay with him, a touchstone. It was a loss still, but a more bearable one.

The boy slept in his arms.

The mist did clear, but not until the middle of the day. Before that they walked between reefs of pink granite which might, for all one could see of their upper reaches, have been Himalayan foothills. The sea had cut the rock into strange shapes; at one time they traversed a twisting gorge, floored with bright sand, where their voices echoed back on them. Billy, discovering this, amused himself with cries, and with listening to the sounds ring round them, dying far away among the mists. But the mists were rising and vanishing: the sun's disk appeared, white at first and then pale yellow, and there were glimpses of spurs and summits dazzling with colour.

Matthew pointed. 'Can you climb that one? See if you can see anything.'

Billy made his way up the side of the reef, sure-footed. From the top, he called down:

'I think . . . I think it's Alderney.'

'I'll come up myself.'

As Matthew climbed, Billy said something which was indistinct. The only word he caught was water. He went on up; at twenty feet the mist was very thin, at thirty non-existent. The sun was hot and golden, the sky an unstained blue. He looked for the horizon. Five miles or more to the south, pinnacles of rock rose out of the gently billowing sea of white. Matthew thought he recognized them, and looked to his left. There was Alderney, a little further away. The pinnacles were the Casquets, the graveyard of the White Ship and countless others.

'Fair enough,' Matthew said. 'We aim for the Casquets, and then a little south of west for Guernsey. We'll make it tomorrow.'

'I thought I saw water,' Billy said. 'The mist opened a bit, but it's closed again now.'

'A pool, probably.'

'It looked big.'

Matthew was scrambling down the rock face. 'Come on, Billy. Almost the last lap.'

They came on the lake unexpectedly, less than a mile south. The ground dipped, and there it was, green and blue with the remnants of the mist clinging to the surface here and there. It was about three-quarters of a mile across, but the impressive thing was its length. It stretched, apparently endless, in either direction.

Billy said: 'Is it the sea, Uncle Matthew?'

There was only one thing it could be. He said:

'Not the sea. The Hurd Deep. A hole in the bed of the Channel. I suppose water stayed trapped in it when the land tilted.'

'Will we have to go round it?'

'I think we'd better. It's a long swim.'

Billy stared at the water. 'Which way, though?'

Matthew was trying to remember a chart he had seen once. The Deep started north of Alderney, and perhaps a little east. It was very long—seventy miles or more. The best plan, he decided, was to head for Alderney after all. They could stay the night there, and then tomorrow it would be a clear run to Guernsey.

'East,' he said. 'We go east, Billy.'

The detour was longer than he had expected; it was something like ten miles before they reached the end of the lake and could round it and head, south-west, towards the island. As he walked, Matthew thought about its size. So huge a body of water, comparable with Lake Geneva, would be years drying out, if it ever did. It might well be self-renewing. And there would be fish in it, for a certainty. He wondered if Miller had discovered it yet. It would be worth building a boat, making nets . . .

The voice startled him. He had thought there was no one within thirty miles of them.

'Mr Cotter! Billy!'

He looked disbelievingly and saw the small ginger-headed

figure emerge from behind the shelter of a rock on their right. Billy called: 'Archie!' and went running towards him. The two figures met and hugged each other. Over Billy's head, Archie said:

'I heard someone, like . . . Didn't know who it might be, so I took cover. Didn't think it could be you, Mr Cotter. Didn't see how.'

Matthew stared at him. A dream? But the scrubby carroty beard, the wrinkled monkey face were real enough.

'For God's sake, Archie,' he said, 'how do you come to be here?'

'Been fishing.' He had a bag with him and he held it open to show what was in it. 'Caught four nice 'uns.'

'But I thought if you left the grotto you were going to the hills?'

'Well, they talked about it, April and Lawrence. They decided this part was best, from what they'd heard from you. Quieter, you know. And they was right.' He gestured towards the bulk of the island, a few miles away. 'There's hens up there, and fish here in the lake. I like fishing, Mr Cotter. Lawrence tells me to come out here and fish. It's a good place.'

It was a long time since Matthew could remember joy shaking him like this.

'The others are there, then, on the island? All of them?'

'Of course,' Archie said. He grinned back, in open simple happiness. 'I reckon they'll be glad to see you.'

The sun was going down the sky, but it had a long way to go to its couch among the distant jagged rocks. It was a cloudless summer's day, with more to follow.

'Yes,' he said, 'it's a good place.'

Something has gone terribly wrong in the
charnel house of science . . . something that
must never see the light of day.

CHIMERA

Stephen Gallagher

Any government cover-up is news but this time journalist Peter Carson
knows he's onto something big. A top research laboratory on the
remote Cumbrian moors is cut off from all outside contact. Rumours of
an accident at the pioneering Jenner Clinic spread beyond the armed
roadblocks and seep through the massive official news blackout.

Dr Jenner's work matters to the government. It matters enough to have
a blank cheque, high security cover and the best technicians in the
country. But something has gone badly wrong. The project that has no
room for mistakes has produced a result so terrible that it must never
see the light of day. And now the evidence must be destroyed whatever
the cost . . .

ADVENTURE/THRILLER   0 7221 3757 5   £1.75

TIME SCAPE

Winner of the 1981 Nebula Award

GREGORY BENFORD

The year is 1998, the world is a growing nightmare of desperation, of uncontrollable pollution and increasing social unrest.

In Cambridge, two scientists experiment with tachyons – subatomic particles that travel faster than the speed of light and, therefore, according to the Theory of Relativity, may move backwards in time. Their plan is to signal a warning to the previous generation . . .

In 1962, a young Californian scientist, Gordon Bernstein, finds his experiments are being spoiled by unknown interference. As he begins to suspect something near the truth it becomes a race against time – the world is collapsing and will only be saved if Gordon can decipher the messages in time.

GENERAL FICTION   0 7221 1630 6   £1.75

I,
SAID THE SPY

by Derek Lambert

Fact: Each year a nucleus of the wealthiest and most influential members of the Western world meet to discuss the future of the world's superpowers at a secret conference called Bilderberg.

A glamorous millionairess just sighting loneliness from the foothills of middle-age . . . a French industrialist whose wealth matches his masochism and meanness . . . a whizz-kid of the seventies conducting a life-long love affair with diamonds, these are just three of the Bilderbergers who have grown to confuse position with invulnerability. A mistake which could prove lethal when a crazed assassin is on the loose . . . a journalist dedicated to exposing the conference infiltrates their midst . . . and intelligence agents from Moscow, Washington and London penetrate Bilderberg's defences to reveal a conspiracy of mind-boggling proportions . . .

I, SAID THE SPY is a novel on a grand scale which sweeps the reader along on a wave of all-out excitement and suspense until the final stunning climax.

ADVENTURE/THRILLER   0 7221 5346 5   £1.75

A selection of bestsellers from SPHERE

FICTION

THE STONE FLOWER	Alan Scholefield	£1.95 □
TWIN CONNECTIONS	Justine Valenti	£1.75 □
YOUR LOVING MOTHER	Deanna Maclaren	£1.50 □
REMEMBRANCE	Danielle Steel	£1.95 □
BY THE GREEN OF THE SPRING	John Masters	£2.50 □

FILM & TV TIE-INS

THE PROFESSIONALS 14 & 15	Ken Blake	£1.25 □ each
E.T. THE EXTRA-TERRESTRIAL	William Kotzwinkle	£1.50 □
E.T. THE EXTRA-TERRESTRIAL STORYBOOK	William Kotzwinkle	£1.95 □
THE IRISH R.M.	E. E. Somerville & M. Ross	£1.95 □

NON-FICTION

THE HEALTH & FITNESS HANDBOOK	Ed. Miriam Polunin	£5.95 □
ONE CHILD	Torey L. Hayden	£1.75 □
GARBO	A. Walker	£5.95 □
BEFORE I FORGET	James Mason	£2.25 □

All Sphere books are available at your local bookshop or newsagent, or can be ordered direct from the publisher. Just tick the titles you want and fill in the form below.

Name _____

Address _____

_____

Write to Sphere Books, Cash Sales Department, P.O. Box 11, Falmouth, Cornwall TR10 9EN

Please enclose a cheque or postal order to the value of the cover price plus:

UK: 45p for the first book, 20p for the second book and 14p for each additional book ordered to a maximum charge of £1.63.

OVERSEAS: 75p for the first book plus 21p per copy for each additional book.

BFPO & EIRE: 45p for the first book, 20p for the second book plus 14p per copy for the next 7 books, thereafter 8p per book.

Sphere Books reserve the right to show new retail prices on covers which may differ from those previously advertised in the text or elsewhere, and to increase postal rates in accordance with the PO.